PRAISE FOR *CLOSELY AKIN TO MURDER*

"Sharp writing in the usual Hess manner provides an exciting trip for the reader."
—*Mystery Lovers Newsletter*

"Another amusing and entertaining story in the Malloy saga." —*Chattanooga Times*

"Clever and snappy. . . . Claire Malloy adds another lively case to her amateur sleuthing resume."
—*Minneapolis Star Tribune*

"A winner. . . . Hess is a master of series writing."
—*Chicago Heights Star*

"If you aren't headed for Acapulco this year, *Closely Akin to Murder* is the next best thing."
—*Mostly Murder*

"Claire Malloy is an appealing heroine: she balances the demands of single motherhood, a small business, a romance, and still finds time to nail the crooks." —*Affaire de Coeur*

"Formidably inventive . . . filled with Hess's trademark guffaws." —*Kirkus Reviews*

"Lively. . . . Hess fans will expect clever dialogue, and they won't be disappointed."
—*Alfred Hitchcock's Mystery Magazine*

"Juicy reading." —*Library Journal*

PRAISE FOR JOAN HESS AND HER CLAIRE MALLOY SERIES

"Lively, sharp, irreverent."
—*New York Times Book Review*

"Intriguing . . . an amusing look at the universal human comedy."
—*Fort Smith Times-Record*

"A winning blend of soft-core feminism, trendy subplots, and a completely irreverent style that characterizes both the series and the sleuth, all nicely on stage."
—*Houston Chronicle*

"Won me over . . . an assured performance that will have me hunting out other Claire Malloy mysteries."
—*Boston Globe*

"Amiable entertainment with an edge. . . . Hess's style rarely flags."
—*Kirkus Reviews*

"Joan Hess is one very funny woman."
—Susan Dunlap, author of *High Fall*

"Hess delivers another tartly told mystery."
—*Publishers Weekly*

MORE PRAISE FOR JOAN HESS AND HER CLAIRE MALLOY SERIES

"Gloriously funny and brilliantly plotted."
—Carolyn Hart

"A breezy and delightful read. . . . Malloy is one of the most engaging narrators in mystery."
—*Drood Review*

"Hess's voice . . . is one of the most distinctive of the current generation of mystery writers—witty, ironic, and biting."
—*Bookpage*

"Whether she's hammering my funny bone or merely passing a feather beneath my nose, Joan Hess always makes me laugh."
—Margaret Maron, author of *Fugitive Colors*

"A colorful kaleidoscope of plotting and clues . . . undeniably funny."
—*Arkansas Democrat-Gazette*

"Joan of Ark. is the patron saint of comic mystery."
—Sharyn McCrumb, author of *She Walks These Hills* and *The Rosewood Casket*

CLOSELY AKIN *to* MURDER

A Claire Malloy Mystery

JOAN HESS

ONYX
Published by the Penguin Group
Penguin Books USA Inc., 375 Hudson Street,
New York, New York 10014, U.S.A.
Penguin Books Ltd, 27 Wrights Lane,
London W8 5TZ, England
Penguin Books Australia Ltd, Ringwood,
Victoria, Australia
Penguin Books Canada Ltd, 10 Alcorn Avenue,
Toronto, Ontario, Canada M4V 3B2
Penguin Books (N.Z.) Ltd, 182–190 Wairau Road,
Auckland 10, New Zealand

Penguin Books Ltd, Registered Offices:
Harmondsworth, Middlesex, England

First Published by Onyx, an imprint of Dutton Signet,
a division of Penguin Books USA Inc.
Previously published in a Dutton edition

First Onyx Printing, June, 1997
10 9 8 7 6 5 4 3 2 1

Printed in the United States of America

PUBLISHER'S NOTE
This is a work of fiction. Names, characters, places, and incidents either are the product of the author's imagination or are used fictitiously, and any resemblance to actual persons, living or dead, events, or locales is entirely coincidental.

Chapter 1

Solitude can be a wonderful thing. It allows one to ponder the perplexities of the universe, to examine one's strengths and imperfections (no matter how infinitesimal), or even to invite a billow of whimsical ideas into one's mind. On the other hand, solitude is not a condition to be treasured when one relies on retail sales to pay the rent, and one's accountant is forever harping about quarterly tax estimates and other dreary things of that nature.

I'd dusted every rack in the Book Depot, my charmingly drafty store beside the abandoned railroad tracks. It's situated on the main drag of Farberville, the home of thirty thousand or so good-natured souls and several thousand industrious college students. After lunch, I'd arranged an artful display of cookbooks and culinary mysteries in the front window, then stood out on the sidewalk under the portico to admire my effort as pedestrians streamed by, seemingly unimpressed. By midafternoon, I'd worked the crossword puzzle and was reduced to trying to decipher the personal ads ("SWCF seeks BMD with IRA") when my solitude was interrupted. With a vengeance, I might add.

"Mother," Caron began as she stomped across the room, her face ablaze with the degree of indignation that only a sixteen-year-old can produce, "before you say anything, I just want you to know It Wasn't My Fault."

Her best friend and co-conspirator, Inez Thornton, soulfully shook her head. "It really wasn't, Mrs. Malloy."

I folded the newspaper and put it aside. Caron was maintaining a belligerent posture, but I could see apprehension lurking in her eyes. For the record, she and I share red hair, green eyes, and a complexion prone to random freckles. Without this physical evidence, I might have believed—or at least suspected—that she'd been swapped in the nursery, and somewhere out there was a child who spoke only in lower case letters and had never stolen frozen frogs from the high school biology department or been taken to the animal shelter in a gorilla suit. Caron has an impressively eclectic rap sheet for her age.

Inez does, too, although as an accomplice rather than a master criminal. She's soft-spoken, when she can get in a word, and she tends to observe Caron with the solemnity of a barn owl. Then again, hawks and owls are perceived differently, but that matters very little to a mouse caught in the moonlight.

"What's not your fault?" I asked reluctantly, assuming we were not about to discuss volcanic eruptions, EuroDisney, or the federal deficit.

Caron sighed. "All I was doing was trying to see who was in Rhonda's car with her. Louis has basketball practice until five, so it couldn't have been him. If she's going steady with him like she claims, then why would she have another guy in her car?"

"It was like in a movie," volunteered Inez "We stayed back so she wouldn't notice us in the rearview mirror. But then—"

"Then a moving van got in the way," Caron cut in, deftly regaining center stage. She gave me a moment to ponder the enormity of this outrage, then continued. "When we got to the corner of Willow and Thurber, Rhonda's car had vanished. I explained it to the cop."

Maternal perspicacity failed me. "Explained what?" I asked her.

"That I had to catch up with Rhonda. If the stupid moving van hadn't pulled out right in front of me, we could have found out who was in her car when they got to wherever they were going. If anyone deserved a ticket, it was the guy driving the van. I practically had to slam on the brakes not to crash into him and end up in traction at the hospital. Or paralyzed for the rest of my life."

I swooped in on the key word, which she'd tried to cloak in the torrent of verbiage. "You got a ticket, right?"

"It wasn't my fault," she said as she drifted behind the science fiction rack. "I may not have come to a complete stop when I turned onto Willow, but it wasn't like I barreled around the corner at fifty miles an hour and ran over some little kid on a bicycle."

I looked at Inez, who had her lower lip firmly clamped beneath her teeth. She aspires to achieve Caron's level of disregard for the facts, but she's not yet a proficient liar. "The ticket was for running a stop sign?"

"He wasn't very nice about it, especially after

Caron pointed out that he'd ruined any chance we had of finding Rhonda."

I tried not to imagine that conversation. "How much does the ticket cost, Caron?"

"Seventy-five dollars," she said, peering at me over the rack to appraise my reaction. "But there's good news, too. If I take some idiotic defensive driving class, then the violation doesn't go on my record and your insurance won't go up too much. The class only costs twenty-five dollars."

"So playing private eye is going to cost you a hundred dollars," I said. "How much do you have in your piggy bank these days?"

"Nowhere near that much. I was thinking you could pay for everything, and then Inez and I can work it off here next month. You're always saying how busy you are in December, and gawd knows you could use some help with the window display. What's there now is pathetic."

"Thank you," I said.

The conversation from this point on did not take on any overtones of jocularity. Once we'd established that I was more perturbed by the cost of the crime rather than its nature, we discussed various financial strategies. The more lucrative possibilities at the mall were summarily dismissed, in that their totalitarian demands might interfere with Christmas shopping. Babysitting was much too tedious, and housework was compared to slavery in the salt mines of Siberia.

I finally gestured at the door. "Your driving privileges are suspended until this is resolved. We'll talk about it tonight."

Caron's lower lip shot out. "But it's Friday night

and there's a football game. How are we supposed to get there?"

"Don't go," I said without sympathy. "If I remember correctly, a year ago you decided football was, and I quote, 'nothing more than a philistine ritual in which the players' IQs are displayed on their jerseys.' "

"That was last year," she said, then shrugged and started for the door. "By the way, some woman called last night while you were at the movie with Peter. She said she'd try again. Come on Inez, let's take the railroad tracks to the bridge and go up the path. If we're lucky, no one will see us and we won't be the laughingstock of the high school Monday morning."

"Who called?" I asked.

Caron paused only long enough to say, "I think her name was Veronica Landonwood."

Seconds later the bell above the door jangled and they were gone. And I was staring at the door, my jaw dangling and my heart beating entirely too quickly. The store was drafty, but the sudden chill that raised goosebumps on my arms came from within me.

Even though I put on a sweater and kicked the rebellious boiler into a semblance of cooperation, I was still shivering when Lieutenant Peter Rosen of the Farberville CID arrived later that afternoon. He was dressed as usual in an exquisitely tailored suit and Italian shoes, courtesy of a family trust fund; he looked as if he would be more at home in a high-powered law firm than in a squad room. Even in baggy gym shorts and a sweatshirt, he's handsome enough to merit a page in a calendar. Curly brown hair, molasses-colored eyes, an aristocratic nose, flawless white teeth, and a cute derriere constitute eligibility.

"I brought capuccinos and chocolate chip cookies," announced my candidate for Mr. November. His smile faded as he looked more closely at me. "What's wrong, Claire? Are you coming down with the flu?"

"You probably should say that I look as though I'd seen a ghost," I said with an unconvincing laugh, "because in a way, I have."

"Has Mr. Grimaldi arisen from eternal rest to demand you stop contaminating his precious bookstore with romance novels, study guides, and sorority stationery?"

"Come into the office and I'll tell you," I said, allowing him to put his arm around me and give me a quick kiss. Peter and I have been working at a relationship for several years, and I regret to say that despite our ages, we tend to approach it with what might be described as adolescent ineptitude. We'd come perilously close to sharing bed and board to determine if we had any hope of long-range compatibility, but he'd been drawn into a sleazy drug case and the issue had been shelved. For the moment, anyway.

I sat down behind the desk and accepted a Styrofoam cup. "According to Caron, last night I had a call from Veronica Landonwood."

"Should I recognize that name?"

"I had a cousin with that name, although everyone called her Ronnie. She was seven years older than I, so we weren't particularly close. She was always very nice to me, though, and I was in awe of her because she lived in Hollywood. Well, technically in Brentwood, but it was close to Hollywood."

Peter took a sip of capuccino, his eyes narrowed as he watched me above the rim. "And she called last night?"

"Somebody called last night, but if it was Ronnie, I'm going to have to rethink my views on the possibility of afterlife. She died thirty years ago, Peter. I was ten at the time, and I was devastated. My only experience with death had been the loss of a nasty yellow tomcat named Colonel Mustard."

"How did she die?"

"She and her parents were in Mexico for a vacation, and their car went off a mountain road. I'd received a postcard from her only a few days before I was told about the wreck. I still have that postcard packed away somewhere."

Peter came behind me and began to massage my shoulders as I blinked back tears. "Then this is just a grotesque coincidence," he said, "or Caron wasn't paying attention and got the name wrong."

"Maybe," I said. Despite my efforts, my hand was shaking so violently I could barely raise the cup to my mouth. A wake-up call from the grave can do that.

I lingered at the bookstore well past closing time, trying to convince myself that trivial chores were, in reality, consequential. By seven o'clock, however, all my pencils were perfectly aligned and the plastic paper clips were sorted by size *and* color. I locked the store and drove home to the duplex across from the Farber College campus. In winter I have a view of the condemned landmark that once housed the English faculty (one of whom had been my deceased husband, Carlton, who'd had an unfortunate encounter with a chicken truck; our turbulent marriage was responsible for my current reluctance to make a commitment to Peter). The downstairs tenants moved in and out on an irregular basis. The current one was a somewhat bald, bewildered retiree from the architecture department whose wife had kicked him out of their house and taken up with her aromatherapist. Neither of us was sure what this implied.

Caron had left a note indicating that despite my hardhearted scheme to destroy her life, she'd found a ride to the football game and would be spending the night at Inez's. I suppose I might have saved it for reference when I got around to writing my memoirs, but I tossed it in the trash and made myself a drink.

Shortly thereafter, I was in my robe and curled up on the sofa with a mystery novel. The muted strains of a Brahms concerto from the first floor mingled with the rustling of leaves outside the window and an occasional car. I was so engrossed in the wily amateur sleuth's exploration of the darkened conservatory that I let out an undignified yelp when the telephone rang.

I finally persuaded myself to pick up the receiver. "Hello?" I said with such timidity that I wasn't sure the word had been audible.

"Claire, this is Ronnie—Ronnie Landonwood."

"If this is some kind of prank, it isn't the least bit amusing. I don't know who you are or why you're doing this, but I can have a trace put on my—"

"On your seventh birthday, I sent you a tutu that I'd worn in a dance recital. You wrote me a stiff thank you note saying you planned to be a detective when you grew up and would prefer a magnifying glass on your next birthday. When you were nine, you fell out of a tree and broke your arm. Later that summer you sent me a poem that vilified Joyce Kilmer. Shall I continue?"

"Hold on a minute, please," I said, then put down the receiver and went into the kitchen to splash some cold water on my face and some scotch in a glass. I sat back down on the sofa and, after a couple of sips, wiped my decidedly damp palms on my robe and picked up the receiver. "Would you care to explain?"

The woman exhaled as if she'd been holding her breath all the time I'd been trying to regain my composure. "It's a complicated story. My parents and I went to Acapulco in December of 1965. My father, who was a second-rate screenwriter, was hoping to cozy up to Oliver Pickett. Oliver was one of the most influential directors in the business, and was scouting locations in that area for his next film. He'd won an Oscar that year for a much-acclaimed medieval epic."

"I'm familiar with the name," I said, "but I still don't understand what's going on."

"Perhaps I shouldn't burden you with this. I chose to disappear all these years, and I have no right to pop up out of the blue and ask for your help. I'm sure you have a busy enough life with your bookstore and your daughter. I was just hoping that your admirable accomplishments in matters of crime—"

"How do you know all that?"

"I hired a private investigator. He didn't delve into your personal affairs, but he found a few articles in the newspaper morgue."

"You hired someone to spy on me?" I said.

"Only to find you," she said in a reproving voice.

"I need someone I can trust. Everything I fought for and attained is in danger. If you'll allow me to finish my story, I think you'll understand the gravity of my situation."

Not at all flattered to have been the subject of a PI's report, I glanced over my shoulder to make sure the curtains were tightly drawn, then said, "I'll listen to your story, but that's all I'm promising to do."

"My father borrowed enough money so that we could stay at the Hotel Las Floritas, where Oliver Pickett was staying. I expected to be utterly miserable all three weeks. My parents were at ease with the Hollywood types, but I was shy and gawky and sadly deficient in social skills. At seventeen, I'd never had a close girlfriend, much less a date. Like many tall girls, I slouched and wore drab clothes to blend into the background. My mother kept enrolling me in cotillions and etiquette classes, but none of them helped."

"I always thought you were glamorous. You knew all the current slang and told risqué jokes." I did not add that I'd never understood them, even though I'd laughed uproariously.

"Younger cousins didn't intimidate me," she said. "To return to the story, the day we arrived, Oliver Pickett's daughter came to our bungalow and introduced herself. Fran was a year younger than I, but much more sophisticated. She had streaky blonde hair, large hazel eyes, and the body of a model. My parents urged me to accept her invitation to go to the beach. From that moment until—until the tragedy, she and I whizzed around Acapulco in her father's limousine, shopping and hanging out at the beach clubs. At night while the adults were partying in hotel bars and private homes, we'd have Jorge drive us to seedy bars in the *Sona Roja,* where we drank margaritas until we threw up in front of the pimps and prostitutes."

"Your parents allowed this?"

"My parents did whatever Oliver said. If he'd told them to dive off the cliff at La Quebrada, they would have put on their bathing suits and started climbing. Oliver had divorced Fran's mother years earlier, and was accompanied by his so-called secretary, an aspiring actress named Debbie D'Avril. She was quite the party animal, as was Chad Warmeyer, Oliver's assistant. The five of them would start celebrating at sunset and stagger back to Las Floritas at sunrise to sleep until noon. Fran and I had virtually no supervision. Occasionally, we were deprived of the limousine when Chad was sent out to photograph a house or beach, but then we took taxis."

I grimaced as I imagined Caron and Inez in a similar situation. "You mentioned a tragedy," I murmured.

"On New Year's Eve, the adults went to a party. A few days earlier, Fran had decided that we should have our own party in her bungalow. She'd invited a dozen kids from the beach, and by midnight, there were three times that many. I drank too much and smoked pot, and eventually passed out in the master bedroom. When I awoke, everybody was gone. My hand and shirt were smeared with blood, and I was holding a knife. Oliver Pickett's body was on the balcony. Two days later I was arrested. Shortly after that, my parents rented a car to drive to Mexico City to get help at the American embassy. I was informed the next day that they'd been in a fatal car accident.

A matron smuggled in a newspaper for me; I couldn't read Spanish, but I could tell that I was presumed to have been in the car with them."

I was too shocked to attempt a response for a long while. The story seemed ludicrous, more suitable for low-budget movies and exploitative true crime novels. My cousin the killer? "I don't know what to say," I said inanely.

"Few people would. I was convicted and sentenced to twelve years in prison. After serving eight, I was released, ordered to leave the country, and given enough money to take a bus to the border. I was too ashamed to make contact with any of the family, so I stayed in San Diego and worked as a waitress and maid until I'd completed my GED and put myself through college. My grades were good enough to get me into medical school. Between moonlighting and student loans, I earned a degree, did further graduate work, and went into research."

"But how could you allow us to believe you were dead? Didn't you feel any obligation to the people who cared about you? Couldn't you have written from prison, or at least after you were released and were back in the country?"

"I killed a man, Claire. I stabbed him in the throat, then tried to escape retribution by throwing his body off a cliff in hopes the police would believe he'd fallen to his death and cut his throat on a sharp rock. I spent eight years wishing I'd died with my parents. When I got out, I wanted nothing more than a new identity and a fresh start. A judge heard me out and allowed me to adopt my mother's maiden name."

I licked my lips. "Why did you kill him?"

"He came back unexpectedly—I think he'd fallen

into a swimming pool and wanted to change clothes—and busted up the party. Fran managed to slip away. Oliver discovered me in his bed, and was attempting to rape me when I grabbed the knife and stabbed him. I kept stabbing him until he collapsed. I still have nightmares in which I'm screaming silently as my arm goes up and down and blood splatters my face. What I did was a monstrous thing. Oliver was too drunk to know what he was doing. He was a hero in Hollywood, and everybody worshipped him."

"Earlier you said that his body was on the balcony. If he assaulted you in the bedroom, how did you and he end up out there?"

"I fought my way out of the bedroom, but he came after me. I grabbed a knife off the bar as I backed toward the balcony. Afterward, I stumbled to the bedroom and passed out again, I suppose this time from the trauma of realizing what I'd done. Fran's scream wakened me. She'd started worrying about leaving me behind, and had Jorge bring her back to the hotel. She was clear-headed enough to point out that I nad no scratches or bruises to back up my accusation of rape, and the police would believe I'd been in his bed to seduce him when he returned. It was such a sick idea that I was ready to throw myself off the balcony."

"But surely the police would have believed you. You were only seventeen, and as you said, unsophisticated. He had to have been at least twenty years older. He'd been drinking, and he was angry about the party. It seems reasonable to assume he might have turned this anger on you, since you were vulnerable."

"And very frightened and confused," she said in a low voice. "Fran convinced me that my only hope was for his body to be discovered at the base of the cliff. Once we'd done that, I wiped up the blood while she disposed of my clothes and the evidence of the party. Then she gave me a sleeping pill, and I went back to my room."

"But the police arrested you?"

"The body was found the next morning, and at first it was assumed that he'd fallen. My parents, Debbie D'Avril, and Chad Warmeyer all admitted they'd been drinking heavily at various parties, and that Oliver could barely walk. Fran went into shock. Her mother arrived that day and arranged for her to be sedated and kept in bed. Then my bloodied shirt was found in a garbage can behind the hotel restaurant. Details came out about the party, and Fran was forced to admit I remained there when everyone else left. The police searched my bedroom at the bungalow and found my diary. It was filled with accounts of sexual encounters, but the police refused to believe they were only the fantasies of an unhappy teenaged girl who'd never been kissed. I finally broke down and confessed. After that, everything was a hideous blur of interrogation rooms, a filthy cell, hearings held in Spanish with no interpreters, and a mockery of a trial in front of a disapproving judge. I was not allowed to testify, and I don't know if my lawyer believed me, either. I'm not even sure my parents did after they were shown my diary, but at that point I was too depressed to care."

"Where was Fran during all this?" I asked.

"I wasn't allowed to see her until the trial, when we were both found guilty. She was glassy-eyed and unwilling to speak to me, and I never saw her again after we were transported to the prison. I tried without success to find out what happened to her. She could have been transferred, released, or buried in the paupers' cemetery just outside the prison wall. Dysentery and tuberculosis were rampant. I had pneumonia numerous times because my cell was so damp. Someone sent me packages of food and medicine every month; without them, I would have starved."

Ronnie's recitation had been unemotional and devoid of details, but it evoked such repugnant images that I felt nauseous. At seventeen, I'd not been obsessed with creature comforts or expensive toys. I wasn't at all sure, however, that I could have survived for eight years in a cell in a foreign country, with no one on the outside to fight for my freedom. Caron wouldn't have lasted eight hours.

"You were very brave," I said. "I don't know if I could have gone through it."

"I didn't call you to start a fan club," she said drily. "What I did in Acapulco was unforgivable. Not a day goes by that I don't say a prayer for Oliver Pickett. I stole his life from him when he was at the peak, and I deserved to be punished. I never married or took a vacation, and I work eighteen-hour stints at the lab. Now, when I'm close to something that will have major significance in the field of drug-resistant viruses, someone's trying to snatch it all away by exposing me. I'll lose my position, my grants, and my credibility in the medical community."

"You're being blackmailed?" I said.

"A week ago I found a message on my answering

machine. The voice was so raspy that I wasn't sure if it was male or female. The message was intelligible, though. If I don't deposit half a million dollars in a shielded bank account in Grand Cayman within the next thirty days, copies of the court transcript will be sent to my colleagues, along with a photocopy of my passport and other proof of my previous identity. I can't let that happen."

Surely the private detective had reported on my financial status, I told myself. "I don't see how I can help," I said. "I barely earn enough at the bookstore—"

"I'm not asking for a loan, Claire. I could borrow the money in a matter of days, but I know it won't stop there. I'll never be sure that this person won't send the evidence out of spite, or make further demands. I can't live with that kind of tension pervading my every thought. I want you to find this person and reason with him—or her. Make some kind of deal in exchange for the money."

"Wait a minute," I said, trying not to gurgle, "I'm a bookseller in a small college town. I have no idea how to deal with something of this magnitude. I may have assisted the police on occasion, but this is way out of my league. Why don't you talk to the private detective? He has the training and resources to track down people. I wouldn't know where to start."

"Acapulco, I should think."

I went ahead and gurgled like a coffeepot. "Call the private detective. He has cohorts in Mexico who can determine who got hold of the court transcripts."

"I don't trust him," she countered, clearly having assembled her arguments in advance. "He knows I'm wealthy. How can I be sure he won't decide to blackmail me, too? You're the only person I can trust, Claire, and as far as I'm concerned, my only relative. I sent that magnifying glass on your eighth birthday; now I'm begging you to dust it off and use it."

Chapter 2

"Think of it as the vacation we can never afford," I said to Caron as the cabin steward removed our untouched lunch trays. "We'll have a suite, a chauffeur, unlimited expenses, and a balcony with a view of Acapulco Bay. All you have to do is lie by the pool or play volleyball on the beach. I'm not going to drag you around with me."

"I am missing the homecoming game," she said, not for the first time, her sullenness having had a distinct impact on my appetite (the appearance of the food itself running a close second). When I failed to respond with adequate compassion, she added, "It was possible that I would have had a date to the dance afterward."

"You didn't tell me that," I said. "Ronnie offered to pay for you to come along and I thought you'd enjoy it, but you certainly weren't under any obligation. You could have stayed with Inez."

"I said it was *possible,* Mother, but the boys at school are hopelessly infantile. I have such a load of homework that all I'll do is sit in some dreary hotel room reading Dickens."

"It's a very nice hotel," I said. "You were going to have to read Dickens anyway. At least you can do it in an exotic setting."

"And if this cousin had been arrested in Bosnia would we have reservations at the Sarajevo Hilton?"

"Buckle your seatbelt, dear."

"I'm serious, Mother. You haven't heard a word from her for thirty years, then all of a sudden she strolls out of the cemetery and you end up agreeing to take up her cause. For all you know, she's totally crazy and made the whole thing up in order to lure you out of the country."

"So she can sneak into the Book Depot and steal a million dollars from the cash register?"

"How should I know? If this is so critical, why is it that she couldn't even bother to come along?"

"As Dr. Vera Gray, she made a commitment a year ago to speak at a symposium in Brussels. From what I could determine at the library, she's one of the pre-eminent figures in her field. She's been director of a research facility in Chicago for more than ten years. She's won all kinds of awards and been nominated twice for a Nobel prize."

Caron yawned. "I don't see how that's going to help you. Your Spanish vocabulary is limited to the menu at the restaurant up the street from the bookstore. Do you honestly think you're going to say 'Enchilada,' and Pancho Villa's going to leap out of the bushes to confess to blackmail?"

I turned my back on her and gazed out the window at the landscape below. The mountains were barren and unfriendly; roads slinked through them like dried tendrils. The pilot had mentioned a volcano, but as fate always decrees, it was visible from the opposite side of the plane. It seemed appropriate.

Peter had been furious when I told him what I intended to do. He'd tried to control his temper, but by the time he'd stalked out the door, bristling like a hedgehog, I had a much keener understanding of the concept of nuclear winter. He'd relented enough to confirm through professional channels the rudimentary facts of the story: Oliver Pickett had been murdered on January 1, 1966; two unnamed American girls had been charged with the crime. Subsequent legal proceedings had been closed because the girls were minors. The Los Angeles newspapers had run a lengthy obituary, but it alluded only fleetingly to a tragic accident and focused on Pickett's cinematic career. His only survivor was a daughter, Franchesca. A much shorter obituary of Arthur, Margaret (nee Gray), and Veronica Landonwood cited the automobile accident; there was no mention of a memorial service or survivors.

Ronnie was picking up the tab, as well as the small salary I was paying the bewildered retiree (aka the downstairs tenant) to mind the bookstore in my absence. She'd mentioned a fee, but I'd changed the subject and refused to return to it. Accepting money for a doomed mission went beyond the pale, even mine. I was much more likely to end up with an infamous traveler's malady than with any inkling of the blackmailer's identity.

Thirty minutes later we stepped off the airplane into blistering white sunshine. My guidebook had stated that the average temperature in November was ninety degrees, and every one of them was ricocheting off the tarmac. We followed worn yellow stripes into the airport and wended our way through the cattle chutes of immigration and customs without undue delays.

"What does that sign say?" asked Caron as we waited by the luggage carousel. "How are we supposed to know what to do if we can't read the signs? We'll accidentally break some law and be locked up in jail. I'm supposed to take the SAT next month."

"This is a tourist-friendly city," I said uneasily. As a devotee of the written word—any written word—I was discomfited by my inability to immediately comprehend the sign under discussion. "Mexico's government is not a repressive communist regime with top-secret defense facilities tucked between scenic photo opportunities."

"Oh, yeah? What about that guy over there by the door? He's been staring at us ever since we entered the airport, and if he's not sinister, then I'm the Farberville High School homecoming queen."

I took a quick look. "You're exaggerating, Your Highness. He's just a businessman trying to remember his schedule. No one has any reason to think we're anything more than tourists on a four-day jaunt. Peter and Ronnie are the only people who know why we're here, and neither would alert the local version of the CIA."

"Don't be so sure," Caron said, already distracted by a group of college boys who'd clearly begun their vacation on the airplane.

We collected our luggage and went out to the street. Everyone else seemed familiar with the drill as they piled into vans, taxis, or cars crammed with beaming relatives. Several drivers held up cardboard signs with names, none of them mine. Within a matter of minutes, the sidewalk was uninhabited, except for a few airport employees sharing a cigarette. In terms of auspicious beginnings, this was not notable.

"I am about to Pass Out," Caron said as she sat on a bench and took a tissue from her purse to wipe her forehead. "If I don't have something cold to drink in the next minute, I'll keel over right here. You'd better look up the Spanish phrase for 'heat-stroke,' because you'll need it at the hospital. Maybe the food's better there than on the airplane."

In that her sinister CIA operative was approaching us, I ignored her. I may have felt a little giddy myself, but I managed an amiable expression. "Yes?"

He was much too young and chubby to have been in a Cold War espionage novel. Despite his conservative gray suit and muted red tie, I estimated his age at no more than twenty-five. The small mustache, no doubt grown to make him appear older, looked as though it might slip off his lip if he smiled. His hair was cropped, his expression wary. His dark eyes met mine briefly, flickered in Caron's direction, and then widened as he took in the extent of our luggage (Caron insists on packing for any and all contingencies).

"I am Manuel Estoban from the Farias Tourist Agency," he said in lightly accented English. "May I ask if you are Claire Malloy?"

"Yes, and this is my daughter. Are you our driver?"

"For the next four days, I am at your disposal." He presented me with a crisp business card, then beckoned to a boy, who began to load the luggage onto a dolly. "The car is down here in the shade. I hope you find it satisfactory, Señora Malloy. I suggest we go first to the hotel so that you can register and unpack. Afterward, I will take you wherever you wish."

His gleaming black Cadillac with tinted windows and a silver logo on the door was quite a bit classier than my battered hatchback. Caron recovered from her stupor long enough to whistle, then scrambled into the backseat and curled up to take a nap. Feeling like a traitor to the bourgeoisie, I joined her.

The trunk slammed, and seconds later, so did the driver's door. "Is this your first visit to Mexico?" Manuel asked as he pulled out onto a flat highway lined with pastel buildings, peeling billboards advertising everything from Pepsi to what appeared to be gratuitous sex, and construction projects. The only hint of exotica came from palm trees. Then again, the Farberville airport is bordered by an auto salvage yard, the Airport Arms apartments, and a convenience store that's robbed on a weekly basis. And there are no palm trees.

"Only a day in Tijuana," I said. To discourage further conversation, I closed my eyes and rested my head on the leather upholstery. At some point Manuel would have to be told I would not be going to the predictable tourist destinations, but instead to the police station, the newspaper office, the courthouse, and the prison compound. I had a list of names of those who'd been involved, although it was likely that many of them would no longer be available.

It could all wait, I told myself as the breeze from the air conditioner eased my headache and dried my damp skin. As the road began to climb into the mountains, I occasionally peeked at the spectacular views of the ocean and rocky cliffs interspersed with stretches of sand. Finally the rigors of the predawn flight did me in, and I fell asleep.

"Here we are," Manuel announced as the car stopped. "The Acapulco Plaza."

I sat up and looked out the window. The hotel was richly landscaped, with an open-air promenade lined with boutiques, groupings of wicker furniture, ceiling fans, and bellmen in pristine white jackets. Behind us was a boulevard with more shops, sidewalk cafes, restaurants, banks, and travel agencies. Traffic flowed around horse-drawn carriages decorated with flowers and balloons. Within a few blocks, mountains rose so steeply it was difficult to comprehend how dwellings could cling to them or cars crawl up them.

I roused Caron, and we waited at the curb as Manuel arranged for our luggage to be unloaded onto a cart.

"Is this where the guy was murdered?" she asked, frowning at the parrots squawking in an atrium. "We're right on the beach. I thought you said they threw the body off a cliff."

"That hotel is no longer open," I said quietly, aware of Manuel's proximity.

He spoke to the bellman in Spanish, then turned to me. "You wish that I return later this afternoon or this evening, Señora? Maybe you like to watch the sunset from one of the bars on the hill?"

"We won't be going anywhere until tomorrow morning," I said, "but I need to set up some appointments and it might be less complicated if you made the telephone calls." I gave him a piece of paper with half a dozen names and a notation after each. "These people lived here thirty years ago. Some of them will have moved away or died, but please do what you can."

"A lawyer?" he said, scanning the list. "A judge? A prosecutor? A police *cabo*? A limousine driver named Jorge? The owner of Hotel Las Floritas? I cannot understand, Señora. I was told you are here in Acapulco to enjoy the sights of our beautiful city. I am unfamiliar with these names, and I have never had an encounter with the police or a judge."

"Not even a traffic ticket?" asked Caron.

"No," he said with obvious distress, his eyes welling with tears. "This is only the first time I have driven for my brother-in-law. He will be displeased if you report to him that I am incompetent and cannot oblige you—but how am I to call a judge and say that an American lady wishes to make an appointment? He will ask why, and then what should I say?"

"Tell anyone you reach that I'm a freelance writer who desires to do an interview for a magazine article," I said. Although I was not accustomed to issuing instructions to a chauffeur, I realized I could get in the habit quite easily. "Please call me at eight tonight in my hotel room to let me know if you have any luck."

We left Manuel twisting his hands and gazing after us with a despondent expression. The desk clerks seemed to feel that the arrival of guests was the least of their worries, but eventually allowed us to register and gave me a thick envelope from Ronnie. Caron and I accompanied a bellman to a one-bedroom suite on the nineteenth floor. I had not yet changed any money, but he seemed delighted to accept American dollars.

Caron explored the rooms in a matter of seconds, then threw herself down on the sofa. "Now what, Mother? Are we going to watch *Jeopardy!* in Spanish, or would you prefer to play gin?"

"I warned you that I have work to do." I changed into shorts and a cotton blouse, picked up the envelope, and tucked my newly acquired (and deeply resented) reading glasses in my pocket. "I'll be at the bar beside the pool if you need me."

There were a few children squealing in the linked oval pools that wound beneath stone bridges. Most of the deck chairs were occupied by inert, sunburned bodies clad in everything from terrycloth robes to string bikinis. A heartening number of them were reading fat paperback books. Beyond the terrace was a moderately populated beach with an endless row of thatched huts.

I found a shady table by the bar. A waiter graciously agreed to provide me with a margarita (I'm more eclectic in my tastes than Miss Marple). I signed the tab, then opened the envelope and pulled out the notes Ronnie had promised to send. She'd warned me that her memory of the people and events was spotty; much of her time in prison had been dedicated to erasing images.

All she remembered of the judge was his last name, Zamora, and his disgusted expression as he listened to the prosecutor, Ruiz, read aloud a translated portion of her diary. Both of them had been gray-haired, so it was likely they would have retired years ago, in one sense or another.

Ronnie's parents had exhausted their financial resources almost immediately, and she had ended up with an inexperienced public defender named Pedro

Benavides. He'd been in his early twenties; if he were still in Acapulco, he might be practicing law. Ronnie had written a comment that he'd needed all the practice he could get.

Jorge, the driver whose last name she could not recall, had been of a similar age, with babyish features, a slight paunch, and a purple birthmark on his neck. His English had been limited, but he'd been cooperative, if sometimes disapproving.

Ronnie described Fran Pickett as petite, with dramatically large hazel eyes, a slender nose, and a small, heart-shaped mouth. Her hair hung to the middle of her back when not swept up in an artful pile. She spoke enough Spanish to share private jokes with Jorge. She lived with her mother, who'd remarried, and her stepfather, a retired army officer and an alcoholic. Ronnie could remember only that the mother's first name was Bea and they lived somewhere in the Southwest on some sort of ranch. Fran had attended a Catholic girls' school (operated, according to her, by the Sisters of the Holy Swine), and infrequently visited her father. She'd desperately wanted to live with him in Beverly Hills, but he'd dismissed the idea. She and Ronnie had spent hours concocting strategies while they lay on the beach and Jorge waited in the limousine.

Debbie D'Avril sounded like a typical starlet, with bleached blond hair, a curvaceous body, and a contrived lisp that Ronnie and Fran found hilarious. Not surprisingly, Fran had been fiercely jealous of her relationship with Oliver, and whenever Fran had been alone with Debbie, the two had bickered. They'd had a major quarrel several days before the party, which Debbie had learned about from an unknown source. She'd threatened to tell Oliver, but obviously had not done so.

Chad Warmeyer, the assistant, had been perhaps thirty, lanky, dark-haired, and with unremarkable features. He'd agreed with everything Oliver said, no matter how preposterous, and ignored the two girls, who considered him a pathetic wimp.

Oliver, in contrast, had been overpowering. Despite his slight stature, he'd dominated every conversation and kept everyone scurrying to follow his orders. His shaggy hair had been brown, his eyes passionate, his laughter loud and contagious, his anger explosive. Ronnie had been terrified of him, but also fascinated.

Ronnie had correctly assumed I had little memory of her parents, and included a brief depiction. Arthur had been forty-one at the time of his death. He'd written scores of screenplays, but none of them had elevated him into the highest levels of the Hollywood hierarchy. When Oliver had invited him to Acapulco to discuss a project, Arthur had packed his bags. Margaret had been thrilled, too. She'd been perfectly suited to a life of cocktail parties, tennis tournaments, lunches at the most fashionable restaurants, and appearances at the right premieres.

I put down the last page and gazed at the bay, trying to envision the dynamics of the group. Oliver at the head of the table, of course, with Debbie and Chad at either side to cater to his fancies. Margaret and Arthur Landonwood, equally solicitous. Fran, hoping for paternal approval. Ronnie, alone at the far end of the table, confused by her awakening sexuality as she watched the man who would attempt to rape her.

I eventually returned to the suite to unpack. Caron was in the shower and I was rubbing lotion on my pink nose when the telephone rang. "Hello?" I said, not sure what I'd do if treated to an effusion of Spanish.

"*Vaya a su casa,*" whispered a voice.

"Excuse me?"

"If you go home now no one will hurt you or your daughter."

"Who is this?"

"A friend."

The receiver hummed in my ear. I'd been in Acapulco less than six hours. I'd checked into the suite, read notes and dozed by the pool, taken a shower—and yet unsettled this miniature universe to the extent that I was being threatened. A personal best, I concluded with a sigh. And although I couldn't be sure of the whisperer's gender, he or she was not a friend.

I nearly tumbled off the bed when the telephone rang again. I picked up the receiver as if it were a pipe bomb and said, "Yes?"

"Señora Malloy, this is Manuel Estoban. I hope your room is nice and you are enjoying your first day in Acapulco, yes?"

"Everything is fine," I said. "Did you get ahold of the people on the list?"

"I tried my best, Señora. Pedro Benavides will see you tomorrow afternoon in his law office, but only for a moment. He has a very important matter pertaining to American investors."

"Very good, Manuel. Who else?"

"Judge Zamora died fifteen years ago, and Prosecutor Ruiz and his family moved away in 1971. Ernesto Santiago has no telephone, but I have learned he continues to live at Hotel Las Floritas, which is now a place where winos and prostitutes rent rooms by the month. The *cabo,* Nicolas Alvarez, is now a *comandante* at the *Ministerio Público.* He is in Mexico City at this time, but will return in two days."

"Señor Poirot could not have done better," I said, wondering if I should tell him about the call. The question was resolved when Caron emerged from the bathroom; if she learned about it, she would be in a cab headed for the airport in a matter of minutes.

"Señor who?" said Manuel.

"I'll explain in the morning," I said. "Please meet me in the lobby at nine o'clock."

"Would you and the señorita like to go to Playa Caleta, known as the morning beach? The water is very warm this time of year, and—"

"I'll see you at nine, Manuel." I hung up and smiled at Caron, who'd turned on the television and was glumly watching CNN. "What did you do this afternoon?"

"I went down to the beach and walked for a long time. You would not believe the people out there. I've never seen so many hairy old men in skimpy bathing suits and pale, dumpy women in bikinis. If I looked like that, I'd have the decency not to parade around. There is Absolutely No Dignity in this world anymore."

"Getting a little conservative in your old age? Will you be joining a group that tries to have books banned from the school library?"

"That's not fair. All I said was that people need to use some judgment before embarrassing the rest of us. There ought to be a law."

And to think that on her first birthday I'd bought her a lifetime membership in the ACLU.

The following morning, I left Caron asleep in the suite, had coffee and a roll in the restaurant, and was sitting on a wicker couch when Manuel's Cadillac pulled to the curb. He opened the back door for me, but I continued around the car and got into the front seat.

Looking very displeased with me, he took his place behind the steering wheel. "Where do we go, Señora?"

After sixteen years of Caron Malloy, I had no difficulty disregarding his petulance. "To the Hotel Las Floritas," I said. "I need to see it, as well as speak to Santiago."

"It is not a safe place. As I told you, it is the home of derelicts. My brother-in-law will be very angry if something happens to this car; it is new and he is very proud of it." He pointed at the dashboard. "See? It has been driven only three thousand kilometers."

"If you refuse to take me there, I'll find a taxi driver who will. When I return, I will call your office and complain to your brother-in-law."

Manuel's pout was quite as impressive as Caron's best endeavors, but he said nothing and pulled out onto the boulevard. Other tourists might have been entertained with a discourse on points of interest and local history, but I was treated only to grumbles.

The road narrowed and the souvenir shops were replaced with grocery stores, racks of shoes, and tiny, smoky restaurants. Branches from mango trees hung over courtyard walls, casting shadows on rusty trucks laden with furniture or boxes of produce. The pedestrians moved slowly but purposefully. As we wound up the side of a hill, potholes began to appear with increasing frequency, until the road looked as if it had been shelled.

"I understand the Hotel Las Floritas was very popular in its day," I said to Manuel.

He kept his eyes on the road, but relaxed enough to say, "Many famous movie stars like John Wayne and Johnny Weissmuller stayed there often. Your President Kennedy and his wife had dinner there while on their honeymoon. Richard Burton drank in the bar while he was making *Night of the Iguana.* My brother-in-law has told me that the parking lot was always crowded with limousines. There were wild parties that lasted all night."

"Did your brother-in-law tell you about the Hollywood director who was murdered at the hotel?"

"A very bad thing, very bad. It happened long before I was born, but . . ." He glanced at me. "Is that why you're here, Señora?"

I wasn't prepared to trust him—or anyone else. "I'm writing an article about it."

"Why?"

"At that time, the details were kept confidential. I want to do the article on the thirtieth anniversary of Oliver Pickett's death, if I can find adequate material. If not, I will have had an enjoyable vacation."

Manuel drove through a gate and stopped in an empty parking lot. "Are you sure it is a good thing to bring alive this old scandal?"

"Yes," I said mendaciously.

The Hotel Las Floritas no longer lived up to its name. The banyan trees were massive, but there were few flowers along the flagstone path to what I assumed was the lobby. Weeds flourished in cracked stone planters. The vine on the wall in front of us was withered. What had been an open-air restaurant contained three or four tables beneath a rotting thatched roof; the shelves behind the bar were empty.

Yet it was easy to imagine the hotel as Ronnie remembered it. Beautiful people in the restaurant, laughing and drinking as the sun set across the bay. Waiters moving unobtrusively, a mariachi band roving among the tables, butterflies drifting over profuse clumps of orange and pink bougainvilleas.

"Shall I accompany you?" asked Manuel.

I reluctantly returned to the less impressive present. "I'd appreciate it if you help me locate Mr. Santiago. If he speaks English, you can come back here and wait for me. I shouldn't be more than fifteen minutes."

Manuel was radiating disapproval as he got out of the car. "Very well, Señora, but please be careful. This is not a place for ladies."

I allowed him to lead the way up the path to a long one-story building with a covered porch. Autographed photos of movie stars hung on the wall; some of the faces were familiar, others not. A beaming man appeared in so many of them that I suspected he was the innkeeper, Santiago.

Manuel knocked on a door. "Señor Santiago?" When there was no response, he knocked again, then looked at me. "He's not here."

"Or he's not in the mood for company," I said as I banged my fist on the door. "Mr. Santiago, please open the door! I can pay you for your time."

"He never creeps out of his grotto before noon,"

said a man as he stepped onto the end of the porch. "If the morning sunshine ever caught him, he'd turn to ashes. The afternoon sunlight suits him much better. He takes a bottle and a glass up to his favorite roost and whiles away the remainder of the day getting sloshed."

"You're American," I said. I could tell little else about him as he stood silhouetted against the sunlight.

"Once upon a time."

Manuel touched my arm. "We should leave, Señora. If you wish, we will come back this afternoon."

"In a moment," I said, then went down to the end of the porch. The man was less imposing at close range; I'd seen more robust specimens coming out of commercial blood banks. He was over six feet tall, but I could have pushed him off the porch with one jab. Greasy gray hair was pulled back in a ponytail. Sunglasses hid his eyes, and an unkempt mustache obscured his mouth. He wore a dingy t-shirt, torn jeans belted with a rope, and plastic sandals. "Once upon a time?" I repeated.

"Just like in the fairy tales," he said as he flashed stained teeth. "Who are you and why do you want to talk to the despicable Santiago? He's not your type."

"I have some personal business with him. My name is Claire Malloy." I waited for a moment, then added, "And yours?"

"Chico will do. Have you ever noticed that no one in any fairy tale has a last name?"

I tried to come up with a contradictory illustration, but at last gave up. "I suppose you're right. Do you live here, Chico?"

"In the honeymoon bungalow, although the mirror on the ceiling fell years ago and the mice have gnawed the stuffing out of the mattress. In bygone days, Santiago charged a hundred dollars a night; I pay less than that a month, so I really shouldn't belittle the accommodations, should I?" He stepped back into a neglected flower bed and lifted his hand in a mock salute. "*Adiós*, Claire Malloy."

"Wait a minute," I said. "I'd like to ask you a few questions."

"And I would like to write a novel that is not only critically acclaimed, but also stays at the top of the bestseller list for a year. We don't always get our way, do we?"

"I'm on assignment for a magazine, and am authorized to pay for information—within reason. Will I get my way for twenty dollars?"

He scratched his chin. "Fifty might be more persuasive."

After some further dickering, we agreed on forty dollars and walked up crumbling concrete stairs to what had been the restaurant. Manuel had taken sanctuary in the Cadillac and was glaring at me through the windshield. I'd never seen a barracuda in an aquarium, but I presumed the effect would be similar.

"I'm afraid the bar is closed," Chico said as he sat down in a rickety chair and propped his feet on a table. "The residents of Hotel Las Floritas are indulgent, as a rule, and would never complain to the management. Disagreements among ourselves are settled with broken bottles. There was a young chap with a fondness for crack who had the impertinence to pull out a gun upon discovering that his backpack had been emptied. Santiago was so offended that he bashed the chap over the head with a crowbar."

I watched an enormous black bug meandering across the floor and decided to remain standing. "How long have you lived here, Chico?"

"As long as I can remember. A wicked witch named Vino Rojo cast an evil spell over me, and I have no memory of my life before Las Floritas. Well, that's not true. Before I moved here, I slept in the streets and panhandled on the beaches. When my economic situation improved, I was able to join Santiago's little community of bottom-feeders."

"Did Santiago tell you about the Hollywood director who was killed here?"

Chico waggled a grimy finger at me. "But not in the honeymoon bungalow. That took place in the bungalow presently occupied by two hookers from Honduras. When they've had a profitable night, they often invite me over for a bowl of black bean soup."

I counted out forty dollars and flapped them at him. "What exactly did Santiago tell you?"

"He's very bitter about it," he said, gazing out at the ocean and shaking his head. "His hotel was a revered destination for the jet set; in the high season, no one could get a room without a referral from a favored guest. The restaurant was one of the most expensive in Acapulco. Santiago ordered champagne from France, Beluga caviar from the black market, and marijuana from Oaxaca. Although there was very little publicity about the case, the word was spread and his beloved movie stars and politicians transferred their allegiance to the Ritz and the Hilton. His wife transferred hers to one of the gardeners. He himself had some sort of mishap that shattered one of his kneecaps, leaving him with a pronounced limp. These days poor old Santiago sits at one of these tables, drinking mescal and staring at the names in the old guest registers. When they fade into nothingness, so will Santiago."

Manuel was probably close to wetting his pants, but I wanted Ronnie's money's worth. "What did he tell you about the crime itself?" I persisted.

"When the body was found, Santiago was more than willing to accept it as an accident. In fact, he paid substantial bribes to the police to convince them to agree with him. But then a bloody shirt was discovered in a garbage can. The police examined the suite more thoroughly and found bloodstains on the rug and the stone floor of the balcony. After they found the girl's diary, she confessed—and that was that."

He hadn't said anything I didn't already know, but I put the cash in his outstretched hand. "If you remember anything else Santiago told you that might be significant, call me at the Acapulco Plaza."

"How deep are your pockets, Claire Malloy?"

"That depends on your information," I said, easing toward the stairs as the black bug veered toward my foot.

"As a reporter, you can protect your sources?"

"Reporters cannot be forced to reveal their sources," I said vaguely. I would have cited the pertinent amendment, but I couldn't think of it and I didn't want to blow my cover with misinformation.

Chico stood up and came across the room, scarcely looking down as the bug crunched under his sandal. "I might be able to provide more information," he said. "I was there."

Chapter 3

Other than promising to call me at the hotel, Chico refused to say anything more and went out the gate to the street. It was still too early to attempt to awaken the somnolent Santiago, so I went to the Cadillac and waited, sweltering and slapping at flies, until Manuel unlocked the door.

Once he was satisfied that I'd locked the door before we were set upon by thugs and bugs, he said, "That is the kind of person I warned you about, Señora Malloy. There are many American expatriates in Mexico because the cost of living is low and they can afford their vices. That man should not be trusted. He would steal his grandmother's wheelchair for enough pesos to buy a bottle of cheap wine."

"He knows something, though," I said.

"He knows who he mugged on the beach last night."

"How old would you say he is?"

Manuel maneuvered out of the parking lot and drove down a curving road that, between onslaughts of trucks, provided a magnificent view of the ocean. "I cannot say. Where are you wishing to go now? Would you like to see La Quebrada, where the young men have been diving into the ocean since 1934? It is very exciting and dangerous. When the surf recedes, the water is only twelve feet deep, so they must time their dives in order—"

"Let's go to the newspaper office," I said. "Perhaps they'll have back copies from the time of the murder. It will be interesting to see if any of the other guests are named."

Once again I was treated to grumbles as we careened down the hill, bouncing over potholes and barely avoiding parked cars and children playing in the road. Manuel was beginning to remind me of Peter, with his stony expression and belligerent attitude. The charming difference was that Peter was in a position to hinder my virtuous, civic-minded attempts to assist the CID; in the past he'd gone so far as to order my car impounded, and, at his most heinous, had me dragged to the police station in the middle of the night for impeding his investigation. Manuel was in no such position.

"You speak English well," I said, feeling magnanimous.

"I worked on a California-based cruise ship for six years."

"How long have you worked for your brother-in-law?"

"For a year. He has the largest tourist agency in Acapulco, with many employees and luxurious cars such as this one. At first I washed cars and delivered our brochures to hotels, then I was given the job of driving the van to the airport. This is my first time to escort someone, which is why it is so important that nothing bad happens to you and the señorita. My brother-in-law has the temper of a bear. If you saw him, you might think he looks like one, too. He is very big and furry."

"Nothing bad is going to happen to us, Manuel. All I'm doing is asking questions about something that took place so long ago that most people have forgotten about it." I paused, thinking about the anonymous call. "When you phoned the people on the list I gave you yesterday, did you mention my name or where I'm staying?"

"No, I said only that you were an American reporter. The daughter of Emilio Zamora told me of his death and ended the conversation very abruptly. The man I spoke to in the prosecutor's office concerning Ruiz was not interested, nor was the *cabo* who told me when to call back to speak to the *comandante.* In the case of Pedro Benavides, I gave his secretary your name, but my office number in case the appointment must be canceled."

"What about the limousine driver named Jorge?"

"Señora, that is a very common first name in Mexico. When I was in school, I had many friends named Jorge. One of my cabin mates on the cruise ship was named Jorge. My landlady's dog is named Jorge. It is impossible to find this man, especially after thirty years."

"Nothing's impossible," I said. "Ask your brother-in-law what limousine companies were in business then, and I'll ask the same of Santiago. He may even remember which one Oliver Pickett preferred."

"As you wish," Manuel said darkly as he parked in front of a red and white building. "Here is the office of *Los Navedades de Acapulco.*"

"You'd better come with me in case I need a translator."

Manuel trailed behind me as I went into a small lobby. A few people sat on a bench, laboriously filling out forms. A receptionist in the rear glanced up at me, then resumed talking on a telephone. Behind a window was a larger room with desks, computers, and listless employees. The newsroom and presses were likely to be in the back of the building.

"Now what?" whispered Manuel.

"I want to know if they have a storage facility with newspapers from the first part of the year 1966. If they do, I'd like to look through them and make photocopies of relevant stories."

He looked as though I'd asked him to twirl around the lobby on his tippy-toes, but he went to the window and waited until a woman approached. While the two conversed in Spanish, I amused myself trying to translate signs on the wall. None of them appeared to be a menu, unless *anuncio* was a variety of burrito.

Manuel tapped me on the shoulder. "The lady says that *Los Navedades* has been in business only since 1969. *Tropico,* the newspaper at that time, is gone, and there is no way to locate old issues."

"Guacamole," I said morosely.

"So, it's almost noon. Will you have lunch with the señorita at the hotel? It's not so far from here. I will take you there, then return when it's time for the appointment with Benavides."

I nodded and went out to the car. It was ridiculous to feel so frustrated, I lectured myself as we drove down the boulevard. I'd known long before I left Farberville that the odds were minute that I'd find out anything whatsoever. The events had occurred when I was in fifth grade, playing kickball, reading Nancy Drew and Trixie Belden books, and fingerprinting my friends. Memories dimmed. Newspapers folded and judges died. Hotels turned into disreputable boarding houses.

And I had made some progress. I would interview Santiago after lunch, presuming he was amenable, and meet with the public defender later in the afternoon. It seemed likely that the pseudonymous Chico had been a guest at Las Floritas when the murder had taken place. Ronnie hadn't mentioned anyone else, but it sounded as if the hotel was booked to capacity during the high season. When she called me from Brussels, I would ask her if she remembered any other guests.

Manuel pulled into the Plaza. "I will come back at four o'clock, Señora," he said as a bellman opened my door.

"Does that give us time to go back to Las Floritas before the appointment?"

He winced. "I will come at three, then."

"Remember to ask your brother-in-law about the old limousine companies." I stopped in the lobby to convert larger bills to pesos, and took the elevator to the nineteenth floor. Caron was gone, as was one of her more modest bathing suits, her sandals, and her copy of *Bleak House*. There was no note; she must have assumed I was shrewd enough to put together the evidence.

Having done so in the twinkling of an eye, I called the desk to check for messages, then wended my way through the clothes strewn on the floor and went down to the bar in the lobby. It was one floor above the pool and the beach; I could hear children and music, but at a civilized distance. After I'd ordered a Bloody Mary, I gave serious thought to the phone call. Whoever had called knew not only my name and where I was staying, but also that I was accompanied by my daughter. Manuel had said he shared none of this information with those on the list; even if he'd let some of it slip (and was too abashed to admit it), all he'd been told before making the calls was that I wished to conduct an interview about an unspecified topic. How had this innocuous request stirred up such a panicky response?

I took Ronnie's notes from my purse and flipped through them in hopes that some remark would titillate my interest, but the only tickle came from the tabasco sauce in my drink.

Caron had not come back to the room by the time I went down to the lobby to meet Manuel. I wasn't worried about her. Having spotted the college boys in the lobby, she'd agreed to stay at the hotel, either at the pool or on the beach adjoining the terrace. Some of her more bizarre escapades had given her a healthy sense of circumspection when approached by strangers.

Manuel was talking to a bellman when I came down the steps. With an expression better suited to an IRS audit, he opened the passenger door for me. "Are we still returning to the Hotel Las Floritas? I told my brother-in-law, and he became upset. Three men have been killed there this year. Many prostitutes conduct business there."

"We'd better be on our way if we're going to be on time at Benavides's office," I said firmly. "It's the middle of the afternoon, for pity's sake. I wouldn't care to prowl around the grounds after dark, but nothing's going to happen at this hour. All I'm going to do is ask Santiago a few questions, pay him if he's cooperative, and leave. I would very much be surprised if Chico shows himself; if he does, I'll arrange another time to speak with him."

When we arrived in the parking lot, no one was loitering beneath the remains of the restaurant. I walked up to the lobby. Keeping an eye on the end of the porch, I knocked on the door, but neither Chico nor Santiago appeared.

I had no desire to keep coming up the steep, pocked road on the chance I'd catch Santiago—and it was possible that Manuel at some point would refuse to bring me. I took out a pad from the hotel and wrote a note promising Santiago fifty dollars if he called me, added my room number, signed it, and wedged it behind the doorknob.

We returned to the main boulevard and crawled through the traffic to a small, tidy building at the far end of the bay. I told Manuel he could wait in the car, then went into an urbanely bland reception room and announced myself to a young woman sitting behind a pristine desk.

"An appointment?" she said in a syrupy voice, brightening at this opportunity to display her petty power. "Señor Benavides is . . . *muy ocupado.* He has important clients arriving by yacht this afternoon."

"My assistant called yesterday and set up the appointment."

"And you are . . . ?"

"Claire Malloy."

She picked up the telephone receiver, murmured a few words, and looked at me with an insincere smile. "Señor Benavides will see you now, Señora. His office is at the end of the hallway."

Pedro Benavides stood up as I entered the room.

He had bronzed skin and black hair combed into a shiny pompadour and streaked with gray at the temples. He was not dressed to meet a yacht; his jacket hung on the back of his chair, his sleeves were rolled up, and his tie was loosened. Unlike the receptionist's desk, his was cluttered with leatherbound books, folders, and thick documents. All of the ornately carved mahogany furniture, including the wall-to-ceiling bookcases, hinted of money (in this case, pesos).

He came around the desk and extended his hand. "Señora Malloy? Welcome to my office. I'm not clear about the purpose of your visit, but I am always pleased to accommodate a reporter. How can I be of service?"

"I'd like to talk to you about Veronica Landonwood," I said, sitting in a padded chair and trying to assume a reporter's air of dogged diligence.

His cordiality evaporating, Benavides sank down in his chair and began to fiddle with a pen, his face lowered to hide his expression. "I was not prepared for this," he said at last. "If I had known that you wished to talk about her, I would not have agreed to be interviewed. What happened so long ago should not be awakened."

"Well, at least you remember the case," I said. "Would you like to know what happened to Veronica after she was released from prison?"

"I don't think so, Señora Malloy. Now, if you will excuse me, I have clients coming later this afternoon and I must make—"

"She petitioned the court to change her name, went on to college and medical school, and is a highly respected researcher." I gave him a moment to grasp all this, then added, "And she's being blackmailed."

"By whom?"

"That's what I'm trying to learn. The press coverage was so minimal that only someone who was involved in the incident would know enough to make a sufficiently threatening demand."

He took a silk handkerchief from his pocket and mopped his forehead. "Are you accusing me?"

"Why shouldn't I? You knew as much as anyone, if not more. You had copies of documents, and probably were informed when she was released from prison. You could have kept track of her over the years."

"I had no reason to do that. She was a client, not a close friend or relative. I did what I could to have her deported instead of sent to prison, but she'd confessed to the police. Perhaps if the issue of marijuana had not been brought up, the judge might have been more lenient. This was in the sixties, however, and Zamora was well known to be severe in drug-related cases. Her diary made her case much worse. Zamora was convinced she was a hardened slut who'd schemed to seduce this older man in his own bed, then changed her mind and killed him. Our system is different than yours. There is no jury or testimony from witnesses. The accused is not allowed to address the court. The judge reads the evidence and makes his decision based on what he believes to be the facts."

"What did you believe?"

"She confessed, so it made no difference what I believed. I spoke very little English at that time, and my office could not afford a translator. On a few occasions, I paid someone out of my own pocket, but

I had a wife, three children, and a small salary. I was assigned so many cases that I worked until midnight almost every night and returned to my office at dawn. Señorita Landonwood was withdrawn, unwilling or unable to answer my questions. I felt very sorry for her."

I'd nursed a degree of hostility toward him because I'd considered him responsible for Ronnie's incarceration. Now I realized how impossible his assignment had been. "Did you arrange for her to receive packages of food while she was in prison?"

"Yes, but not with my own money. Every month for eight years, I received a small sum from the United States. I used it to make sure the señorita had adequate food, bottled water, vitamins, and medicine. When the checks stopped, I inquired at the prison and learned she was no longer there. I assumed she'd left the country as quickly as possible."

"Who sent the money?"

"There was no name or return address on the envelope. The first one contained a terse note as to its purpose. After that, there was only the money."

"How strange," I said. "What about the postmark?"

Benavides shrugged. "I have no memory of it. Even if I had glanced at it, it would have meant nothing to me because I knew very little about your country."

"What happened to Franchesca Pickett, the victim's daughter? Ronnie told me that they were transported to the prison together, but never saw each other after that."

"She was found guilty of conspiracy because she helped to throw the body onto the rocks. Zamora was outraged that she would do that to her own father, and sentenced her to . . . I'm not sure, maybe four years. Her lawyer told me that her mother was determined to save her daughter from prison, and after the trial went back to the United States to find the necessary money to bribe certain parties. It's possible she succeeded; judges, prosecutors, and prison officials were paid no better than public defenders."

I was increasingly fond of good old Pedro. "This is the first link I've found to Fran's mother. What was the lawyer's name?"

He thought for a moment, then said, "Aurelio Perez, but he died of cancer some years ago."

"Oh," I said, my optimism deflating as quickly as it had inflated seconds earlier, as if I were a manic-depressive balloon.

"It is possible his files can be found," Benavides said. "As soon as I have time, I will call his firm and ask if they can locate them. However, this took place a long time ago, and it's unlikely he would have continued to save any records. Even if he had, his widow might have disposed of them." He stood up and again extended his hand. "I will do what I can, but I must prepare for my clients, who will be here shortly. My secretary or I will call you if I have any luck."

I shook his hand. "Thank you for your time, Señor Benavides."

I was halfway to the door when he said, "Why are you involved in this?"

"Because Veronica Landonwood paid for what she did. Oliver Pickett was attempting to rape her when she attacked him. In the United States, this would have been considered self-defense. Instead, she lost her parents and spent eight years in hell. She survived and got on with her life—and now someone's trying to take that away from her." I realized I was trembling and my voice was loud enough to be heard on the street. I took a deep breath. "Did you call me at my hotel last night, Señor Benavides?"

He was too unnerved by my outburst to do more than shake his head, and he was still doing it as I left his office. The reception room was uninhabited; the receptionist must have taken refuge in another room.

I certainly would have.

Manuel scrambled out of the car and opened the door for me. "Did you find out anything, Señora?"

"A few things, but not enough," I said. "It sounds as if Fran Pickett may have avoided much time in prison and returned to the United States. If Fran's mother is alive, she'll be in her late sixties or early seventies. Of course it's a bit tricky to locate her, since I don't know her last name or where she lives. Señor Benavides may be able to help me, but I doubt it. There's still Santiago, I suppose, and Chico."

"So we go back to the Hotel Las Floritas again? It is late in the day, Señora, and you were told Santiago starts drinking at noon. By now he cannot remember what he ate for lunch, much less things in the distant past. Would it not be better to sit and watch the sunset, listening to music and having something cool to drink?"

"I suppose it can wait until early tomorrow afternoon," I said, aware that I hadn't connected with Caron all day. "You may drop me off at the hotel, and pick me up at nine tomorrow morning. We'll start at the courthouse. If the records still exist, they'll be sealed, but maybe I can find out if someone managed to get copies of them."

"Very good," Manuel said unenthusiastically, clearly unwilling to take on the role of Dr. Watson. As we stopped in front of the hotel, he added, "Nine o'clock, then?"

I nodded, then climbed out of the car and left him to imagine the wrath that would be rained down on him by his ursine brother-in-law. As I went past the bellman's desk, I noticed that he was staring at me with an oddly curious expression. Wondering if Caron had done something to garner the animosity of the staff, I hurried toward the elevators.

"Señora Claire Malloy?" barked a voice.

I halted and turned around, but instead of an antagonistic hotel manager, I found myself confronting a policeman in a dark blue shirt and badge. The gun at his side looked more appropriate to a battlefield than the lobby of an expensive hotel.

"Yes?" I said warily, spotting his colleague nearby.

"You come with us," he said, his accent so thick that I could barely understand him.

"Why?"

"You come with us."

"I don't think so," I said as I assessed the distance to the elevators. The doors of one of them slid open, and two white-haired men in garish print shirts and shorts emerged, took in the scene, and scampered toward the bar like terrified bunnies. Before I could make my move, the doors slid closed. "I don't know what this is about, and I'm not going anywhere until I do."

He placed his hand on the holster of his weapon. "You come with us."

"No," I said, perhaps a bit shrilly. "Since that's how one says it in Spanish as well as English, you should have no difficulty understanding it."

"You are under arrest, Señora. You come with us."

"Under arrest for what? I haven't done anything the slightest bit illegal. I wasn't even driving a car, so you can't try to frame me for a traffic violation."

"You come with us."

The menace in his tone was getting harder and harder to overlook, and the second officer was edging toward me. The bartender, waiters, and customers were all watching with wonderment, as were the incoming guests at the front desk. I was unfamiliar with Mexican police procedure, but I wasn't confident I wouldn't be shot in the back if I fled.

I attempted a pinched smile. "Please explain what this is about, Señor. I'm sure there's been a mistake, and I prefer to clear it up right here."

"Señora Malloy!" called Manuel as he hurried across the lobby. "The bellman says the police . . ." He caught sight of my companions and froze in midstep.

"Are looking for me?" I suggested, so relieved to see him that I wanted to kiss his cheek. "As you can see, they've found me, but we're having a tiny problem communicating. Ask him what's wrong."

Manuel reluctantly joined us and began a low, incomprehensible exchange with the officer. The other joined in with much gesturing in my direction. Terrified that something had happened to Caron, I struggled to catch pertinent words, but they were all speaking so rapidly that only one made sense: *homicidio.*

I grabbed Manuel's arm. "What are they saying? Has someone been killed? Is my daughter all right? Damn it, what's going on, Manuel?"

"It does not concern the señorita. These officers want to question you about a homicide that took place today."

"Me?" I said numbly. "Who was murdered?"

"Ernesto Santiago. He was found in the lobby of the Hotel Las Floritas, with his throat slashed."

"I've never even seen him. Did you tell them that?"

He fluttered his hands. "Yes, but they insist you come with them to the *Ministerio Público*—the police headquarters. I do not know what to do, Señora. My brother-in-law will be so angry that he will slash my throat. This is a *pesadilla,* a nightmare. Why did I give up my job as a cabin steward? The tips were very good, and I had the opportunity to visit many ports. I—"

"This is not the time for vocational angst," I said, hoping it wasn't the time for handcuffs and cattle prods, either. "We both know I did not slash Santiago's throat. This is a misunderstanding that can be resolved as soon as I speak to an officer in charge." A dire thought popped into my mind. "If he speaks English, that is. Stop blubbering and listen, Manuel. I want you to find Caron out by the pool or on the beach, and tell her to stay in our suite with the door locked until she hears from me. Have her paged if necessary. She can order room service, but she is not to open the door to anyone else. Then come immediately to the police headquarters."

"Okay, okay," he said as sweat trickled down into his already watery eyes.

I made a face at the policemen. "Shall we go?"

Chapter 4

I was escorted to a cramped white car and thrust into the backseat, where the splattered upholstery suggested the past presence of gastrically challenged passengers. A barrier of scratched plastic precluded conversation with the officers in the front seat (had it seemed the polite thing to do). Apparently, I was not a worthy enough desperado to merit sirens and flashing lights, but although we drove only a dozen blocks before turning up a steep hill, I felt as though every tourist on the boulevard had seen me cowering in the backseat and judged me guilty of *homicidio,* or worse. Pedro Benavides's earlier remark resounded in my mind like a dirge: "Our system is different than yours."

The police headquarters consisted of a large walled compound with a hodgepodge of buildings, ancient trees, and parking areas. The walls were topped with barbed wire, the gate protected by armed guards. Cars and trucks were on racks beside what was presumably a mechanical shed. A one-story building with barred windows squatted beyond an expanse of cracked concrete; two guards sat at a table by the door, their weapons conspicuously displayed in front of them. Other officers lounged in the shade or stood in lines, receiving instructions.

Civilians were going in and out of the unimposing building into which I was taken. Unlike the Farberville police station, there was no front office with a pretention of welcome, but merely a vast, dingy room with benches for whispered conferences. Yellowed posters featured the visages of surly men. The pay telephones along one wall were all in use. Ceiling fans did little to disperse the sour odor of anxiety.

We continued into a small room with a table and a few chairs. The walls were bare, the floor filthy, the window covered with heavy mesh. The officer pointed at a chair and demanded a *pasaporte*. Having used a voter registration card as identification to enter the country, the best I could produce was my driver's license.

Once I was alone, I propped my head on my hands and attempted to assimilate what had happened. I'd been heading for the suite to see if Caron wanted to join me in the bar (for a virgin strawberry daiquiri that would cost as much as the real thing, but Ronnie was footing the bill), and now I was in a nasty little room waiting to be questioned about the murder of a man I'd never met. I could hardly call Peter and ask what he knew about the machinations of the Mexican legal system. If nothing else, he'd pitch a self-righteous fit, replete with I-told-you-so and I-warned-you-not-to-get-involved. Hardly productive. Calling Pedro Benavides made a lot more sense, but he was likely to be drinking martinis on a yacht. I desperately wanted to call Caron and make sure she was obeying my order. Any of the above would require a telephone or telepathic ability, neither of which I possessed.

After ten stressful minutes, a middle-aged man entered the room. He wore a short-sleeved dress shirt rather than a uniform, but he had the wintry demeanor I knew so well. His mustache was straight out of a movie, his complexion out of a pineapple advertisement.

He tossed my license on the table and addressed me in Spanish. I shrugged in response.

"My English is no good," he said, sounding not at all apologetic. "*Me llamo* Comandante Quiroz. I investigate the *homicidio* of Ernesto Santiago."

I decided to maintain the pose of magazine reporter, and had managed to communicate little else (I was never a champion charades player) when Manuel arrived. "Did you find Caron?" I asked him as he edged around the table, staring fearfully at the comandante.

"Yes, she was by the pool. She said she will do as told. She also said several things about the food, but perhaps they are irrelevant at this time."

"I should think so," I said. "Now will you please tell the officer the purpose of my presence in Acapulco? Reporters do not murder the people they wish to interview—and I never made contact with Santiago."

Manuel and the comandante took off in Spanish. I listened for a while, picking out a key word now and then, but finally gave up and let their voices swirl around me like the vicious Santa Ana wind that torments California. At one point, the comandante slammed his fist on the table, and Manuel whimpered a reply. It was not encouraging. Oliver Pickett's and Ernesto Santiago's names were mentioned several times, as well as that of the Hotel Las Floritas. When Manuel mentioned Chico, the comandante shook his head and growled like a mastiff.

Finally the comandante quieted down. Manuel looked at me. "Late this afternoon they had a tip that someone had been murdered in what was once the lobby of the Hotel Las Floritas. They discovered Santiago's body. They also found a note with your name and an offer of money."

"Behind the doorknob," I said, trying not to glare at Comandante Quiroz.

"They found it under the body," Manuel said in a squeaky voice. "It had blood on it. They think Santiago called you and set up a meeting. For some reason, maybe related to a drug deal, you killed him. *El pesquisidor*—I don't know in English—has determined that Santiago died only a few hours ago. I had to tell the comandante that I took you back to the Plaza at noon and did not return until three o'clock."

"And during that period I went to the hotel and killed him? That's ludicrous, Manuel. Does he think I took a cab—or hijacked a horse and buggy to get there? Did the bellman carelessly fail to notice the blood on my clothes when I returned? Wouldn't the people by the pool have said something if they'd watched me scale nineteen stories?"

"What about the note, Señora?"

I explained, then watched Comandante Quiroz's expression as Manuel translated what I'd said. It eased only marginally, but he was less emphatic as he launched into another spate of Spanish. Manuel responded as best he could, but his voice was increasingly hoarse and his hands were so tightly clenched that his knuckles were apt to burst through his skin. I wondered if Ronnie had felt the same apprehension when she watched Pedro Benavides plead for leniency.

"You told me there have been three murders at the hotel this year," I inserted when I had the opportunity. "Doesn't it seem more likely that one of the criminals who lives there killed Santiago? What about Chico or the prostitutes or their pimp?"

"He says when the *cabos* arrived, all of the bungalows had been vacated. Those who live there are like cockroaches. Blue lights send them scuttling into the *Sona Roja.* Only when the lights go away will they return. He does want you to describe this American who was living there, however."

After further disjointed communication, Comandante Quiroz admitted that the only evidence they had was the note—and, yes, it was possible that someone else had taken it inside the lobby. I offered to allow him to search the suite at the Plaza for bloodied clothes or a knife, as long as Manuel, the hotel manager, and I were present. He appeared to be so unimpressed with my generosity that I decided search warrants were less than obligatory in Mexico, if the concept existed at all.

I was on the verge of demanding to call the American consulate when the comandante stood up, lectured Manuel with such intensity that spittle flew out of his mouth, then gave me a parting scowl and left the room.

Manuel gulped. "Let's go, Señora. The comandante says you must make yourself available until you have permission from the *Ministerio Público* to leave the country. They will try to find this Chico; if they do, you and I both will be required to identify him."

"That could take days," I said as I grabbed my purse and headed for the door. "Or weeks, or years. What if he hopped on a bus for Mexico City to lose himself among twenty million people? This is a lovely place, Manuel, but I wouldn't want to live here for the rest of my life."

He steered me through the front room and out into the blessed evening breeze. Without speaking, we hurried past the smirky guards at the gates of the compound. The Cadillac was parked several blocks up the hill, and I was gasping for breath as I dove into the front seat. Manuel jammed in the ignition key, backed into the street, and sent the car squealing around the corner as if we'd just held up the neighborhood tequila store.

Eventually, he eased up on the accelerator, but his hands were still gripping the steering wheel hard enough to leave indentations. "I myself have no influence here in Acapulco. I will take you to the hotel, then go to the office and speak to my brother-in-law. He knows politicians and men of wealth. Many of them rely on his discretion when they wish to have companions other than their wives. He will do what he can."

"Thank you," I murmured. I couldn't decide if my head was more likely to explode or implode, but I was certain my blood pressure exceeded the sum of the temperature and the humidity, with the price of the suite thrown in for good measure. Twenty-four hours earlier I'd been threatened on the telephone. Had the caller attempted to frame me for murder? Ronnie's would-be blackmailer had stirred up the embers of the case, but it seemed I'd incited a first-class inferno.

"Are you okay, Señora?" asked Manuel. "Your face is very white."

"No, I'm not okay. I've put myself into an exceedingly awkward position—and I've put my daughter in a dangerous one. How soon can she get a flight to the States?"

"There are no more flights today. The first one in the morning is shortly after nine o'clock. I will call to find out if there is a seat for her. If there is, I will drive her to the airport and stay with her until she is on the airplane. It would not be wise for you to be seen at the airport, Señora. Comandante Quiroz will have men there, watching for you."

He agreed to call me as soon as he'd called the airlines. Regally ignoring the stares of the Plaza staff, I took the elevator upstairs and knocked on the suite door. Several seconds passed during which I assumed I was being scrutinized through the peephole in case I was a skillfully disguised homicidal maniac.

I'd found my key when the door opened and Caron dragged me into the room. "What Is Going On?" she demanded. "All Manuel would tell me was that you'd been taken to the police station. I have been sitting here for Three Hours, fully expecting to be arrested by hairy goons with machine guns. They'd take me away to prison and nobody would ever know what happened to me!"

I hugged her until she calmed down, then went into the bedroom and fell across the nearest bed. It was quite a bit softer than a cot in a clammy cell. When Caron sat down on the other bed, I told her everything that had happened.

"Yuck," she said, capturing my sentiments as well. "Why don't we have Manuel drive us to another town with an airport?"

"I'd still have to show identification at the airline counter, and it might set off all kinds of alarms. The last thing I want to do is cross Comandante Quiroz."

"What if they can't find this guy?"

"I'll send you a postcard every week and learn how to say 'bookstore' in Spanish. In the meantime, let's order dinner from room service. I need to stay here in case Manuel calls with the airline particulars."

"I don't want to leave you here by yourself."

Surprised by her concern for anything other than her hide, I sat up and presented persuasive arguments until she agreed to leave on the morning flight. I called room service, took a shower, and was drying my hair in the bathroom when the telephone rang.

"It's probably Manuel," I called to Caron. "Be sure and find out what time he's picking you up in the morning."

A moment later she called back, "It's not Manuel, Mother, but some man who won't give his name."

I went into the bedroom and took the receiver from her. "Who is this?"

"I don't think it's wise to mention names. Why don't you call me Prince Charming?"

"Brother Grimm might be more accurate," I said, recognizing Chico's voice. "What do you know about Santiago's murder?"

"What's it worth to you?"

"Meet me in the lobby bar and we'll negotiate a fee based on what you know."

"That's a poor idea, Claire. It's been made known

to me that the police are looking for me. As flattering as that may be, I'm not eager for them to find me. I've avoided making their acquaintance thus far. From what I've been told, the cells at the *Ministerio Público* are overcrowded, and the prison proper is not at all the sort of place to relax and catch up on one's reading."

If he'd been in the room, I would have clobbered him with the hair dryer. Reminding myself that he might be a crucial figure in both Oliver Pickett's case and Santiago's murder, I said, "Then where do you suggest we meet?"

"Why don't you go down to the bar in your hotel at midnight? Have a drink, listen to the band, chat with the salesmen from Los Angeles and their wives. After a while, take the stairs down to the ground floor and go for a stroll along the beach. If I can be certain you're not being followed, I'll join you."

"So you can cut my throat? I'm willing to talk to you, Chico, but I'm not going to risk my life to do it." I glanced up and saw Caron in the doorway, her eyes round with dismay and her lower lip extended so far she resembled a small, wan camel. I gestured for her to go into the living room, then said, "Any other brilliant suggestions?"

"This is what is called a Mexican standoff, I believe. It's much too risky for me to be seen with you in public; Quiroz has a squad of undercover men at his disposal, and he's likely to have assigned some of them to follow you. Then again, I'm not your typical tourist, and I understand your reluctance to meet me in a desolate spot."

"That's perceptive."

"Well, allow me to think about all this. How much longer will you and your daughter be in Acapulco?"

"I'll be here until Comandante Quiroz gives me permission to leave," I said levelly. "My daughter is leaving on the next flight. She'll be under constant protection until she's on board the plane, so don't get any stupid ideas. I quite agree with you that there are undercover police officers in the hotel—and I gave them a very detailed description of you."

"Hasta la vista."

I called room service to add a bottle of scotch to the order, plumped the pillows, and made myself think. Chico knew that I was poking around the Oliver Pickett case and wanted to interview Santiago. Pedro Benavides had learned of my objectives late in the afternoon, when the police were already at the crime scene. I hadn't spoken to anyone else on my original list. The Hotel Las Floritas was a veritable haven of iniquity, but it was impossible to ignore the fact that Santiago, who'd been surviving for better or worse for thirty years, was murdered on the very day I knocked on his door. Chico was seeming less and less an innocent observer, I concluded as I listened to Caron respond to the arrival of room service.

It consisted of a squealed: "You call this a taco? Don't you people know how to fix Mexican food? Where's the sour cream?"

For some reason, I found this infinitely comforting.

At seven-thirty the following morning, the bellman escorted Caron and her suitcases down to the lobby. Although I was reluctant to say goodbye in the suite,

I had no desire for Quiroz's men to spot me alongside a luggage cart, heading for the Cadillac. A misunderstanding on their side might well lead to another distasteful session at the police compound.

Manuel had thought he would be back at the Acapulco Plaza by ten—if the flight left on time. He'd sounded doubtful. I called Inez's mother and asked her to pick Caron up at the airport, paced, listened to CNN, and bawled out the room service waiter when the coffee took forever to arrive. I stood on the balcony, watching sun worshippers court skin cancer and suicidal parasailors being towed through the sky. I contemplated dropping ice cubes on the children in the swimming pool. I tried to read, but the book might as well have been written in Spanish.

When the telephone rang, I snatched up the receiver, hoping Manuel was calling to report that Caron had left. It was not Manuel . . . or Ronnie . . . or even Chico.

"So, how's it going?" Peter said.

"The hotel's lovely, and the weather is ideal. How's everything in Farberville?"

"Oh, everything's fine *here.* Tell me how your investigation is coming."

There was an edge to his voice that caused the coffee in my stomach to slosh. "I've spoken to a few key people," I said, "but I'll tell you all about it when I get home. I wouldn't want to burden the CID's long-distance bill with a lot of irrelevant chatter. By the way, Caron decided to fly home today so she won't miss the homecoming game festivities. She's remarkably unpredictable, isn't she? I'd assumed she would have been thrilled to lie by the pool and read—"

"Then you've done one intelligent thing since you arrived there."

"What's that supposed to mean?" I said, feigning indignation while I tried to guess what was coming next.

"I have in my hand a printout of a query passed on to us from the National Crime Information Center. It's from a law enforcement agent named Quiroz, who would like to know if you have a criminal record or a history of mentally disturbed behavior. I haven't decided how to reply, but it's possible I'll say yes to both."

"That may not be a good idea," I muttered. In the ensuing silence, I could easily imagine his expression, and almost hear his teeth grinding. "Comandante Quiroz has this absurd idea that I was involved in some unpleasantness yesterday. I wasn't, of course, and as soon as the suspect is taken into custody, I'll leave."

"You're under house arrest?"

I forced out an incredulous laugh. "Heavens, no. He politely asked me to stay in Acapulco so that I can identify the suspect. I'm just cooperating in order to foster international goodwill."

"Sort of a one-woman Olympic team? If the event you've entered has anything to do with meddling in a murder investigation, you're likely to bring home the gold medal."

"Or the silver," I said modestly.

Peter's voice flattened. "Do you need me to fly down there, Claire? Things are hectic around here, but I can take a couple of days of sick leave. Getting involved with the police down there can mean serious trouble."

"No, I can handle this. If Quiroz gets ugly, I'll hire a lawyer." I changed the subject to a more intimate one, and after a few endearments from both ends, I promised to call him in the evening with what would surely be a lengthy accounting of the situation.

Noon came and went without a communiqué from Manuel. I called the local office of the airline, and after being put on hold for ten minutes while an agent who spoke English was located, learned only that the nine o'clock flight had taken off on time—except for an unspecified delay due to mechanical problems. The list of passengers could not be revealed under any circumstances. I pointed out it was a little late to plant a bomb or arrange for a hijacking. The agent terminated the call.

By midafternoon I'd left furrows in the carpet from pacing and I could no longer understand the CNN reporters as they dithered about trivial issues like wars and floods. Caron had promised to call me from the Dallas airport if she had time between gate changes, but even if she hadn't, she should have arrived in Farberville an hour earlier. It was not likely that Manuel had been recruited by the maintenance crew and was at the airport gluing on wings. If I took a cab to the airport, I might be arrested as a fugitive.

I realized that if I remained in the room, I was in danger of losing my mind and leaping off the balcony. This would not be good, even if I landed in the pool. Manuel had given me a business card when we'd met; I dug it out of my purse, gave the telephone one last chance to ring, and went down to the lobby.

There were some rowdy vacationers in the bar, and several couples seated on the wicker furniture. No one leapt to his feet and pointed an accusatory finger at me, but I could sense that my infamy had spread throughout the hotel. I hurried out to the curb and asked the bellman to summon a cab. As I waited, I noticed two men in plaid shirts and khaki trousers come out of the lobby and stroll toward a dirty black car that did not blend in well with the line of limousines, vans, and expensive cars favored by the hotel's clientele. In that Chico might be cowering behind the foliage, I did not object to what I surmised was an official tail. It occurred to me that if Chico called again, I could agree to meet him, and tip off Comandante Quiroz. An affront to my integrity, disloyal to a fellow national—but also the most expedient way to catch the next flight to Farberville.

I gave the cab driver the address of Farias Tourist Agency, sat back, and tried not to speculate about the whereabouts of Caron and Manuel.

We drove down the familiar boulevard, then along a winding road into the mountains. There were pockets of poverty interspersed between modest middle-class neighborhoods. Any tourist on the street was there because he or she was lost; this was not the Acapulco in the travel guides and slick brochures.

"How much farther?" I asked the driver.

"Not far," he said cheerfully. There was no meter in the cab, but I could hear one ticking in his head as he continued to navigate sharp turns, double-parked trucks, and debris from construction projects.

Fifteen minutes later, I was about to repeat my question when he turned through into a compound at least as large and complex as that of the police. Parked irregularly around the various buildings, however, were Cadillacs, Lincolns, and limousines of both unassuming and outrageous lengths.

We stopped in front of what might have been a humble family home, complete with a porch bedecked with flower pots and curtains at the windows. A pretty young woman in a white sundress came outside as I gathered my courage to inquire about the fare. She squinted at me, then gestured for the cab driver to roll down his window.

After a short discussion in which the Acapulco Plaza was the only phrase I caught, she said to me, "May I help you, Señora?"

"I hope so," I said. "I'm Claire Malloy, and Manuel Estoban has been driving me for the last three days. A problem has arisen, I'm afraid, and I need to talk to his employer. Would you please ask this gentleman about the fare?"

Their exchange suggested that the driver had been planning to engage in a contemporary version of highway robbery. Finally they arrived at a compromise. I handed over a thick wad of pesos and climbed out of the cab.

"Should I have him wait?" I asked the woman.

"Oh, no, someone from the agency will take you back when you are ready. This is most extraordinary that a client should come here, Señora Malloy. Has Manuel done something to make you so angry with him that . . . ?" Her brown shoulders rippled as she gave me a weak smile. "He is the last of many children, and his oldest sister is my mother. He and I grew up together and we are close. My father will be unhappy if you have a complaint."

"I have no desire to get Manuel in trouble," I said,

noting the black car parked by the gate. "Shall we go inside so that I can explain what's happened?"

"Yes, of course. I am Gabriella Farias."

I followed her into the front room, which was crowded with two desks and numerous filing cabinets. Religious paintings hung beside framed licenses and family photographs. At one desk, a middle-aged woman with bright orange hair snarled into a telephone receiver. Someone in an adjoining room was typing at an admirable pace; a boy who was ten or eleven years old dashed into the room to drop an armload of folders on top of a cabinet, then dashed away. It was by far the busiest place I'd visited in Acapulco.

"We have just begun the high season," Gabriella said. "Many tourists are arriving every day, and we try our best to accommodate them, even when they have changed their plans at the last minute. We are very proud of our reputation."

"I'd like to speak to Señor Farias," I said.

"One moment, please." She went through a doorway.

I sat down on a scratchy sofa and waited, less and less sure of what I hoped to accomplish by facing Manuel's purportedly ruthless brother-in-law. If I'd been a more religious person, I might have attempted to communicate with the dewy-eyed depiction of the Virgin Mary regarding me across the room. When Gabriella returned, I said, "Before I speak to Señor Farias, would you please call my hotel and ask the switchboard if I have a message from Manuel?"

She flipped through a Rolodex, dialed a number, and spoke in a low voice. "A person named Dr. Gray called, but that is all," she said as she replaced the receiver. "My father will speak with you in his office, where it is quieter. Will you be so kind as to come with me?"

Señor Farias did not rise as I entered his office, but I was not offended. He was so obese that standing up might have required assistance, as well as life-endangering exertion. Small dark eyes and a feminine mouth were almost lost in folds of fat, and his jowls hung beneath his jaw. Thin black hair covered his scalp like a shoddy paint job. He wore a short-sleeved shirt, exposing lower arms thicker than hams and pudgy fingers adorned with rings. The top three buttons of his shirt were open; the visible expanse was as hairy as Manuel had sworn. I decided it was daring of him to risk involuntary depilation by wearing gold chains. Apparently, he did not share my concern.

He waved at a chair. "Please sit down, Señora Malloy, and tell me what is wrong that has led you to come here. If Manuel has done something to upset you, we have many other escorts available. I will gladly assign another driver, and upgrade you to a limousine at no extra charge. We are at your service."

I sat down, a bit puzzled by the contrast between his words and the hostility he was scarcely able to conceal. I could tell from Gabriella's sudden intake of breath that she too was aware of his forced smile and slitted eyes.

"No, I'm not upset with Manuel," I said. "He's done a splendid job thus far. Last night he arranged for my daughter to take the first morning flight out of the country. He picked her up at the hotel at seven-thirty, and I've not heard from either of them since then. Has your office heard from him?"

"I will find out," Gabriella said.

Farias waited until the door closed. "My daughter is very efficient. One day I will retire and she will take over the agency. Already she is talking about opening offices in Ixtapa and Puerto Escondido."

I was not interested in the Farias family fortune. "Is it like Manuel not to stay in touch with you?"

"If he had car trouble, he should have reported it to us so we could send another vehicle immediately. Never has a client missed a flight due to incompetency on the part of Farias Tourist Agency. He has standing orders to check in every three hours. I agree that you and I both should have heard from him long before now."

"Did he tell you what happened yesterday with the police?"

Nodding curtly, he said, "He did. I know Comandante Quiroz's supervisor. I have already left a message for him to call me as soon as he arrives back from an appointment in Chilpancingo. He will see that you are allowed to leave at your convenience. Quiroz is taking this case much too seriously. Santiago was a pimp and known to deal in drugs. It's not important that his murderer is brought to trial."

"I'm sorry that you've been asked to use your influence, Señor Farias," I said, wishing I could dimple disarmingly at him.

The door behind me opened.

"Papa," said Gabriella, "we have trouble."

I barely heard her, in that I was mesmerized by the purple birthmark on his neck.

Chapter 5

"What is it, Gabriella?" demanded Farias.

"I called Manuel's apartment. When there was no answer, I called his landlady and asked her to check on him." She pressed her hands together and touched her fingertips to her chin as if to steady it. "Manuel has been hurt. She has already called for an ambulance, Papa. We must go to the hospital now."

It took a few seconds for the implication of what she'd said to sink in. "What's going on?" I said as I shoved myself out of the chair and took a step toward her. I tried to blurt out another question, but all I could do was stare at her as if I were in icy water and she had the only life jacket.

"Manuel is unconscious. He suffered a bad head wound, and his hands and ankles were secured with wire. The Cadillac is not parked in the garage where he keeps it when he needs it early in the morning."

"What about Caron?"

"I do not know," she said. "Papa?"

Farias reached for the telephone and jabbed at the buttons as though squashing ants. He muttered rapidly in Spanish, spat out what I assumed was an oath, and slammed down the receiver. "This morning shortly before seven-thirty a Cadillac with our insignia appeared at the Plaza. The bell captain did not recognize the driver, but assumed we'd hired a new man. The señorita's luggage was placed in the trunk, and she was driven away."

The walls and ceiling closed in, expelling all the oxygen and light. My eyes flew open when I felt something cold on my forehead, and I looked up to see Gabriella with a washcloth in her hand. I realized I'd fallen back into the chair hard enough to cause my ears to ring. "We have to find Caron," I said. "Call the police."

Farias had made it to his feet and was tucking a gun under his belt. "No, that may not be wise," he rumbled as he put on a white jacket and straw hat, then picked up a walking stick with a brass knob. "Gabriella, have Tomas bring around my car. Tell Alfredo to stand guard at the hospital. Juan Federico is to go to Manuel's apartment and wait there. Have Aurora call the airline and determine if Miss Malloy was on the morning flight."

Gabriella ran out of the room. I took a few measured breaths, then stood up. The move was premature, and only Farias's grip on my arm kept me from doing further damage to my head.

"We will find the señorita," he said. "I will consider her as my own daughter, and deal with the bastard accordingly. There is no place he can hide in all of Acapulco."

"Are you sure?" I said as I allowed him to guide me out to the porch. In the compound, car engines were coming to life and armed men were darting about. For a dazed moment, I felt as though I was at the *Ministerio Público* as the riot squad prepared for a fray.

"I am sure." He took my elbow and helped me down the stairs as a grandiose silver limousine pulled up in front of us. He opened the door, waited until I'd climbed in, then wedged himself through the doorway with a few muffled grunts. "I know not only our esteemed mayor and honorable public servants, but also the bartenders in the *Sona Rosa,* the drug dealers, the pimps, and most importantly, those who will betray their acquaintances for a bottle of mescal." He leaned forward and opened a cabinet. "You must have a drink of brandy to calm yourself Señora."

I accepted a snifter as Gabriella got into the front seat, which seemed to be miles away from our broad leather throne. The limousine rolled out of the gate. Farias and I were obscured behind the tinted windows, but my two watchdogs must have seen us come out of the office. In any case, they fell into line behind us.

"*Agentes de policía,*" announced the driver.

"Let them come along," Farias said without interest. "It is like Quiroz to be more worried about you than this man called Chico. Manuel's description was not good. If you will tell me what you remember of him, I will see what can be learned about him."

"He's about six feet tall, emaciated, with a yellowish complexion, stained teeth, frizzy gray hair pulled back in a ponytail, and a wispy mustache," I said. "You might have met him in the past, Señor Farias. He claimed to have been a guest at the Hotel Las Floritas thirty years ago."

"I can assure you I was not a guest at Hotel Las

Floritas thirty years ago. My salary was so small that I could not have afforded a drink in the bar."

"I didn't mean to imply you were a guest,' I said, watching him. He stared straight ahead, his expression as unruffled as that of a concrete frog in a rock garden. I wasn't sure he'd react if I emptied the snifter in his lap, but I took my best metaphorical shot. "What I meant was that you might have driven him around Acapulco in the same manner you drove Fran Pickett and Ronnie Landonwood."

"So you have made the connection. Very good, Señora. Manuel seemed to think you were a little loco, but I see now that he underestimated you. I will not make the same mistake." He opened yet another cabinet and took out a cellular phone. "Please excuse me while I speak to Aurora."

The limousine was slicing through the traffic like a silvery shark, never braking in deference to potential hazards. Outside, horns were blaring, machinery grinding, dogs yapping, children shouting; inside, there were only the sounds of Farias's low voice and the gentle drone of the engine. I could see Gabriella's mouth moving and her hands fluttering as she spoke to the driver, but the partition muted her words.

The brandy was apt to be expensive, but it burned my throat and left an acidic taste in my mouth. Jorge Farias's sinister declaration that no one could elude him had kept me a few feet away from the brink of hysteria, but no farther than that. Chico had seen the agency Cadillac at the Hotel Las Floritas; a few pesos might have persuaded a bellman at the Plaza to provide Manuel's name. I'd been the one who told him that Caron was leaving on the next flight. Such a strong flood of loathing came over me that I almost doubled over on the seat. The previous day he'd irritated me; now I would have succumbed to a primitive instinct and gone for his carotid artery.

Farias set the telephone on his knee. "Your daughter was not on the flight to Dallas. Please be so kind as to repeat everything you can of your conversations with Chico."

I recounted what I could, feeling as if I were feeding data into a massive computer. Only when I mentioned the hookers from Honduras did Farias's eyes flicker.

"There are not so many women from Honduras," he said as he retrieved the telephone. "Let us find out where they are at the moment, and what they know about Chico."

"The one thing I know is that he's desperate for money in order to get out of Mexico before the police arrest him," I said. "I'm dreadfully sorry about Manuel, but I'd better go back to the hotel and wait for Chico to call with his ransom demand."

He considered this, then nodded. "Yes, that is best. Gabriella will stay with you so that she can keep me informed. After I go to the hospital, I will continue to the *Sona Rosa* to speak with those who are indebted to me. It is not so easy to conceal a Cadillac in an alley or behind a bar, or even up in the hills in one of the villages. You would have equal difficulty concealing a burro in your town, yes?"

"I suppose so." I gazed out the window as Farias made another call, forcing myself to review everything from Ronnie's first call to the present. When he snapped the phone closed, I said, "You must have realized I wanted to talk to you about the Oliver Pickett murder. Manuel certainly did; he was very careful not to mention your name when he was trying to convince me of the futility of finding a man named Jorge. He did drop something about how you'd described the parking lot of the Hotel Las Floritas in its halcyon days, but I failed to pick up on it at the time."

"It was a long time ago."

"Yes, it was," I said, "but it was not a minor incident that would be easily forgotten. You spent a great deal of time with the two girls, driving them to bars, waiting in the car while they swam at the beach, listening to them while they talked in the backseat. You weren't much older than they were, and from what I was told, you had a crush on Fran Pickett. You were at their New Year's Eve party when Oliver barged in and threw everyone out, weren't you?"

"I knew at the time it was risky to be there, but Fran was very determined to have her way. Early that night after Señor Pickett and the others left, she sent me to buy cases of beer and tequila. By the time I returned, there was much marijuana smoke and loud music. Santiago came to the bungalow several times to beg her to be discreet, but she laughed at him. She went into the bedroom with many different men that night." He paused to pour himself a scant inch of brandy. "She told me things about her life. When she was with her mother, she was made to be a prim schoolgirl, to wear a modest uniform, to braid her hair, to take music and sewing lessons from the sisters at the convent school. Many times when she was supposed to visit her father, her mother would find an excuse to refuse to allow her to go. Her father was not so dependable, either. He would tell her she could come, then at the last minute call to tell her he had other plans. It was all very difficult for her."

Gabriella pushed back the partition. "Papa, I have spoken with someone at the hospital. Manuel has been taken to the X-ray room for tests."

Farias sighed. "This Chico is a dangerous man, Señora. I agree that he will call you to demand money in exchange for releasing the señorita. It would be foolish of you to meet him without allowing me to arrange for your protection. He has little to lose by committing another murder, and if Manuel does not survive, you will be the only person who can identify Chico. You and your daughter, that is."

I averted my face and bit down fiercely on my lip. Farias handed me a handkerchief, then tactfully shifted his attention to the uninspiring scenery along the street. There was no way to put any of this in perspective, I told myself as I dabbed my eyes. The only perspective was the buck-naked reality: Caron had been kidnapped by a man who might be a murderer. Who he was and how he fit into the scenario was impossible to determine. My responsibility, on the other hand, rang as loudly as the bells in the Farber College campanile.

I crossed my fingers. "Okay, I won't go rushing off to meet Chico, even with Comandante Quiroz's men behind me."

"I will deal with them," Farias said. "Should we feel it necessary, something will happen to divert them long enough for you and Gabriella to slip away."

"What happened after you and Fran slipped away from the confrontation with Oliver Pickett?" I asked abruptly.

Farias's face darkened as if he were an erumpent volcano. He was neither smoldering nor belching sulphurous fumes, but it was obvious I'd floundered onto something he found distressing. "He ordered me to leave. Everyone else disappeared like sand fleas, but I sat in the limousine in the parking lot, praying to all the saints I could think of that I would have my job in the morning. Fran came stumbling down the path and got into the car. She told me to drive along the beach, which I did while she cried and said many harsh things about her father. Most of what she said was in English, but I could tell how angry she was and I made no attempt to converse with her. Eventually, when we had driven for fifteen or maybe twenty minutes, she remembered that Ronnie was asleep in the bedroom and told me to go back to the hotel. I was too cowardly to do more than watch her go up the path before I drove away."

"Oliver and his entourage weren't relying on you for transportation that night," I said. "How did he get back to the hotel?"

"There was a taxi idling in the parking lot. Santiago's rule was that those taxis hoping for a fare had to line up out on the street until signaled by the concierge. The fact that this one was inside the gate indicated to me that the driver had brought a passenger there and been instructed to wait."

"If the passenger was Oliver, the driver should have still been there yesterday," I said as the limousine pulled to the curb in front of the Acapulco Plaza.

I fidgeted on the sidewalk while Farias issued instructions to Gabriella, who then joined me as the limousine sped away.

"I guess there is nothing I can do at the hospital,"

she said sadly. "Manuel will be heavily sedated until the morning. My mother has made sure family members will be there throughout the night, and Alfredo will remain outside Manuel's room. I am so sorry about your daughter, Señora Malloy. Papa will find her."

I once again had to bite my lip to hold back tears. "I'm sure he will," I said as we walked past the jewelry shops and designer boutiques. The pair of undercover officers followed at a circumspect distance, looking so incongruous in the expensive surroundings that I was surprised they weren't challenged by a hotel security guard.

"I'm going straight to the room," I said to Gabriella. "Will you please go by the front desk and find out if there are any messages or packages?"

For the first time since we'd arrived two days ago, I had the elevator to myself. As I unlocked the door of the suite, I noticed that I'd inadvertently left the DO NOT DISTURB sign on the knob. The maid had abided by it; the trays from room service were piling up and the leftover food was beginning to ripen. I was considering the logistics of moving everything out to the hall when the telephone rang.

I answered it with a terse, "Yes?"

Chico's voice was even oilier than I remembered. "So, you're finally back, Claire Malloy. I've been calling every few minutes for three hours."

"Let me speak to my daughter."

"That's not possible at the moment. She has quite a vocabulary for one so young, doesn't she? I finally grew tired of her incessant complaints and put tape across her mouth. I can assure you that she is surviving, if not thriving. How much cash do you have?"

"Close to five hundred American dollars and maybe

a hundred dollars' worth of pesos. Please let me speak to Caron for one minute."

"Are you alone?"

I glanced at the door. "At the moment, yes."

"Take the stairwell to the ground floor. When you get to the beach, turn left and walk to the El Presidente Hotel. Go through the lobby, get a cab, and tell the driver you wish to go to Calle Madero 124. There is a bar there, although not as nice as the one in your hotel. Sit down and order a drink. If you are unaccompanied, you will receive further instructions—but if there is the slightest indication that the police or anyone else is with you . . . well, use your imagination."

I replaced the receiver, scribbled the address he'd given me, and grabbed my purse. The hallway was empty. As I skittered down the stairs with all the grace of a ping-pong ball, I tried to convince myself that I was doing the right thing. My promise to Jorge Farias was irrelevant when placed alongside Chico's threat to harm Caron.

The sun was setting as I hurried past the pool and down the steps to the sand. The beach was populated by a few sunbathers, most of whom were packing towels, paperback books, and suntan lotion into mesh bags. I glanced back at the Acapulco Plaza, but no one appeared to be following me. By now, Gabriella no doubt had discovered that I was not in the suite and was on a phone with her father, who would not be happy with either of us. I didn't care.

I forced myself to walk at a more decorous rate through the lobby of the El Presidente to the sidewalk. As at the Plaza, taxis were waiting. I climbed into the backseat of the nearest one, uncrumpled the piece of paper in my hand, and told the driver the address.

"Not so good a neighborhood," he said, clucking his tongue. "I know many nice restaurants where the señora can have a margarita and listen to music."

I repeated the address with enough urgency to convince him to pull away from the curb. Manuel had been correct when he accused me of being a little loco, I decided as I hunted through my purse for a potential weapon. The best I could come up with was a bent nail file; it would hardly suffice if Chico pulled out a knife.

The narrow streets were unfamiliar, but I was aware we were headed toward the vicinity of the Hotel Las Floritas. Surely Chico was not so brazen as to return there the day after the murder, when the police might be keeping it under surveillance. Surely not.

The taxi driver slowed down, peering at numbers above doorways in the increasing gloom. "Señora," he said, "I do not think you should come here by yourself. Please let me take you back down to Costera Miguel Aleman, where there are many safe places to eat and drink. You will not have to pay me anything."

"The address I gave you is that of a bar," I said. "Could that be it up there on the left?"

He pulled up in front of an open doorway through which loud Latino music blared. A woman in a tight dress that exposed considerable cleavage and covered only the tops of her thighs staggered out onto the sidewalk, braying with laughter. A man came after her and nudged her into an alley. Inside the dim, smoky barroom I could see faceless figures shifting like shadows on an uneven wall. A group of men played cards at a table beneath a flickering lightbulb. A young man came to the doorway, lit a cigarette, then gave me a cool look before retreating. All in all, it lacked the sanitized ambiance of the bar at the Acapulco Plaza.

I took out my wallet, but the driver held up his hand. "No, Señora, I will accept no money to bring you here."

"Thanks," I said as I got out of the taxi and waited until he drove up the hill. There were no vehicles approaching from either direction; I was on my own—and a lot loco.

The interior of the bar smelled like a restroom at a grungy gas station. My entrance garnered only fleeting curiosity; the business of the hour was drinking. I eased into a chair in the corner of the room and scanned the faces for that of Chico. I didn't spot him, but if he'd shaved off his mustache, cut his hair, and changed into less disreputable clothes, I might not have recognized him.

A woman in a stained apron came to the table and put down a handwritten menu. I shook my head and said, "Nothing, *gracias*. I'm, ah, waiting for someone."

She retrieved the menu and shuffled away, apparently inured to the idiosyncracies of tourists. A dwarfish man at the next table gave me a toothless smile; I looked down at the scarred tabletop and reminded myself that bolting out of the bar would jeopardize Caron.

I was beginning to fear I was in the wrong bar when a hefty woman with bleached hair dropped a note on the table as she brushed past me. She was already out the door before I realized what had happened and swung around to get a better look at her. I unfolded the note, took out my reading glasses, and tried to make out the cramped print.

The note instructed me to walk up to the next corner, turn left, and continue for three blocks. At that point, I would find myself in front of the Hotel Las Floritas. I was to go to the restaurant, where I would find a bag on the bar. After I put the money in the bag, I was to return to where I currently was. Caron would be released shortly thereafter.

I had no idea if Chico had a network of unsavory spies, but no one seemed interested as I wound among the tables and went out to the sidewalk. Peering nervously at dark recesses and clutching my purse as if it were a parachute, I followed Chico's directions to the gates of Las Floritas. Unlike the crime scenes in Farberville, which were always decorated with yellow tape and signs forbidding trespassing, there was nothing to indicate that the police had been there the previous day. There was enough light from the houses across the street for me to see that the Cadillac was not in the parking lot.

I crept up the path to the lobby, half-expecting a policeman to emerge from behind a tree and begin shouting—or shooting—at me. The door where I'd left the note was ajar, but I had no desire to take a peek inside so that at a later time I could share my insights with Comandante Quiroz. Peter was never appreciative of my contributions, even when I tied up his case in a pretty pink bow and demurely declined any credit. Quiroz wouldn't hesitate to have me dragged off to a cell.

The steps to the restaurant were treacherous in the

dark. I eased my way up them and continued into the relative protection of the thatched roof. The rafters were likely to be home to a colony of bats; the best I could hope was that they were fonder of fruit than of blood.

A plastic bag lay on the bar. I put the cash in it, dropped it, and retraced my way to the steps. I stopped to listen for some hint that Chico was nearby, but all I heard was distant music and the rumble of a truck struggling up the steep hill. He could be anywhere—inside the building, perched on a branch like a vulture, crouched behind any of the bushes. Wherever he was, he had the advantage.

I let out a squeak as something scurried across the path and disappeared into the weeds, and I was trying to persuade myself that it was nothing more than a vole when I heard male voices at the gates. Flashlights illuminated the cracks in the parking lot, then flickered toward the lobby. As the two men came inside, I could see the outline of their hats and the bulge of holsters at their waists. Badges glinted in the moonlight. Would Chico assume I'd tipped them off and carry through with his threat?

They came up the path toward the lobby. The restaurant was a logical destination on their itinerary. Forcing myself to move slowly to avoid catching their attention, I went back to the bar, stuffed the bag into my purse, and tested a door on the far wall. It was locked. The restaurant was too close to the edge of the cliff to risk concealing myself behind the low wall; one loose rock and I'd be found in the same spot where Oliver Pickett had been thirty years ago.

The voices were growing louder. Whatever they were saying to each other sounded good-natured, but

I had a feeling they might not be inclined to banter with me. I was not a gymnast who could grab a rafter and swing into the shadows with the bats. I took a step toward an overturned table, reconsidered, and dropped behind the bar seconds before the policemen arrived at the top step.

The floor was sticky, but it was not the time to criticize the lack of adherence to the municipal health code. I crawled as far as I could, then curled up under the counter and held my breath.

The beam of a flashlight splashed across the empty shelves and cracked mirror. A conversation concerning tequila and whiskey ensued; I tried not to imagine what would happen if one of them decided to search for an overlooked bottle behind the bar. I wiggled further into the niche—and bumped into a warm body. A hand clamped across my mouth, cutting short my involuntary gasp. I tried to jerk away, but a second hand pressed against the back of my neck, holding my head in a vise.

Clearly, I was a whole lot loco.

Chapter 6

The policemen lingered for a few more minutes, then left. When their voices were no longer audible, my head was released with such suddenness that I would have fallen forward if space permitted. I crawled out from under the counter and took several gulps of air, then stood up as Chico emerged. Manuel's characterization of the residents as cockroaches seemed *à propos,* although in this case blue uniforms had been as effective as blue lights.

I stomped on his hand to get his attention. "Where's Caron?"

"Hey," he whined, "there's no need for violence." He tried to pull his hand free, but I increased the pressure until I heard bones creak. In that I needed his cooperation, I did not attempt to find out if I could make them crack. Then again, at that moment I would not have described myself as a mild-mannered bookseller.

"Where's Caron?" I repeated.

"She's all right," he said.

I removed my foot, allowing him to crawl out into the narrow aisle. When he attempted to stand up, however, I kicked his shoulder hard enough to knock him onto his scrawny rear. "I want to see her now."

He sat up and massaged his hand. "Jeez, it feels like you broke something. How am I gonna type the definitive American novel with broken fingers?"

"Now."

"Okay, okay," he muttered, watching me warily as he got to his feet. "But you have to give me the money first. We made a deal."

"This is not a television game show, and you don't get what's behind curtain number two until you produce Caron—and tell me what you know about the Oliver Pickett case."

"You have to promise not to turn me in," he said sullenly. "I never killed anybody, including Santiago. He and I got along just fine." He pushed past me and headed for the steps, his sandals slapping on the floor like apathetic applause. "Your daughter's in the last bungalow. I've met bikers' chicks with cleaner mouths. How old is she, anyway?"

"Old enough to object to being kidnapped," I said, wondering what she'd been reading lately. Mr. Dickens would never have used anything spicier than a "Balderdash!" or a "Pshaw!" Making a mental note to inquire into this at a later time, I followed Chico past the lobby and down a path lined with a few white rocks. There were six bungalows on each side; the ones away from the cliff were set high enough on the hillside to provide a view over the roofs of those opposite.

"If you didn't kill Santiago, who did?" I asked.

"Someone who didn't want you to question him," he said without looking back at me. "He knew more than he let on about the night the girl killed the other girl's father. I don't know who was paying him to keep quiet, but after thirty years, he was still getting money in the mail every year. He'd wave it around and talk about how he was going to restore this dump, but then he'd buy a bottle of tequila to celebrate. Within a week, the money would be pissed away. *Qué será, será,* I suppose."

"Did he ever say who was sending the money?" I asked, frowning. Santiago did not sound as if he had had the wits or the wherewithal to track down Ronnie after she returned to the U.S. and changed her name. If by some miracle he had and she'd been sending money once a year, his name should have come to mind when the half-million-dollar demand was made.

"Once he and I were sharing a bottle when the letter arrived, and while he was chortling and counting the money, I happened to pick up the envelope. No return address, but it was postmarked here."

He turned down a short path to a cliffside bungalow. The glass in the windows was held together with strips of peeling tape, and the door hung aslant on a single hinge. Moonlight illuminated broken tiles, bottles, tin cans, and what appeared to be the frame of a baby stroller.

He pushed aside the door and stuck his head inside. "Your mother's with me, so don't try anything funny."

"I'm here," I called. "Everything's going to be all right, dear."

The inside of the bungalow was as black as the boiler at the bookstore. Chico stepped back and gestured for me to precede him, as if he believed Caron might come flying at him with a makeshift weapon of some sort.

"She's in the back bedroom," he said. "I tried to make her as comfortable as possible. I don't have the chance to talk to my fellow compatriots very often, you know. We could have had a pleasant conversation if she'd ever quit carrying on like she was strapped on a rack in a dungeon."

I tripped on some unseen object, but caught myself and reached the far side of the room. It took my eyes a moment to adjust to the minimal light. Finally I made out a bed and a figure on it. I encountered no obstacles as I hurried over to the bed, sat down, and began to tug at the tape across Caron's mouth. The ripping sound was painful, but I kept at it until the tape came free in my hand.

"Kill him," she croaked.

"Let me get you untied," I said, working on the wire around her wrists.

"It's not like we have dinner reservations. I really don't mind waiting while you kill him."

Her exhortation had merit, but I put it aside for the moment and twisted the ends of the wire until I'd removed it. "Are you okay?" I asked as I started on her ankles.

"Oh, I'm dandy, considering I was brought here with a knife poking my back and have been on this filthy, stinking mattress all day long." She sat up and examined her wrists for signs of permanent scarring. "All I've had to eat since breakfast was a bag of some kind of vile banana chips. I refused to drink the water he gave me in a rusty cup, so he got me a bottle of orange soda that Wasn't Even Cold. Then he brought me this pathetic sandwich that tasted like week-old dog food. I am malnourished and dehydrated—but other than that, I'm just dandy."

I unwound the wire around her ankles, then turned around and hugged her so tightly she groaned in protest. I felt wetness on my cheeks, but I wasn't sure whose tears they were. Images of her infancy and childhood scrolled past me: bibs and bonnets, pigtails, scabby knees, birthday cakes and ice cream, petitions printed in crayon, the gathering thunderheads of puberty. When I could trust myself, I said, "Do you need me to help you get up?"

"Give me a minute," she said. "My feet are numb from lack of circulation. If you hadn't found me tonight, you'd have to be looking up 'amputation' in your Spanish phrase book."

"It's *amputación,*" Chico said, "and the wire wasn't all that tight. It's your own fault, anyway. If you hadn't tried to kick me in the face, I wouldn't have had to put the wire around your ankles."

Caron sneered at him. "Well, excuse me. I guess I haven't read the Dear Miss Demeanor column on being held hostage."

"Hush, dear," I said, patting her knee. Chico had not yet pulled out a knife, but there was no need to provoke him into doing so. I glanced back at him and was disturbed to see he'd edged into the room, and now was within a few feet of the end of the bed. Doing my best to laden my tone with the menace of a gangster, I said, "Listen, Chico, you implied you know something significant about Oliver Pickett's death. Tell me what it is and I'll pay you. What you do after that is your own business."

"The night he died, I was in the bungalow right across from his. I'd come to do some deep-sea fishing with a guy from work. I hadn't bothered with suntan lotion during the day, and the sunburn combined with a bad hangover kept me in. Most of the evening I sat out on my porch, nursing a beer, smoking dope, and watching the party get wilder and wilder. Santiago kept flapping down the path like a wounded parrot to plead with Pickett's daughter. From what I could hear, she wasn't receptive. I must have dozed off, because the next thing I heard was the mighty Pickett himself bellowing so loudly they should have heard him down at the Hilton. The kids took off every which way. He went inside and bellowed some more; I heard his daughter's name more than once. It was so entertaining that I stepped inside to answer the call of nature, get another beer, and settle in for the show, but when I came back out, everything was as dark and peaceful as a cemetery."

"Cemeteries aren't dark during the day," Caron inserted acerbically. "No wonder you can't sell your so-called literary novels to anyone."

I squeezed her leg to shut her up. "Go ahead," I said to Chico. "Then what happened?"

"I opened a beer just as Pickett's daughter came out of the bungalow and ran toward the restaurant and parking lot. She was making all sorts of unholy noises. If she hadn't been running so fast, I would have wondered if she'd been stabbed in the gut. I was contemplating all this when I saw someone else come out of the bungalow."

"Someone else?" I said. "Who?"

"Whoever it was did not have the common courtesy to come up to the well-lit path, but instead stayed in the shadows alongside the bungalows. It's a shame you can't ask Santiago for details. He was standing at the top of the path, and had a much better view of the person. Of course, he might have been disinclined to talk about it even after all these years. Be sure and mention all this in your article."

"Mother," Caron said, "I am the victim here. Whatever happened thirty years ago is history. My blood sugar is dangerously low and I feel dizzy. Could you and this worm turd continue your conversation at a later time?"

Chico shook his head. "There's no reason to be verbally abusive. I explained to you why it was necessary for me to do what I did. In reality, this is your mother's fault for refusing to meet me on the beach last night."

"Maybe you can explain it again at Manuel's funeral. I'm sure the family will be thrilled."

I stood up and positioned myself between the two. "You'd better leave town as soon as possible," I said to Chico. "Jorge Farias is very unhappy with you, and he seemed to think he would have no difficulty finding you. I don't think he wants to hire you as a chauffeur."

"He drives worse than Rhonda Maguire," Caron contributed from behind me, "and she flunked drivers' ed three times. After she ran over Coach Witbred's foot, he told her—"

"Let's be on our way, dear," I said. "I'm sure Chico needs to start on his travel arrangements."

"Farias?" he said, sounding as though he needed to start on his funeral arrangements. "He practically runs this town from his hillside mansion. He'll have men crawling all over the *Sona Rosa* by now. I'd planned on being in Mexico City before Manuel was found. Is he going to be okay?"

"You're damn lucky someone found him before he bled to death."

"All I did was tap him on the head so he couldn't yell for help," Chico said as he edged toward the door. "Before you leave, you might want to go out on the balcony and look around."

"Why would I want to do that?" I asked.

"It's where Pickett's body was tossed."

I was too startled to reply as he disappeared into the darkness of the front room. Moaning piteously, Caron got off the bed and said, "Well, at least you didn't give him any money. He should have to pay me for all my pain and suffering."

I'd dropped my purse on the floor when I saw Caron. I located it and determined that the plastic bag had been removed while I'd been occupied with the tape and wire. "If we see him again, I'll mention it," I said, mentally cursing myself for my carelessness.

We went out into the front room. Earlier I'd been too frantic to notice anything, but now I could see an opening that led to a balcony. Beyond that, the bay was outlined with tiny lights. It would have been quite romantic in a different situation.

"You're not really going out there?" Caron said in a shocked voice. "What if Chico's waiting to push you over the rail?"

"He's halfway to the border by now." I managed to avoid any lurking obstacles and went out onto a spacious balcony. Two chairs implied the current occupants, allegedly the hookers from Honduras, still enjoyed the view, if not room service and the solicitous attention of Ernesto Santiago. The railing was four feet high. Throwing a body over it wouldn't have been easy, but Ronnie and Fran had been operating on a mixture of alcohol, marijuana, and adrenaline.

"Mother," called Caron, "can we please go to the hotel? Being held hostage All Day Long has given me a headache."

As I came back across the room, I realized that I'd been too worried about Caron to consider the consequences of putting all my cash in the bag. I had only a few coins, mostly pennies and nickels. Furthermore, taxis were no longer lined up in the street to take guests down the hill to the beaches and nightclubs. It would take more than a signal from a phantom concierge to bring a taxi to the gate of the Hotel Las Floritas.

"We need to find a telephone," I said to Caron as we trudged up the path. "I'll call Farias's office and ask for a car to be sent."

"Or we can drive. As far as I know, my luggage and purse are still in the trunk of the Cadillac. I'll get into all kinds of trouble if I don't return the Dickens book to the school library. Being held hostage for a day is one thing, but Miss Ferrenclift will make sure I have detention every morning until I graduate."

"Do you know where the car is?"

"Yeah, but I can't promise the keys are in it. I was a little distracted by the knife that moron kept waving at me."

Instead of going out the gate, she led the way across the parking lot to a road that curled behind the restaurant to a service entrance. The Cadillac was partly concealed by a shed that was likely to have contained lawn equipment. I was about to open the driver's door when I saw the beady red glow of a cigarette above us on the terrace.

I hissed at Caron to be quiet and gestured for her to duck behind the car. We converged at the trunk.

"Now what?" she whispered. "I have no desire to stay here the rest of the night."

"I don't know." I slumped against the bumper and regarded the moon. Considering how the trip had gone thus far, I was surprised the craggy face wasn't spitting at me. The police had been here less than an hour ago to conduct a cursory inspection; they would not have returned so soon. Chico would not have lingered to admire the view one last time. The most probable explanation was that one of the other residents had decided it was safe to move back into a bungalow. And what an upstanding group they were.

Caron jabbed me. "Why are we sitting here? I am going to Absolutely Die if I don't take a shower before too long. That mattress was so nasty that I can feel things crawling all over me. What if I have fleas?"

"Did you see anybody else when Chico took you to the bungalow?" I asked.

"Don't be absurd. Did you hear what I said? I am infested and in danger of catching the bubonic plague. I want you to promise that you'll have my body flown back to Farberville so Inez can put flowers on my grave every Sunday." She paused to savor the macabre scene, then sighed. "She's kind of forgetful, though. Maybe it would be better to have me cremated so you can keep me in an urn on the mantel."

"We don't have a mantel," I pointed out, "but I

could make a shrine on the bookcase in my bedroom . . . or in the front window at the Book Depot."

"It would be an improvement."

The appropriately bizarre conversation might have continued had a male voice not said, "Senora Malloy, we have been searching everywhere for you. I see you have found the senorita. Is she unharmed?"

"Mother!" Caron gasped, clutching my hand.

"It's all right, dear," I said as I stood up. "This is Señor Farias, known on an informal basis as Jorge. I suppose he would like us to move so he can collect his Cadillac."

Farias nodded at Caron, then glared at me. "Only a few minutes ago was I informed of your arrival at the bar on Calle Madero. It seemed obvious that you would come here. Adolfo arrived in time to see you and your daughter walk across the parking lot and down this road. Rather than approach you, he waited for me. Please explain what has taken place."

I gave him an abridged version, concluding with, "Chico left the bungalow ten minutes before we did. Knowing that you were looking for him, he must have felt it was risky to take the Cadillac." I was too embarrassed to mention what he *had* taken—from my purse.

Farias rumbled under his breath. "You should not have violated our agreement, Senora, but all has turned out well. You have your daughter, I have my car, and Manuel will have a vacation in the hospital. I will assign another driver to take you to the airport in the morning. Unlike Manuel, who is inexperienced and at times negligent, this driver will be armed."

"I'm not sure we're leaving in the morning," I said

with such crispness that I startled myself. Seconds earlier I might have asked to be taken directly to the airport, abandoning my luggage at the hotel. "There's still the problem with Comandante Quiroz. Besides, I may decide to take a closer look at what happened the night Oliver Pickett was killed. Ronnie's version of the events may not be as accurate as she thinks. In any case, I'll keep you informed of my plans. Could you please arrange for us to be taken to the Acapulco Plaza? Caron is hungry and in need of a shower."

"Of course," Farias murmured. He signaled the figure on the terrace, who leapt over the wall and came jogging toward us. He was older than Manuel, more muscular, and presumably more experienced. "Adolfo will take you there immediately. Please accept my apologies for all that has happened today. If Manuel had been less eager to open his apartment door early this morning, none of this would have occurred."

Caron and I got into the backseat. As we headed for the hotel, she continued to describe her ordeal, requiring of me only sympathetic clucks and tut-tuts. Adolfo glanced at her in the rearview mirror several times, puzzled by her increasingly melodramatic narrative. I myself winced when she characterized Chico as a demented neo-Nazi troglodyte with a track record to rival that of Genghis Khan, but I kept my mouth shut.

It was after nine o'clock when we entered the suite, once again accompanied by a bellman. He may have expected a tip, but all he received was a warm expression of gratitude. Caron selected an impressive number of items from the room service menu, then headed for the shower. After I'd placed the order, I called the desk to ask for messages. The list was long: Dr. Vera Gray, Gabriella Farias, Pedro Benavides, Comandante Quiroz, and Peter Rosen. It was too late to try Benavides, impossible to deal with Quiroz due to our inability to communicate (charades are tough on the telephone), and unnecessary to call Gabriella, since her father would have given her an update by now.

It wasn't too late to call Peter—in the literal sense, anyway. He and I were both fond of watching old movies or reading until midnight. Despite some lapses in my short-term memory, I was aware I'd promised to call him with a more extensive accounting of my investigation. So he could lecture me. So he could condescend. So he could demand that Caron and I catch the next flight back to Farberville. The conversation would be as appetizing as a taco without sour cream.

My remark to Farias that I might not leave in the morning had arisen from bravado, at best. In my mind, Acapulco was hardly a potpourri of posh hotels, sunny beaches, mariachi bands, and frozen margaritas; it was a frightening place. It was tempting to call Peter and meekly listen to him, then slink home. I could still try to help Ronnie somehow or convince her to rely on the private detective. Sure I could.

I decided to delay making that decision until I'd returned Ronnie's call. Brussels was six or seven hours ahead of the local time. She would be in her hotel room, although not necessarily delighted with my timing. After half a dozen rings, she answered with a hoarse, "Hello?"

"This is Claire," I said. "I have some questions for you, but first—do you have information for me?"

"Yes, I do. Let me turn on the light and get the faxes."

I waited patiently, since the cost of the call was covered by her credit card.

"Here we are," she continued, her voice more distinct. "I had a report from a private investigator in Los Angeles. He ran Chad Warmeyer's and Debbie D'Avril's names past the Screen Actors Guild and dug up what he could. People in the industry were more superstitious than any aboriginal tribe, and the two were tainted by their association with Oliver's death. Chad never again worked in Hollywood. Debbie was reduced to making porn movies. In 1973, the police raided the set—a motel room—and found a large quantity of cocaine. She skipped bail and has not been heard of since."

"How tall was Chad Warmeyer?" I asked.

Papers rustled in the background as Ronnie thought. "It's hard to remember, but he was shorter than Oliver Pickett. I don't think Oliver would have hired an assistant taller than he. Like Zeus, he preferred to look down on his flunkies. I'd have to say Chad was no more than five-seven. Why do you ask, Claire? Have you encountered him in Acapulco?"

"Not unless he had a secondary growth spurt," I said, reluctantly discarding the tiny blip of a theory. "Do you have any memory of the people staying in the bungalow directly across from Oliver's on the night of the murder?"

"That would have been the last one on the right. Ours was on the right, too, but closest to the restaurant. The last one . . ."

I struggled not to prompt her with Chico's description or his story about deep-sea fishing. "Yes?"

"Oh, I've got it. It was a Mexican movie star well past her prime. She wore tight sequined dresses and paraded around the hotel with a hairless little dog that resembled a rat. I'd never heard of her, and there's no way I could produce her name after all these years."

"Who accompanied her?"

"Various men went in and out of her bungalow, but the only other person staying there was her personal maid, a young woman, maybe twenty years old."

"And on New Year's Eve?"

"The movie star left with one of her escorts. The only reason I noticed was that she was wearing a mink coat and sweating. Later, Fran made several vulgar remarks about the maid glaring at us from the porch. She was going to invite her over for a drink, but I managed to talk her out of it. We were having enough problems with the hotel manager. Have you located him?"

"In a manner of speaking, but he wasn't helpful," I said tactfully, since there was little point in alarming someone who was over seven thousand miles away and more skilled in analyzing mutant viruses than murder. "Do you remember any of the other guests?"

"Not with any clarity," Ronnie admitted. "A honeymoon couple was next to us; they rarely came out of the bungalow. Chad Warmeyer had his own, while Debbie stayed with Oliver and Fran. There was a young French family . . . the wife kept trying to persuade Fran and me to babysit. We never did. An hoary old toad who ogled us when his wife wasn't watching. It's so hard to remember, Claire, especially at four o'clock in the morning."

I held back a retort concerning the difference between major and minor inconveniences. "Those packages of food and medicine that you received while in prison—did you ever wonder who sent them?"

"You have to understand my state of mind back then. I was barely functional, mentally and physically. I did my assigned work, sometimes weeding in the garden, sometimes scrubbing clothes in the laundry, and then I sat in my cell and wished I were dead. The only respite was on Sundays, when we were taken to mass and allowed out for an hour in an exercise area. I always looked for Fran so I could beg her forgiveness, even when it became preposterous to think she might still be there."

"Fran's mother may have bribed officials in order to get her out of Mexico. I'd like to talk to her and Fran, but I have no idea how to find them on my own. Oliver Pickett's estate went through probate, and Fran may have received the proceeds. Can you have an investigator go through the court records to see if there's an address?"

After a moment of silence, Ronnie said, "I can't risk arousing the investigator's curiosity. Oliver Pickett is still considered one of the most prominent directors of this century. Chad and Debbie were insignificant, and their presence in Acapulco was hardly newsworthy. These days they'd have sold their stories to the tabloids—and my yearbook photo would have been on the cover with a headline about a Hollywood Lolita's obsession with a famous director. It still may happen if you don't find this blackmailer."

I was frustrated, but I understood her paranoia. It was as if she'd been in the witness protection program for more than twenty years, perpetually worried that she might let something slip out about her past. She'd been obliged to create a fictionalized childhood and never contradict herself, never forget what she'd told this or that person, never panic when asked an innocuous question. No wonder she'd taken refuge in a laboratory, where formulas and equations were more important than nostalgia.

"I have a tenuous lead here," I said. "If it doesn't come through, I'm pretty much at a dead end. I haven't talked to the police officer who investigated the crime, but I doubt he'll have any useful information."

"Did you find Jorge?"

"Through a stroke of luck, yes. He certainly didn't come forward voluntarily, even though he was aware I wanted to interview him."

Her voice thickened with hesitancy. "Then do you think—could he—could he be the one? He seemed so nice back then. No matter how imperious Fran was, he smiled and nodded and followed her orders."

"He issues the orders these days," I said, mulling over her accusation. "He owns a very large and prosperous tourist agency and lives in a mansion. It's always useful to have an extra half million dollars, I suppose, but he has plenty of potential blackmail victims right here in Acapulco."

"I'm glad he's done well for himself," Ronnie said with a shaky laugh. "I must get some sleep now. My keynote presentation is tomorrow, and my work is so controversial that I'll have to defend myself all afternoon. What you're doing means a great deal to me, Claire. If you hadn't agreed to help me, I might have . . . taken the cowardly way out."

I wished her success with her presentation and replaced the receiver. Great, I thought as I flopped back on the bed and closed my eyes. My cousin, recently returned from the grave, had placed her life in my fumbling fingers. Her research center probably had more lethal potions than Acapulco did street vendors.

Caron came out of the bathroom. "I washed my hair until I ran out of shampoo. You'd think a hotel like this could provide more than one little bottle of some weird Mexican brand that smells like cactus sap. Has room service arrived yet?"

"It should be here any minute," I said. I listened to her go into the living room and open the minibar. "If it's okay with you, we're going to stay another day and go home as planned."

Cellophane crinkled as she opened one of the world's most expensive bags of potato chips. "No, I don't care. I was so busy being held hostage all day that I didn't have any time to read. Mr. Simpson's such an old fart that he'll probably give us a pop quiz on Monday." The television set came on. "What is wrong with these people?" she added tartly. "Can't anybody speak English?"

It was good to know she'd survived the day without any permanent psychological scars. Or even temporary.

On that note, I dialed the number of the Farias Tourist Agency, wondering if Jorge would renege on his promise to upgrade me to a limo. The woman who answered spoke no English, so our conversation was brief.

Then, after a craven delay while I called Inez's mother and apologized for Caron's failure to appear at the Farberville airport, I squared my shoulders, scowled at myself in the mirror, and called Peter.

Chapter 7

The following morning, I spread out my notes on the coffee table in the living room where I wouldn't disturb Caron. Martyrs need their sleep. Meddlers need their caffeine (and their fresh croissants), but I was at the mercy of room service.

I called the Farias Tourist Agency and asked for Gabriella. When she came on the line, I cautiously inquired about Manuel. Jorge Farias had blamed him for what had happened, but I knew where the culpability lay—on the table in front of me. Chico had not assaulted Manuel out of random spite or a yearning to drive a Cadillac, nor had he kidnapped Caron in order to discuss contemporary trends in literature.

"He's doing well," said Gabriella. "He suffered a mild concussion and loss of blood. He has a terrible headache and remembers only a little of what happened, but the doctor said that was to be expected. Papa and I will visit him later this morning. I am told you and your daughter are not leaving today. Adolfo is parked outside your hotel should you wish to go somewhere."

"I will before too long," I said, looking at the list

of messages from the previous day. "Comandante Quiroz called, but he doesn't speak English and I don't see how I can call him back. Will you please find out what he wants?"

"Yes, Señora."

"And while you're on the line with the police department, arrange an interview for me with a comandante named Alvarez. He's supposed to be back today."

Sounding less enthusiastic, she agreed. Room service arrived while I was waiting, and I scribbled a tip at the bottom of the bill. My credit card had neared its limit during the back-to-school sales, but I could probably squeeze a hundred dollars out of it. We were leaving in twenty-four hours, and there were four restaurants in the hotel if we couldn't face room service.

Gabriella called me back ten minutes later. "Comandante Quiroz offers his apologies for the distress he may have caused you. The undercover officers who followed you yesterday have been reassigned, and you are free to leave Acapulco at any time."

Jorge Farias may have been bragging when he'd mentioned his influence in local matters, but he hadn't been exaggerating, I thought with a flicker of apprehension. "Did you speak to Comandante Alvarez?"

"He was reluctant at first, but I asked him to have a word with Quiroz. He returned to say he will be at the courthouse all day and can see you whenever it is convenient for you. His English is adequate."

I thanked her, then poured myself a cup of coffee and carried it with me as I opened drawers until I found a telephone directory. There were two listings for Pedro Benavides; I brilliantly deduced that *bufete* was more likely to be the word for "office" than for "salad bar," and dialed that number.

The receptionist, perhaps out of boredom as much as anything, tried to deter me with a snivelly discourse in Spanish, but I repeated my name until she relented and put me through.

"Señora Malloy," Benavides said briskly, "it is as I warned you. Perez cleaned out his office before he died, and his widow had no place to store the many boxes. She had them taken to a dump. I am sorry."

"So am I," I said, then made him wait while I refilled my cup and thought about our earlier conversation, when he'd been rattled by the nature of my mission. "I spoke to Ronnie last night," I continued. "I asked her if she'd ever wondered who arranged for the packages she received while in prison. It was quite a burden on you, wasn't it? You had a tremendous workload, yet every month for eight years you took the time to find a box, fill it with food and medicine, and take it to the prison. That was very generous of you."

"The money came in the mail for that purpose. I may not have been an effective public defender, but I was an honorable man."

"Do you realize you made almost a hundred deliveries?" I said. "How far was the prison?"

"It took an hour to drive there," he said guardedly, as if he believed that I could catch him in a lie. For all I knew, the prison could have been a block away from his office or two hundred miles away in Mexico City. One of the first skills a nosy amateur sleuth needs to perfect is the ability to bluff. Peter had provided me with ample opportunities to practice, and, frankly, I was a pro.

I took a deep breath. "Señor Benavides, you had a motive other than honor. Isn't it true that you were promised an additional payment if you faithfully delivered the packages until Ronnie was released? Isn't that how you were able to leave the public defender's office and set up a private practice? If so, it would have been very naive of you not to know the name and address of this benefactor in the United States. Were you that naive?"

He hung up.

Demoting myself to the minors, I drew a dollar sign next to his name. Ronnie's crime had destroyed the Hotel Las Floritas, so Santiago certainly wouldn't have arranged for the packages to express his gratitude. Jorge Farias had claimed that thirty years ago he'd have been unable to afford a drink in the bar of the Hotel Las Floritas; if he'd managed to scrape together the money every month to provide Ronnie with provisions, he could have taken them to the prison himself rather than set up an elaborate ploy. It was hard to imagine that Fran Pickett would have sent money to her father's murderer; if she had, why the need to pay Benavides for anonymity? Debbie D'Avril and Chad Warmeyer would have felt resentment, not compassion, for the girl who'd sabotaged their careers. Ronnie's parents were dead, and no one else in the family knew what had happened.

I was out of players, which was most annoying. I cannot tolerate mystery novels in which the villain wanders into the plot in the penultimate chapter. Of course, in this case the murderer had confessed to the crime two days after she committed it, and was currently defending her research in Brussels and fantasizing about a Nobel prize. Santiago might have been killed by an unhappy tenant or a dissatisfied junkie. Coincidences happen. Then again, if I bought Chico's expensive and at least partially mendacious story, Santiago *had* seen someone sneak out of the bungalow, and *had* ended up on someone's payroll.

It all kept coming back to Chico, I realized as I ate a croissant and finished the last of the coffee. I reviewed all of our encounters, forcing myself to visualize his grimy face and remember precisely what he'd said. It did nothing to aid digestion, but I came up with an idea, albeit feeble, to uncover his identity.

I called Gabriella and said, "Please let Comandante Quiroz know that I'm going to the Hotel Las Floritas to have a look at the lobby. If he has a problem with that, tell him to speak to your father."

"Oh, Señora, it is not a good thing for you to do. Here in Mexico we honor the dead. We even have a festival called *Día de los Muertos,* when the children eat candy skeletons and families have picnics in the cemetery. But Santiago's death should mean nothing to you. Comandante Quiroz is satisfied that you were not involved. Would it not be better to forget all this and go home?"

"I have no doubt about that, Gabriella, but I'm still going to the Hotel Las Floritas. My estimated time of arrival is thirty minutes from now. Shouldn't you be on the phone with Quiroz?"

I awoke Caron and badgered her until she promised not to go one foot past the hotel pool, not even out to the beach or into any of the nearby shops. Presumably, she would be in no danger of anything more life-threatening than a sunburn. I was convinced Chico had left Acapulco; I hoped Farias's bloodhounds were snapping at his heels—or chewing on his ankles.

The white limo at the curb wasn't of preposterous length, but it would dwarf the Cadillac. Adolfo opened the door for me, and instead of taking the egalitarian attitude, I climbed into a leather, brass, and ebony chamber. Various buttons on a panel activated a tiny television, reading and overhead lights, and climate control; I finally found one that caused the partition to glide open.

"Yes, Señora?" Adolfo said promptly.

"I would like to go to the Hotel Las Floritas."

"Gabriella called me a few minutes earlier and said Comandante Quiroz does not object. Please help yourself to the bar with Señor Farias's compliments."

I'd always wondered who rode in such cars, and now I knew. The only credential required was the willingness not to gag when presented with the bill. I sipped chilled mineral water as we purred down the boulevard on yet another wild goose chase. My success rate was such that I had no need to take a correspondence course in taxidermy.

The Hotel Las Floritas was less menacing in the daylight, back to its shabby, neglected ambiance. No one was visible, but I asked Adolfo to accompany me in case I bumped into a tenant with an attitude.

The door of the lobby was still ajar. I eased it open, paused to allow the indigenous vermin to take cover, and then went into the main room. In the past, it may have had charm, but now the primary decor consisted of mildew, dust, and cobwebs. The bloodstains on the threadbare rug had dried to a dull brown; the stench in the air was that of violent death.

On the walls were more photographs of celebrities with capped teeth and professional smiles. Someone schooled in the history of Hollywood would have had a grand time hunting for familiar faces, but Bette Davis was the best I could do, and only after some thought.

"Now what, Señora?" Adolfo said, trying with limited success to keep the bewilderment out of his voice.

"You can wait here." I opened a door and found a smaller room with a mattress on the floor, a chair with little of its original upholstery, and an array of empty bottles amidst dingy T-shirts and dingier boxer shorts. The room beyond that was apt to be a bathroom, but I was not inclined to explore it, since I had a feeling that Santiago and I had different standards when it came to hygiene and porcelain.

"What I'm looking for," I said as I came back into the lobby, "are the old guest registers, specifically from the last part of 1965. Supposedly, Santiago saved them in order to relive his better days. I didn't see them in the other room." I went behind a counter and began opening cabinets, sneezing periodically as three decades of mold drifted out. My eyes were streaming by the time I found a drawer filled with large, thin books that originally had been bound in leather and embossed with the name of the hotel.

I stood up and beckoned to Adolfo. "Would you please carry these out to the porch?" I asked. "If I stay in here any longer, I'm liable to sneeze off my nose."

After Adolfo made three trips, we had well over forty guest registers in a precarious pile. He offered to bring me something to drink from the limo, and left me to ponder where to start. I put on my reading glasses and took the top one. The ink had faded to a watery beige, but I made out a date, sneezed, and reached for the next one.

There were only a few remaining when I spotted the pertinent year. I carefully turned the brittle pages until I found a December date, then eased my finger down the page until I came to Oliver Pickett's scrawled signature. Below that was Debbie D'Avril's name, embellished with tiny hearts above the I's. Chad Warmeyer had printed his name with anal-retentive precision. I continued down the page: Arthur and Margaret Landonwood, and daughter; Jeannine Diego Delgado, possibly the Mexican actress; Henri and Madeline Delacroix, the French couple.

I took out my notebook and copied all the names of those who'd been in residence on New Year's Eve, then set aside the register. Four of the couples had Hispanic surnames. Two women had shared a bungalow; I recognized one of the names as that of a fleetingly famous striptease queen. The final two couples had Swedish and German names, respectively.

According to my list, none of the bungalows had been occupied by two men, unless one of them had a serious identity problem.

Chico had done it again.

I asked Adolfo to drive me to a bank, and then to the hospital. At my request, he stopped next to a flower vendor and I bought a bouquet to brighten Manuel's room—and appease my conscience. The fragrance reminded me of the sickly sweet stench in the lobby of Las Floritas; I'd encountered it in the past, but it still made me queasy. Maybe it truly was time to retire my magnifying glass and hang up my deerstalker hat. Peter had certainly thought so the previous night, when he'd sputtered like a burst water main for more than an hour. My responses had grown increasingly perfunctory, until I finally hung up on him.

Our relationship was not something I cared to think about, so I resumed brooding about Chico. Had everything he'd told me come from Santiago's maudlin memories? Chico could be nothing more than what he seemed: a broken-down scavenger scraping by on a little money, drinking himself to death while he wrote and rewrote the first sentence of the Great American Novel. Clearly, he was an opportunist. What was odd, though, was that after he'd stolen the money from my purse, he'd stayed long enough to give me his fabricated story about watching the party progress into an orgy—and seeing someone come out of the Picketts' bungalow. He'd told me to be sure to mention it in my article. Why did he care?

When we arrived at the hospital, Adolfo told me how to find Manuel's room, then let me out at the entrance and went to park in the shade. The exterior of the building was of the same faux-adobe stucco utilized all over the city. The lobby was much like that of the hospital in Farberville: cheap furniture, plastic plants, serious faces, and well-worn linoleum.

I took the elevator to the third floor and walked down a hallway to Manuel's room. From inside I heard voices, but I didn't bother to eavesdrop (okay, so the conversation was in Spanish) and opened the door. Jorge Farias was seated in an oversized chair that must have been brought to the room especially for him. His eyes were closed and his hands rested on the knob of his walking stick; the effect was rather regal, although this Old King Cole was by no means a jolly old soul. Gabriella stood by the window. She was wearing a pink sundress, but had covered her bare shoulders with a shawl out of deference to the solemnity of the occasion.

Manuel's head was wrapped with gauze and his cheek was discolored, but he gave me a wan smile as I approached the bed. "You did not need to come, Señora," he said. "A hospital is not a place for tourists."

"I'm really sorry about this," I said awkwardly.

Manuel glanced at his brother-in-law. "No, Señora, it was all my fault. I have been told that the señorita suffered much indignity because of my error. When I opened the front door of my apartment, Chico shoved me backward. Before I could regain my balance, he hit me with a piece of pipe and I lost consciousness. The key to the Cadillac was on the kitchen table."

"I heard that you went to the Hotel Las Floritas this morning," Farias said.

I handed the bouquet to Gabriella, then turned around to face him. "Yes, I did. It seems that no one is stepping forward to volunteer any information, so I'm obliged to dig it up for myself. For instance, I now have a list of everyone who was staying at the hotel on New Year's Eve. Chico was not among the guests."

"Then he lied to you. Does that surprise you?"

"Not really," I said as I sat down on a chair designed for mere mortals. "And it's hard to decide what, if anything, he told me is true. He claimed to have seen someone leave the bungalow after Fran did, and he also said Santiago had seen this person. Did you?"

He pursed his mouth for a moment, regarding me with the same ill-disguised hostility he'd shown the previous day. "I told you everything that happened, Señora. I was in the parking lot when Fran ran up to the car and got in the backseat. She ordered me to drive away, and so I did. I saw no one else. Chico told you his story because he wanted money from you."

"He is a very bad man," added Gabriella. "Look what he did to poor Manuel." She put the bouquet on the window sill and reached down to stroke his shoulder with her finger.

Poor Manuel nodded. "I warned you about him when you first encountered him near the lobby."

"I'm not attesting to his character," I said, more interested in the sweat forming on Farias's forehead and the nerve twitching in his eyelid. "But for some strange reason, he wanted me to know that someone else was in the bungalow just before Oliver Pickett was killed."

Farias tightened his grip on the walking stick. "There were more than thirty people at the party. When Pickett burst into the room, there was much confusion. I cannot swear that everyone ran out the front door immediately. Maybe one of the boys had to pull on his pants before he could escape."

"While Oliver patiently waited?" I said. "If he was as outraged as everyone says he was, I can't imagine anyone asking his permission to get dressed or finish a cigarette. How long were you in the parking lot before Fran appeared?"

"Ten minutes, perhaps fifteen."

"Did you see Santiago heading toward the bungalows?"

Farias hesitated, then said, "When one prays, Señora, it is traditional to close one's eyes. I opened them only when Fran got into the limousine."

"Papa," said Gabriella, "Manuel has fallen asleep. We should leave now so he is not disturbed."

I nudged her toward the door with the subtlety of a rogue elephant. "Let's go ask the nurses if there's a vase we can use. It would be a shame if the flowers are wilted when Manuel wakes up."

"We will be back in a minute, Papa," she called as I dragged her out into the hall. "Why do you ask Papa all these questions?" she continued, frowning at me. "You have caused him to be tense and bad-tempered. This morning he spoke so sharply to my mother that she cried, and our only driver who speaks French has threatened to quit. Morale is very bad at the agency when Papa is like this."

"I'm sorry to hear that, but what began as a straightforward story has taken more twists than the drive along the coastline." I patted her arm and gave her what I hoped was a supportive smile. "I'm leaving in the morning, and everything should be back to normal at the agency. I've been told it is the largest and most reputable in Acapulco."

"Oh, yes," Gabriella said, then spoke to a nurse behind a desk. The woman nodded and glided down the hallway, presumably to find a receptacle for the bouquet.

I widened my smile until my ears wiggled; if we were near the psychiatric ward, I might have been accused of being an escapee. "How long has the Farias Tourist Agency been in business?"

"Two years ago we celebrated its twenty-fifth anniversary. We had a lavish party at one of the hotels, with much food and music. The mayor presented Papa with a brass plaque."

"Your father has come a long way from the day he was only an employee, hasn't he?"

She nodded proudly. "After he bought the agency, he worked very hard to expand the fleet of limousines and vans. We accommodated over three thousand tourists last year with less than two dozen complaints." She took an ugly green vase from the nurse and started back toward Manuel's room. "Many of the complaints were not our fault. In several situations, the groups were larger than we had been led to expect. One of your famous authors was drunk when he got off the airplane, and insisted—"

"How was your father able to buy the agency from its previous owner?" I said quickly. "He himself told me his salary was tiny back then."

She stopped and looked back at me. "He worked hard, Señora. Do you have any more questions before we go into the room?"

"Did he send a check every year to Ernesto Santiago?" I asked out of desperation as she reached for the doorknob.

She gaped for a second, as if startled by a distant connection, then moistened her lips and said, "I can think of no reason why he would. Goodbye, Señora. Please enjoy your last day in Acapulco. There are many lovely places you have not yet visited. You and your daughter should tour the *Casa de la Cultura de Acapulco*. They have a very nice display of pre-Columbian artifacts and Mexican handicrafts." She went into the room and closed the door.

So Jorge Farias was on the payroll, too, I thought as I went down to the lobby and out into the sunshine. He'd not only accepted hush money, he'd also offered it to Santiago. There seemed to be more questionable financial transactions (past and present) than in the Cayman Islands on an average day. Benavides, Farias, Santiago, and even Ronnie had been the recipients of someone's generosity.

Someone with resources, like the person who'd inherited Oliver Pickett's estate. Regrettably, I had no idea how to find her.

"Where would you like to go?" asked Adolfo as he opened the limousine door for me.

"To the courthouse," I said.

I'd assumed it would be somewhere in the vicinity of the downtown area, but I was wrong. Once again we went up into the hills, passing shops, bars, markets, and the omnipresent construction sites. I finished a second bottle of mineral water and was starting on a third when we came down into an industrial zone of derelict warehouses and what appeared to be abandoned factories.

I tried a button marked INTERCOM. "Are you sure the courthouse is around here?"

"Yes, it is next to the *Centro de Rehabilitación*, the prison. There have been protests about its location. It is not convenient for the lawyers and judges to drive out here, nor for the families of the prisoners."

He turned down what might qualify as an alley, apparently unconcerned that the limousine might sustain damage from the cars parked on the sidewalk. Shortly thereafter, we were on a country road of sorts, with arid expanses of dirt and scruffy plants. I'd seen Adolfo make more than one call on a cellular phone; I hoped Farias had not been issuing orders to dispose of the passenger's corpse in a rock quarry.

Towering gray walls came into view, forming forty-foot barriers on two sides of a grassy parking lot. They were topped by concertina wire, and above the one in front of us I could see a guard box. The scene was oppressive, to put it mildly, and I was doubting my wisdom in requesting to be brought there as Adolfo parked.

"You must walk from here," he said, pointing at a whitewashed booth. "Only those with official passes can drive past the guards."

If I'd had a lace hankie, I would have been wringing it in my admittedly sweaty hands. I knocked back the rest of the mineral water to fortify myself, then allowed Adolfo to open the door for me.

"You'll need to come with me," I said. "We're looking for Comandante Alvarez."

Adolfo shrugged. "As you wish."

We trudged across the field to a tunnel where the walls met. Inside were two drowsy guards on wooden chairs and a sign that Adolfo obligingly translated: no weapons, no alcohol, shirts and shoes required. Claustrophobia was optional, I supposed, trying to ignore the walls on either side of us.

Adolfo led the way through a maze of corridors and courtyards, then up a flight of stairs to a large room with an aura of bureaucratic lethargy. On one side were closed doors; across from them were cubicles with desks in front of meshed windows. The typewriters and telephones were silent, and only a handful of employees were reading files. At least one was filing her nails.

Adolfo gestured at the doors. "Those are the chambers. When a judge has decided on a verdict, he comes out to one of the tables and the prisoner is brought to the window to hear his sentence."

"Aren't there courtrooms?"

"Only in special cases. This way is faster and saves money."

I asked him to locate Comandante Alvarez, then went into a cubicle and gazed through the mesh at the narrow walkway. Through the opposite windows I could see a parched garden and an orchard of gnarled, leafless trees. To my relief, I couldn't see the cemetery Ronnie had mentioned when speculating about Fran's disappearance. I would have more luck finding her there than I would somewhere in the United States. As everyone was so fond of reminding me, thirty years was a long time.

My morose thoughts were interrupted by a gray-haired man with a creased face and a nose that had been broken more than once. I'd been expecting a version of dear old Quiroz, but this man gave me a civil, if not heartwarming, smile. "I am Comandante Alvarez. I have been told you wish to speak to me, Señora Malloy. I am sorry you had to come so far, but I must be here today for depositions. We can sit at this table."

"I want to ask you about the death of Oliver Pickett," I said, taking out a notebook. "I was told you were involved in the investigation."

"Yes, I was."

"When the body was first discovered, you believed his death was accidental. Later you found evidence to incriminate Veronica Landonwood, right?" When he merely nodded, I added, "Someone found a shirt with blood on it?"

"One of the maids found it in a garbage can on the hotel grounds. The girl's name was on a tag sewn in the collar. She became very emotional when asked to explain it, and this led us to search the bungalow where she was staying with her parents. I myself found her diary in her suitcase. The entries made it clear that she desired a sexual encounter with Pickett and had been scheming to arrange it. She confessed to his murder and also of her attempt to cover up the crime with the assistance of his daughter. The daughter then acknowledged her role. There was no need for further investigation."

"Did you question the others in Pickett's group?"

"We asked them what happened that night. I don't remember their names, but they all agreed that while at a party, Pickett fell into the swimming pool. He was angry because he thought he'd been pushed, but he was also drunk. He announced he was taking a cab back to the Hotel Las Floritas to change into dry clothes. One of the women offered to accompany him, but he refused. They all stayed at the party, dancing with each other, and only several hours later did they begin to worry about Pickett's failure to return. When they went to the bungalow, it was dark and the daughter was asleep. She said she'd heard nothing. It was agreed that Pickett might have run into someone at the hotel and gone to another party somewhere in Acapulco."

"Did any of them leave the party?" I asked.

"They swore they were together from the time he left until they returned as a group to the hotel," Alvarez said, glancing at his watch. "I have a meeting in a few minutes, Señora. If you have a final question . . ."

"Did you question the other guests at the hotel?"

"As a formality, yes. There was one couple, young and recently married, who were in their bungalow and saw nothing. All the rest of them were out at parties, with the exception of a maid who said she went to bed before midnight."

"Santiago claimed he saw someone sneak out of the bungalow," I said.

"Santiago," said Alvarez, "was a reluctant and unreliable witness. At first he refused to tell us of the party. Later he admitted he'd seen Pickett get out of the taxi and discreetly followed him. Once the party had been disbanded and things were quiet, Santiago went back to the restaurant. A few days later, he suffered a fall and spent some weeks in a hospital in Mexico City." He paused to give me a sharp look. "Quiroz accepted your testimony that you never spoke to Santiago, Señora. Were you lying?"

I put my notebook away and stood up. "No, I was told this by a third party. Would it be possible for me to see the court records?"

"You will have to send a written request to the authorities in Chilpancingo, which is the capital of Guerrero. It will be reviewed within ninety days and you will be informed of the decision. To be honest, Señora, I would be surprised if the records still exist. If they do, the likelihood of being allowed to review them is very small because the case involved juveniles."

"Is there any way to find out if someone has been given access to them in the last year?"

Alvarez thought for a moment, then sighed and said, "I have been instructed to cooperate with you, so I will see what I can learn. It may take several weeks, though. Often the person with the pertinent information is out of his office for various reasons, or must put the request through the appropriate channels."

I wrote down the telephone numbers of the Book Depot and my apartment and tore the page out of the notebook. "You can call me at the Acapulco Plaza until tomorrow morning," I said, "or afterward at one of these numbers." I thanked him for his time, then beckoned to Adolfo, who was entertaining a secretary.

"Did you find out what you needed?" he asked me as we escaped from the stifling grayness.

"All I found out," I said as I flicked a fly off my arm, "is that I'm better suited to selling books than meddling."

Chapter 8

Since I was out of ideas, brilliant or otherwise, I had Adolfo take me back to the Acapulco Plaza and arranged for him to pick us up the next morning to go to the airport. What a bizarre four-day trip it had been, I thought as I went up to the suite. Caron had been held hostage, Manuel had been assaulted, Santiago had been murdered, and I'd been dragged to the police station as a suspected knife-wielding drug dealer. I couldn't remember a time when I'd personally been responsible for so many catastrophes. Santiago was the only one who had suffered irreparable damage; Manuel would recover, and in the past, Caron and I had found ourselves in stickier situations.

I left my notebook on the bed and took a paperback down to the pool. Caron was cuddled up with Mr. Dickens on a chaise longue, her grimace indicating she was not especially enamored of him.

"We need to pack tonight," I said as I sat down next to her. "You'll have quite a story to tell when we get back home, won't you? I wish I did."

She peered at me over the top of the book. "You

sound awfully discouraged, Mother. I told you before we left that the whole thing was stupid. Why would anybody even remember a bunch of stuff that happened so long ago? By middle age, there is a measurable reduction in neural activity and a corresponding decline in the ability to retrieve information."

"The information I need to retrieve is in the Los Angeles County Courthouse," I said, "and I'd probably have as much luck there as I would in Chilpancingo. I guess I should call Ronnie before it gets too late in Brussels." Instead of doing so, I beckoned to a waiter and ordered a margarita, then leaned back and examined each dead end for a tiny fissure. Miss Marple had waited in her cozy cottage for fresh information to be served alongside tea and scones. Maud Silver and Hildegarde Withers snooped more vigorously, and heaven knows Cordelia Gray went after her prey. Alas, they knew what they were doing; I felt as if I were all dressed up with nowhere to go . . . except home, shrouded in failure.

Caron closed the book. "I can't concentrate if you're going to sit there and wheeze. I'm surprised the sky hasn't clouded over out of deference to your mood. This is My Last Day to work on a tan, you know."

"You'll be relieved to learn I have very little impact on the weather," I said.

"I wasn't holding my breath." She discarded the book, dabbed lotion on her nose, and lay back to capture whatever ultraviolet rays remained in the late afternoon sunlight.

I sipped the drink and watched the brightly colored parasails drift across the sky. It was easy to ignore the cables linking them to boats far below and imagine them to be fanciful tropical birds gliding in the breeze. Two bikini-clad girls walked by, pointing at the parasails and chattering excitedly in Spanish. A man on a nearby chaise longue pulled off his sunglasses to ogle them; the acceleration in the rhythm of their hips suggested they were aware of him.

Fran Pickett would have garnered such looks, I thought idly, but not stooped, gawky Ronnie. Fran had been compared to a fashion model, petite and perfectly sculpted. Wearing a bikini must have been quite a contrast after a semester of plaid skirts and blazers—or whatever convent school girls wore. According to Ronnie, Fran had loathed the school and the stringent supervision of what she'd called "the sisters of the holy swine."

The convent would be a good place to start trying to locate Fran and her mother, but I doubted I could go to the public library in Farberville and track down the order in *Know Your Nuns.* I couldn't see myself on the doorstep of the local Catholic school, asking if anyone there knew of "the sisters of the holy swine." As a child, I'd always worried what the voluminous black habits might conceal; the anxiety lingered despite the modernization of their attire.

"Holy swine," I muttered.

"What's the matter?" Caron said without raising her head (and possibly deflecting a ray). "Have pigs taken to playing volleyball on the beach?"

" 'Holy swine' is a crude nickname."

"I told you some of these people are disgusting. They ought to wear black plastic garbage bags instead of bathing suits. They certainly have no business playing volleyball; they'd be better off praying at a shrine dedicated to Our Lady of Liposuction."

"Shrine," I said, my lips barely moving.

"Will you order me a lemonade? It is so incredibly hot here that I can feel my flesh melting."

I distractedly waved at the waiter as I envisioned myself on the doorstep of the Catholic school, this time inquiring about a convent in the Southwest that was staffed by the Sisters of the Holy Shrine, most likely of something or other. Eyebrows might be raised, but offense would not be taken. And I might get an answer.

"She'll have a lemonade," I said to the waiter, my face aglow with the rosy rapture of a novitiate. "What the hey—make it a double."

The following afternoon, Caron and I arrived home without incident. Caron dropped her luggage in the living room and dashed into her bedroom to call Inez to find out what unprecedented and deeply momentous events had taken place during the last four days. She was probably hoping to hear that Rhonda Maguire was impregnated or imprisoned. Either would be acceptable.

I put on clothes more suitable to the blustery November weather, made a pot of tea, and sorted through the mail. Praying that Peter's schedule had not changed, I craftily called his house and left a message on his answering machine. I could have tried the police department, of course, and I knew I couldn't avoid him indefinitely. Comandante Quiroz had not been told about the kidnapping, and there was no reason to think he'd been in further communication on whatever computer system had culminated with the printout on Peter's desk. Unless Caron insisted on appearing on the nightly news or holding a press conference to breathlessly describe her ordeal, Peter might never find out about it. I would be spared a lecture accentuated with dejected sighs and avowals of frustration at his inability to convince me of the folly of my ways. Despite his intelligence, the man was a slow learner in certain matters.

I looked up the telephone number of St. Martin's Academy, then decided that calling was cowardly. It would also require me to convince Caron to surrender the phone—not an easy process. I went down the back staircase to the garage, brushed a spider off the windshield, and drove toward Thurber Street.

The Book Depot was open, but as usual there were no customers with a lust for literature streaming through the doorway. The bewildered retiree was sweeping the brick expanse beneath the portico; he looked so despondent that I was tempted to stop and assure him that his temporary tenure was drawing to an end. However, I continued toward the school, where I dearly hoped I would encounter Sally Field instead of Rosalind Russell.

Classes had ended for the day, and only a dozen or so students were in the paved playground adjoining the three-story red brick building. The girls wore knee socks and dark skirts, but their winter coats hid the rest of the ensemble. The boys wore slacks rather than blue jeans, and their hair was uniformly short. This did not guarantee that these neatly dressed youth would not grow up to be professional wrestlers and trailer park queens, but it was an improvement over the slovenly attire at other schools in town.

I parked, rehearsed my story until my teeth started to chatter, and walked up the sidewalk to the main entrance. Through the glass I could see two women conversing in the hallway and a hunched figure pushing a mop. I went inside and hesitated, unsure how to address women who might be undercover nuns.

One of them smiled at me and said, "Are you looking for the office? It's at the end of the hall just beyond the trophy case."

"Thanks," I said, then scooted past them without being forced to resolve my quandary. The awards in the trophy case were based on academic achievements instead of more physical endeavors; St. Martin's had won the parochial equivalent of the College Bowl four years in a row. A framed photograph of moppets commemorated the planting of rosebushes at a nursing home. Red and blue ribbons from science fairs added a festive touch.

The office was large and equipped with all the technology of the day, including a droning photocopy machine, multibuttoned telephones, and computers. I was struggling to envision Rosalind Russell bent over a keyboard when a middle-aged woman in slacks and a sweater came out of a back room. Surely nuns did not wear makeup, I told myself as I went to the counter.

"Are you here about our second semester enrollment?" she asked. "We still don't have the application forms, but I can take your name and address and mail it to you."

It was tempting to give out a false name and flee, but I stiffened my spineless back and said, "I'm trying to get information about a convent school in another state. This seemed like the logical place to start.

I was hoping there might be some sort of catalog with listings."

"If there's a catalog like that, I've never heard of it. Let me see if Sister Mary Clarissa is still in her classroom." The woman went back into the inner sanctum, leaving me to perspire ever so discreetly and wish I were at the bar at the Acapulco Plaza. I doubted St. Martin's Academy would offer me a margarita and a bowl of pretzels.

The woman returned and gave me directions to the biology lab. The corridors were similar to those at Farberville High School, but the lockers were unblemished and the graffiti was absent. A poster announced an upcoming choir concert, and taped on the wall outside what I presumed was a kindergarten classroom were drawings of coneheaded Pilgrims.

The lab was on the second floor; the astringent odor of formaldehyde was unmistakable. As I came inside, Sister Mary Clarissa stepped out from behind a lab table. She was gray-haired and dauntingly stern in an odd combination of gray skirt, white blouse, gray cardigan sweater, and high-topped athletic shoes. The only manifestation of her vocation was a small gold cross on a chain around her neck.

"You wanted to speak to me?" she began in a tone that must have squelched many an impertinent question about the racier aspects of the procreation of the species *homo sapiens*.

A candid response would have been that I most assuredly did not want to speak to her, but it would not have been constructive. I swallowed and said, "I'm trying to find out about a convent school run by an order called the Sisters of the Holy Shrine."

"Holy Shrine of what?"

"I don't know. A daughter of an acquaintance attended classes there thirty years ago, and I'm hoping I can locate them through school records. All I know is that it was in the Southwest and was very strict."

Sister Mary Clarissa gave me a pitying look. "All convent schools were very strict thirty years ago. We here at St. Martin's have come to tolerate some progressive theories, but we fill our classrooms because we offer a well-structured program in a disciplined environment."

"I apologize for taking up your time," I said, edging toward the door.

"I didn't say I couldn't help you. I seem to think Sister Thomasina attended a retreat at a convent with a similar name. When she returned, she bored us to tears with descriptions of cacti. Wait here while I try to catch her before she leaves for her tennis lesson."

Sister Mary Clarissa charged out of the room like a gray and white tornado. I could not have moved my feet if a fire alarm had gone off. I'm sorry to say this paralysis was caused more by Sister Mary Clarissa's command than the possibility I might actually have a new lead. It occurred to me that if I ended up in possession of the address of the convent school, there were apt to be a goodly number of nuns in my future.

I was examining a poster concerning the life cycle of sponges when Sister Mary Clarissa returned.

"Although Sister Thomasina's mind is as mushy as a bowl of oatmeal, she remembered the retreat. It was run by the Sisters of the Holy Shrine of San Jacinto at their convent outside of Phoenix. I'd be surprised if the school were still in operation. It used to be popular to pack off one's daughters to the vigilant guidance of the sisters, but these days girls are allowed to do as they wish." She leaned forward, staring at me. "Are you the mother of a teenaged girl?"

I cravenly shook my head, thanked her for the information, and hurried to my car before my knees dissolved. Only then did I realize that my quest had been successful, that I knew the name and location of Fran's school. It was challenging to drive and pat myself on the back at the same time, but I managed.

Caron had left a note stating that she was walking to Inez's house since someone had driven away in the only vehicle without so much as advising other parties who might be in need of transportation. These other parties, the note continued, had not acclimatized themselves to the brutal local weather conditions and might come down with frostbite, hypothermia—or worse.

I dropped the note on the kitchen table, made a drink, and called Ronnie.

She sounded more chipper than she had at four in the morning. "Hello?"

I explained that I was in Farberville, but had not yet conceded defeat. Before she could blurt out any questions, I added, "I have to ask you more about the night Oliver Pickett attacked you. It may be painful for you to try to remember the details, but you need to do it if you want me to get to the bottom of all this."

"I'll do my best," she said dully.

"You were unconscious in the master bedroom when Oliver broke up the party. You awoke to find him on top of you, and fought him off into the living room, where you grabbed a knife off the bar and stabbed him."

"That's the part I wish I could forget, but it's all too vivid in my mind. There was a surreal quality to the scene, as if it were a macabre dance choreographed by some fiend. Neither of us spoke; the only sounds were his grunts and my whimpers. When the blade plunged into his neck, we were both so startled that all we could do was gape at each other as blood splattered my shirt. He crumpled onto the floor of the balcony, and I staggered into the bedroom and collapsed."

"Is it possible," I said, "that someone else could have been there at that time?"

"Was someone else there?" she demanded.

"I have no idea. I met a man in Acapulco who claimed he saw a figure come out of the bungalow well after the guests had dispersed. He lied to me more than once, however."

"What was his name?"

I sighed. "He used a pseudonym, and there's no real evidence he was at the Hotel Las Floritas that night. In any case, he's disappeared. Let me ask you something else, Ronnie. After the stabbing, you went back into the bedroom and passed out. When Fran's scream awakened you, you saw the blood on your clothes and the knife near your hand." I paused, aware I was about to say something that might have a profoundly upsetting effect on her. "Did Fran tell you what you'd done, painting such vivid images that your mind could have seized on them and incorporated them into your memory?"

In the ensuing silence, I could hear the clock ticking in my kitchen and footsteps in the downstairs apartment as the tenant returned from a less than arduous day at the bookstore. A motorcycle drove down the alley behind the duplex. I pressed the receiver more tightly to my ear and listened to traffic on a Brussels street.

"No," Ronnie said at last. "I'm familiar with the concept of false memories, and I realize people can be convinced of their validity, especially when a traumatic event is the focus. What you hypothesized is not what happened at the bungalow. As soon as I opened my eyes, I remembered exactly what I'd done. Fran didn't tell me; I told her. Even now I could relate every step I took, every punch I tried to throw, every hysterical thought that raced through my brain. The way his fingers dug into my shoulder. My bewilderment that his clothes were wet. The crazed look on his face. It was over in less than two minutes, and I can recall every second."

She'd sounded so tortured that I had no reservations about her sincerity. I waited a moment, then said, "But you were under the influence of alcohol and marijuana that night. If you'd had so much that you passed out, how could you remember anything with that kind of clarity?"

"Having someone rip off your clothes can be sobering. It may have taken me a few seconds to figure out what was going on and begin to struggle, but I did. Bear in mind I'd had more than an hour to sleep off the ill effects of the alcohol. I wasn't a drinker, so my tolerance threshold was low and I doubt I had more than two or three drinks."

"That makes sense," I conceded.

"I should hope so," Ronnie said. "You said earlier that you have a new lead. What is it?"

"Those packages you received in prison may have come from Fran's mother. I haven't learned her last name, but I think I know the location of the convent school that Fran attended."

"How could you have found that out?"

I'd been expecting an expression of admiration for my deductive mastery, but I reminded myself that she'd just been forced to relive a murder. I told her about the conversation with Caron and my subsequent visit to St. Martin's Academy. "I don't believe the extortionist is in Acapulco," I continued. "Either Chad Warmeyer or Debbie D'Avril could be involved, I suppose, but this would require one of them to locate you after you changed your name twenty-two years ago. Has your photograph been in a newspaper or magazine recently?"

"I have never permitted any formal photographs of me to be published. I'm a scientist, not a media-hungry celebrity. Even if Debbie or Chad happened to glance through a medical journal and find a group photograph taken at a conference, neither would recognize me. They had no interest in me thirty years ago. I was nothing more than an extra bag Arthur and Margaret Landonwood brought to Acapulco."

"Fran's the most likely suspect," I said. "She certainly has the strongest motive, and her mother seems to have known when you were released from prison. The only hope I have of finding her is to go to Phoenix and make inquiries at the convent."

"I'm beginning to wonder if I shouldn't simply pay the money. I'd assumed one of the Mexicans involved in the case was the guilty party. I'm not so certain I want you to continue this investigation in the United States, where the danger of having it made public is so much greater."

"I'll do whatever you wish," I said as graciously as I could, "but I've put a lot of energy into this and I'd hate to give up while I still have a lead."

"Why do you believe the sisters at the convent will tell you anything? They're apt to be in their eighties or nineties and unable to place an unremarkable student from thirty years ago."

I was a bit annoyed with her abrupt capitulation. She'd begged me to go to Acapulco, and I'd obliged despite my misgivings. Caron's life had been endangered. My nightmares might not be as gory as Ronnie's, but I knew I wouldn't easily forget the terror that had gripped me during the ordeal.

"Okay," I said. "I'll resume selling books and you can start saving up for the next call from the extortionist."

"And you believe that's Fran?"

"You killed her father, whom she loved. Because of what you did, she ended up spending an unknown number of years in a filthy prison. Perhaps she's decided to punish you, or has spent her inheritance and needs money. In either scenario, she won't quit with a single payment."

"Locating her won't do any good, then," Ronnie said with a sigh.

"You might be able to reason with her. If not, at least you'll know what you're up against and can decide how to proceed. You may have to go public with the story yourself. Three decades can blunt the impact of almost anything."

"Call my travel agent in Chicago and have her make arrangements for you to go to Phoenix, and also wire you whatever cash you need. Please keep me informed of any progress you make. I'll be home at the end of the week."

My elation faded as I hung up the receiver. More nuns more sun more bad airline food, and more dead ends. And this time it was my own doing.

I had a feeling Peter would not be amused.

Chapter 9

"But you don't believe Fran Pickett killed Santiago, do you?" Peter asked after I'd finished a carefully edited rendition of the previous four days.

When he'd returned my call earlier in the evening, his voice had been so silky (read: seductive) that I'd put aside my misgivings and invited him over for a drink. Now I was wondering if I should have listened to my head instead of my hormones.

"No," I said reluctantly. "I first spoke to Chico at about ten o'clock in the morning. Santiago was killed no later than the middle of the afternoon. Unless Fran was already in Mexico, I can't see how she could have done it—or why, for that matter. The identity of a second person who may have been in the bungalow is irrelevant. Ronnie stabbed Oliver Pickett."

"Maybe she concocted the confession in order to protect someone else," he said. "That, or she's unbalanced. All police departments deal with people who are so desperate for attention that they'll confess to any crime worthy of front page coverage. There's a local guy who comes into the station once a month to confess to the Lindbergh baby's kidnapping. We make the rookies take turns writing up the report."

I craned my neck to look up at his face. After an indulgent moment to marvel at his profile, I said, "Ronnie's emotional development wasn't enhanced by her stint in prison, but she sounded as though she'd dealt with it. Besides, if she knew someone else stabbed Oliver Pickett, why wouldn't she tell me the truth before she sent me blundering around Acapulco?"

He gave me an innocent smile. "You and she are cousins. Does a propensity for fabrication run in the family?"

Before I could respond, Caron burst through the front door. "Rhonda Maguire is a bitch," she said as she flopped into a chair and regarded us with a beady look until we'd moved to a more decorous distance. "She had a slumber party the night of the homecoming game, and I wasn't invited."

"You weren't in town," I said.

"She didn't know I wouldn't be when she sent the invitations out a week beforehand. According to what Inez heard, all the girls brought their dates over after the dance for a midnight breakfast. They had fruit cups! Doesn't that make you Totally Nauseous?"

Peter and I nodded like a pair of marionettes, then I said, "Did Inez ever learn who was in Rhonda's car the day you had the costly encounter with the police officer?"

Caron rolled her eyes at the ceiling. "No, and Rhonda wouldn't even tell Emily and Merissa when they were at the mall on Saturday. You'd think it was some kind of top-secret meeting with a spy from one of those Eastern European countries that nobody can pronounce. They need to go on *Wheel of Fortune* and buy some vowels." She stalked into her bedroom and slammed the door.

Peter risked putting his arm back around me. "When are you leaving for Phoenix?"

"I'll call Ronnie's travel agent in the morning and try for a flight as soon as tomorrow afternoon. Caron's staying with Inez, and the downstairs tenant agreed to run the store for a few more days. He's taken to reading romance novels when there are no customers, which means he has almost limitless opportunities. Azalea Twilight's his favorite author thus far. Do you remember what a turmoil she stirred up with *Professor of Passion?* I truly thought you were going to arrest me for her murder."

Peter ignored my flimsy shot at a diversion. "I'm not going to do my usual song-and-dance routine about exposing yourself to danger, but I want you to remember that someone stabbed a pitiful old man in the throat. It could have been a fluke—or it could have happened because *you* inadvertently pinched a nerve."

"Are you suggesting that I should check into the convent until the case is solved? What if one of the Sisters of the Holy Shrine of San Jacinto is a serial killer on a religious retreat? There I'll be, sleeping on a straw pallet in a tiny cell when the door eases open and in creeps Sister Ted Bundy."

He failed to appreciate my wit. "If you actually find out where Fran Pickett's mother lives and start questioning her, she's liable to inform Fran. You brought up the likelihood that Fran is behind the blackmail demand."

"It was merely a theory," I said, trying not to sound overly defensive. "If Fran is alive, she's forty-six years old."

"And therefore incapable of doing grievous bodily harm? Would you care to think back over your illustrious career as a meddlesome snoop? Right offhand, I can name two middle-aged women who packed pistols in their handbags and tried to shoot you. I'm sure there have been more. When I have some free time, maybe I'll make a list."

Not pleased with the tenor of his remarks, I banged down my empty glass on the coffee table and retreated to the far end of the sofa. "Don't start with the sarcasm, Peter. If you can't accept that I do not enjoy being patronized, find someone who does. Try the personal ads in the newspaper; there seem to be plenty of people eager to be abused in one way or another."

"I apologize," he said.

"You do?"

"Go to Phoenix and find the convent. If this leads you to Fran's mother and ultimately to Fran herself, I'm confident you can deal with her in your own unorthodox fashion. Is there anything I can do here to help you?"

I eyed him suspiciously. In general, he was forthright, which meant I'd become adept at predicting his behavior. I'd memorized some of his more insufferable lectures. I knew how to interpret the sudden tightening of his jaw that warned me I'd gone too far. I probably could have assessed his blood pressure with the accuracy of a sphygmomanometer. "Help me how?" I asked.

"Whatever you want. I can take you to the airport,

swing by on Thursday and put out the trash, wallpaper the bedroom, assign Jorgeson to identify the mysterious passenger in Rhonda's car." He made an elaborate production of yawning, then stood up and picked up his coat. "Call me before you leave if you think of anything. I don't guess you know when you'll be back, do you?"

"It depends on what develops in Phoenix," I said, still puzzled by his amicability. His jaw should have been tighter, and his brow lowered enough to accentuate a faintly etched furrow that I found adorable. Instead, his expression was relaxed, as if he were preparing to watch a favorite movie. Or was off to visit someone with a less acerbic tongue, I thought as he bent down to give me a perfunctory kiss and then left.

"Oh my gawd!" Caron howled from her bedroom. "You've got to be kidding! We can't have a test on the Dickens book tomorrow. I've only read three chapters!"

Some things never change.

I was in Phoenix by six o'clock the next afternoon, settled in a cushy hotel room and armed with a drink from the minibar. I found a telephone directory in a drawer alongside a Gideon bible, took out the former, checked to make sure Fran wasn't listed (I'd called information from Farberville), and then flipped to the yellow pages. There was no heading for "Convents, Catholic," so I retreated a few pages to "Churches, Catholic." The substantial Hispanic population was reflected by the number of listings, many of which included times for masses held in Spanish.

I randomly selected one of them, and quickly

learned that church offices not only have voice mail, but also close at five. I could have attended one of the numerous evening masses, I supposed, and lurked in the vestibule afterward in hopes of encountering a well-informed nun or priest.

On that note, I took a shower, ordered room service, and spent the evening pleasantly entertained with a mystery novel.

My first telephone call in the morning was to St. Francis of Assisi—or to his church, anyway. His secretary wasn't in, but my fourth call (St. Sebastian) elicited the information I needed. Although the school was closed, the Convent of the Holy Shrine of San Jacinto was indeed in operation in a small town in the Tonto National Forest.

I'd had the foresight to rent a car at the airport. I stopped at the hotel desk for a map and directions, and after a maddening fifteen minutes during which it was made clear that hotel desks were not staffed by moonlighting brain surgeons, went out to the parking lot with a map and some idea of how to proceed.

The traffic in Phoenix was typical of any sprawling city; the only evidence I wasn't in Atlanta or Dallas was the occasional swollen cactus holding up its arms as if the victim of a mugging. The artificial greenery of the city gave way to the browns and siennas of the high desert, and then to piñon and ponderosa pines as I drove into the mountains. Here there were streams, some rushing and some trickling, and forests with shadowy tunnels. I found a country music station to distract myself from worrying about coming face-to-face with another Sister Mary Clarissa.

Buckneck turned out to be seventy-five miles from Phoenix. The town was no more than a single street lined with dilapidated houses, trailers, and a couple of all-purpose stores. A gas station seemed to be the social hub; half a dozen trucks were parked nearby and a bench out front was occupied by a row of stubbly old men, oblivious to the bony yellow dog sniffing at their khaki trouser cuffs.

The convent was at the end of the street. I parked in front of an adobe wall and mindlessly stared at the cracks, riveted by the same ridiculous anxiety I'd felt outside St. Martin's Academy. When my cowardice became unbearable, I checked my hair and lipstick in the rearview mirror and climbed out of the car.

The wooden gates were open wide enough to permit pedestrians, bicycles, and emaciated burros. I continued into a courtyard landscaped only with asymmetrical flagstones. In front of me was a simple church, done in a style reminiscent of the architecture of Acapulco; fences on either side made it obvious that the only approach to the convent was through its doors.

This was my last chance to find Fran Pickett, I told myself as I entered the church. Two sections of a dozen pews were divided by an aisle sloping down to a pulpit. On the wall behind it hung a massive, elaborately framed painting of the Virgin Mary with a baby in her lap and a pair of celestial attendants. On a side wall was a shallow recess with another painting that I presumed involved San Jacinto; candles set in small glass dishes flickered on a railing in front of it.

The pews were uninhabited. The doors on either

side of me did not have signs that invited admission. Since I'd arrived, I'd not heard one noise that indicated there was anyone currently in residence within the walls. People had been here earlier, unless the candles had lit themselves through spontaneous combustion.

I could either sit passively in a pew, or conduct myself like a reasonably assertive forty-year-old woman and take action. It was a tough call, but I finally went to one of the doors and determined it was locked. The other door was locked, too, but beside it was a faded, hand-printed card that advised visitors to push a button. I did so, and heard a buzz somewhere in the distance.

That was about as assertive as I could be, so I sat down in the back pew and waited. Several minutes later, the door opened and a wizened figure emerged. She was dressed in an old-fashioned black habit that brushed the floor as she scuttled toward me.

"Yes?" she said, looking at me through rheumy eyes so clouded with cataracts that I doubted she could see me.

"Are you the Mother Superior?" I asked.

"Oh, heavens no. I'm Sister Jerome. I'm supposed to tend the door today. You haven't been waiting too long, have you?"

She sounded so distressed that I said, "I just came inside a second ago, and was admiring the church."

"Shall I take you to the Reverend Mother?"

"Yes, please." I followed her through the doorway and down a hall to a closed door. Sister Jerome opened the door with a leathery hand, stepped aside, and poked me in the back.

"Thank you," I said to her, then went into what

proved to be a rather standard office. The woman behind the desk wore the same black habit as her colleague, and she was at least as old and worn. The look she gave me, however, was a good deal sharper.

"Yes?" she said in a steady baritone.

"I'm trying to find a girl who attended the convent school about thirty years ago," I began in a somewhat higher voice.

"The school has been closed for twenty years. We do not hold class reunions, and few of the girls bother to keep in touch these days. But why should they? There are only six of us left in what is basically a retirement home. His Holiness has given us permission to live out our days here. Despite appearances, I suspect Sister Jerome will be left to turn out the lights and lock the door."

"Oh," I said, disconcerted.

"Sister Ursala has developed a very bad cough," the Reverend Mother continued. "I doubt she'll survive the winter. I can't think how many times I told her not to tend to her bees without a proper wrap, but she's as rebellious as a schoolgirl."

I seized the opportunity to steer the conversation back to Fran. "As I mentioned, I'm trying to locate one of your former students, Franchesca Pickett, who attended classes in the sixties. Her mother had remarried, and I was hoping you might have records that reflected her name."

"Even if that were available, it would not be appropriate to give it to anyone who asked for it. We have a policy of strict adherence to the laws of confidentiality. Over the years, I've turned down numerous requests such as yours."

I'd run into dead ends before, but I felt as though

I'd smacked into this one with enough force to make my head reel. The woman had the demeanor of a judge who'd been on the bench well past retirement age, who'd never fallen for a contrived alibi or an outlandish excuse, who had no qualms about handing out the most severe sentences. She might have intimidated Sister Mary Clarissa.

I tried to sound confident as I said, "What a shame. I have some wonderful news for Franchesca, but no way to share it with her."

"Do tell," commanded the Reverend Mother.

I sank down on a chair and crossed my ankles while I groped for a suitable story. "I'm also governed by the laws of confidentiality, but I can tell you that there's half a million dollars at stake. If Franchesca were to collect it, she might be so grateful to you that she would make a substantial donation to the convent."

"So that we can put in tennis courts and a hot tub?"

"Or a medical clinic for your parishioners."

The Reverend Mother rocked back and folded her arms, staring at me as if I'd been caught with a cigarette in the restroom. "Franchesca was very unhappy here. She'd be more likely to buy the property from under us and have it bulldozed."

"Then you remember her?"

"I remember all the troublemakers. Franchesca was very intelligent and industrious about her studies, but she was also stubborn. She and I had many long discussions in this room about her failure to conform to our rules. She would sit in that chair with her ankles crossed like yours, her hands in her lap and her eyes wide with repentance, readily accepting penance in the chapel and additional chores in the kitchen. Hours later a deputy sheriff would spot her trying to hitchhike into Phoenix and bring her back. At her mother's insistence, we did all we could to instill in Franchesca a sense of respect and obedience, but we had no success. The heart of her problem lay in her parents' divorce."

"Her father's death must have been devastating," I said, wondering how the Reverend Mother defined the concept of confidentiality. I wasn't about to interrupt her to discuss it, though. Maybe twenty years of conversation with Sister Jerome and others of a similar age hadn't been especially engrossing.

"She never returned to us after her ill-fated vacation to Mexico. Her mother refused my calls and sent back my letters unopened. Franchesca's clothing and personal possessions were stored in the basement of the dormitory; to the best of my knowledge, no one ever came for the suitcases and the trunk."

"I guess that's that," I said with a polite smile. "Thank you so much for your time, Reverend Mother."

She nodded dismissively and picked up a pen. I returned to the church proper, where I found Sister Jerome napping in the first pew. I sat down next to her and gently shook her shoulder.

"Sister Jerome," I said, "there's something I'd like to ask you before I leave."

Her eyes fluttered open. "You were here earlier, weren't you? Did you have a nice visit with the Reverend Mother?"

"Very nice," I said. Ignoring the fact I was about to lie to an elderly nun under the scrutiny of the Virgin Mary and her crew, I added, "She said something about one of the sisters keeping bees. I'm an avid bee enthusiast, and it would mean a great deal to me to see the hives."

She recoiled so abruptly that I had to catch her arm to keep her from sliding off the pew. "Oh, no, that would never be permitted. Several of the sisters have chosen to lead cloistered lives, including Sister Ursala. On mornings like this, she often sits in the garden and watches her little bees buzz merrily among the flowers."

"Could I see the dormitory where the students lived?" I asked.

"The dormitory and the classrooms are directly across from our living quarters. Dear Sister Ambrose would have another stroke if she happened to see an outsider, and she's so very frail that she might not survive. It's out of the question, my dear." She stood up as if to scuttle away, then clasped her hands and gave me a doleful look. "But I do hate to disappoint you. I don't suppose there would be any harm in allowing you to peek through the window in the sacristy."

"That would be wonderful," I said. The Reverend Mother knew perfectly well what she'd said about Fran's belongings. She hadn't issued an open invitation to break into the basement, but she must have suspected I would consider the idea. It really was unfortunate there was no book entitled *Know Your Nuns,* because this one was quite an enigma.

We went up the aisle. Sister Jerome took a key ring from an invisible pocket and unlocked the door opposite the one with the buzzer. The hallway on this side of the church was narrower, and there were no doors except the one at the end. With her head lowered and her sleeves swishing, she hurried along like a bat returning to its belfry after a busy night.

The sacristy turned out to be nothing more than a mundane storage room with an exotic label. The window gave a limited view of a garden, stucco buildings forming the back three quarters of a quadrangle, and what Sister Jerome assured me was the apiary. It looked like a bunch of gray crates to me, but I murmured appreciative noises as I tried to determine a route to the dormitory.

"Is there any sort of service this evening?" I asked as I watched one of the sisters rise from a bench in the garden and move very slowly toward the building that Sister Jerome had told me was their living quarters.

"We gather to recite the rosary at seven, but we don't permit visitors. Father Filicales comes on Saturdays to hear confessions and conduct mass." She gestured at a black robe on a hook. "That's his cassock. It's been mended so often that one of these days it's liable to fall apart. So is Father Filicales, I'm sorry to say."

An exceedingly wicked idea came to mind. "Oh," I said, tilting my head like a robin within range of a worm, "I believe I heard someone come into the church. Shouldn't you see who it is?"

"We've been waiting for days for a plumber. If he leaves without fixing the leak in the kitchen, the Reverend Mother will be beside herself."

I resumed gazing out the window with a rapt expression. "This is so peaceful and inspiring. Would you mind if I stayed a few minutes longer?"

After a moment of indecision, Sister Jerome

handed me the key ring. "Please lock the door and return the keys to me before you leave."

Seconds later, I had the cassock rolled up into the smallest bundle possible. I tucked it under my waistband in the middle of my back, arranged my shirttail over it, fastidiously locked the door, and returned to the church, where I found my guide looking out at the empty courtyard.

"There's no one here," she said. "Whatever shall I say to the Reverend Mother if the plumber is already on his way back to Phoenix? It's so difficult to get anyone to come all this way."

"I must have been mistaken," I said soothingly. I handed her the key ring and eased around her, all the while thanking her for her hospitality. The bulge in my back might have been noticeable to someone with keener eyesight, but I felt fairly confident as I walked across the courtyard and out the gate.

One of the two stores had bolts of fabric. I bought a yard of black cotton, a packet of bobby pins, and a disposable flashlight, then stopped at a cafe and bought the makings of a primitive picnic. I drove back to a stream that had been particularly picturesque and spent the afternoon dabbling my toes in the water, munching crackers and cheese, and reading the paperback I'd cleverly thought to put in my purse. And plotting a commando raid on the convent, of course.

As the sun set, I pulled on the cassock and drove into Buckneck. The men on the bench in front of the gas station had departed for the day, as had the yellow dog. The stores were closed, the street deserted. I parked half a block from the convent. The cassock lacked pockets, so I put my purse under the seat, then draped the fabric over my head and pinned it in place. The effect was minimal, but so was the light.

There was a glow from inside the church, but the courtyard was empty. I slithered along the wall until I reached the fence, searched unsuccessfully for a gate, and then, amid muffled curses and admonishments to myself to take care of Father Whatever's cassock, clambered over the fence and landed on my derriere in what I supposed was hallowed dirt. When no alarms went off or armed guards appeared, I headed for the vacant dormitory, hoping that the sister with the history of strokes had not decided to skip the service.

No one had thought to lock the building. I went inside, switched on the cheap flashlight, and glanced around what had been a communal living room. The furniture that remained was stark and clearly selected for function rather than comfort; the only decor on the walls was of a religious nature. I prowled down a hall, opening doors and illuminating a kitchen, an office, a closet, and eventually a flight of stairs descending into utter blackness.

Gulping, I slowly went down the steps, feeling as though I should have been wearing a negligee and carrying a candle. The air was stagnant. The beam of my flashlight flickered on cardboard boxes, broken chairs, an ancient bicycle, and an impresssive collection of dusty jars. In one corner I spotted several suitcases and a worn trunk from a much earlier era.

Trying not to chortle (and perhaps end up in hysterics), I knelt next to the trunk and examined it for an identifying label. When I found none, I shifted my attention to the suitcases. The last one had a small piece of paper held in place by tape. The writing had faded, but I was able to make out Fran's name and what I dearly hoped was a home address: Rt. 3, Box 77, Phoenix.

"A hot tub might do much to ease Sister Jerome's arthritis," said a baritone voice at the top of the stairs.

I decided not to congratulate myself on the breadth of my resourcefulness just yet. "I'll keep that in mind," I replied.

"You may leave Father Filicales's cassock by the door of the church."

"Yes, ma'am."

"With a donation for the indigent of the parish."

"Yes, ma'am."

The floor creaked as she left, and only then did I enjoy the luxury of a deep breath. Being accused of murder in Acapulco didn't begin to compare to being caught red-handed (as well as red-faced) in a cloistered convent.

Fran Pickett had been one tough cookie to defy the Reverend Mother, I thought as I sharted up the stairs.

Chapter 10

After breakfast, I called the main post office and asked for the location of Route 3, Box 77. I was advised that the route consisted of Old Madrid Road and the identity of the boxholder was none of my business. I debated whether or not to pack and check out of the hotel. If the road was now lined with convenience stores and parking lots, I'd have no choice but to head for the airport to catch the next flight back to Farberville.

I left my suitcase in the room as a gesture of optimism. After all, I had tracked down the address, which at one time had seemed a task of Herculean magnitude. I'd been humiliated in the process, but I'd survived with a shred or two of dignity left intact—and the Sisters of the Holy Shrine of San Jacinto were fifty dollars richer.

According to my map, Old Madrid Road originated in the south part of Phoenix and at one time might have been the primary route to Tucson. I plotted my course and in less than half an hour spotted the pertinent street sign.

Old Madrid Road didn't dally inside the city limits.

Within minutes, I was squinting at numbers on mailboxes in front of isolated houses. It was easy to understand why Fran had been so desperate to live with her father in Beverly Hills and hang out with mall rats rather than kangaroo rats.

I was running out of mailboxes when I saw a billboard heralding the proximity of the Tricky M Ranchettes. The half-acre "ranchettes" were available for a low down payment and affordable monthly payments. Friendly agents were awaiting my family's arrival with complimentary coffee, tea, and lemonade. No appointment necessary.

I drove through a gate made of railroad ties adorned with horseshoes and antique oddments. The street was as broad as a boulevard, but not clogged with mothers in station wagons and children on bicycles. I quickly deduced this was due to the scarcity of houses; the sole completed one didn't appear to be inhabited. A dozen others were in varying stages of construction, from skeletal frames to half-completed exteriors. There were no workmen or trucks, however, in what amounted to a suburban ghost town.

I followed signs purporting to lead the way to the office, where I was most likely to encounter a friendly agent, a complimentary cup of coffee, and perhaps a clue as to the location of Fran Pickett's home of thirty years ago.

Several streets later, I saw a battered silver trailer under the only tree I'd seen thus far. The tree was not comparable to the stately elms commonplace on the Farber College campus, but it provided a small amount of shade. Beyond the trailer was a lunar landscape of rocks and jutting hills. High above me, buzzards circled, monitoring that which would be lunch when nicely ripened.

As I parked, a pickup truck whipped in beside me in a cloud of dark, odoriferous exhaust fumes. The truck looked as though it had been painted to blend in with the desert behind it, but a closer scrutiny indicated that time and nature were the culprits. The gun rack in the rear window was well equipped with what I supposed were shotguns or rifles.

The woman who got out of the driver's side had not fared much better than her vehicle. She had cropped gray hair and a face so heavily wrinkled and spotted that it resembled a piece of dried fruit. Her tight jeans emphasized her ample rump, and her worn boots and dusty leather hat were not frivolous fashion accessories. I expected to hear the theme song from *Bonanza* as she hurried around the hood of the car.

"Welcome to the Tricky M," she said as she yanked open my door. "I was over at the barn trying to get that lazy son of a bitch to do some work when I saw your car. As I'm sure you noticed, we've temporarily halted construction, but by a year from now, we'll be our own little community of nearly four hundred families on a thousand acres of God's country." She bent down to peer into the rental car. "You by yourself?"

"Yes, and I'm not a prospective buyer."

"That's what they all say," she said, stepping back to allow me to get out of the car. "I've been selling real estate for more than twenty years, and my motto's always been, 'Buyers are liars.' I worked once with a woman who insisted she needed five thousand square feet, a separate apartment for her mother-in-law, and a pool." She took my arm and propelled me toward the trailer. "Well, I spent months showing her houses all over Phoenix and Scottsdale. One didn't have adequate closets, another was too close to a busy street, and so forth. Then she turned around and bought a two-bedroom condo from another agent. I sent her a decapitated jackrabbit for a housewarming present."

The interior of the trailer was crowded with two desks and numerous straightbacked chairs. The walls were covered with depictions of houses surrounded by verdant grass, flowers, and patio furniture. A fan on a filing cabinet rustled loose papers and rolled-up blueprints. Ashtrays overflowed on each desk, and a wastebasket had reached its capacity at some point in the distant past. Black gunk coated the bottom of the glass coffeepot. As far as I could tell, there were no friendly agents lurking in the corner.

"I don't believe I caught your name," she continued. "Mine's Trixie. My partner's name is Maisie, so we stuck 'em together and came up with Tricky M."

"I'm Claire," I said. "I'm trying to locate an address, but haven't had any luck. Box seventy-seven is all I know."

"Seventy-seven," she said, sitting behind one of the desks and resting her boots on the rim of the wastebasket. She took out a charcoal brown cigarette and lit it. "That'd be out this way, but I'm not sure where it is. Who're you looking for, Claire?"

"Part of the problem is I don't know the last name," I admitted. "A married couple, probably close to seventy years old, who lived here thirty years ago. The woman's first name was Bea. They had only one child, a girl named Franchesca Pickett. She was from the woman's first marriage and kept her father's surname. She'd be in her late forties."

Trixie blew a ribbon of smoke at the ceiling. "Nobody comes to mind. The Calvos are that old, but the wife's name is Amalia and they had a whole passel of kids. So did Maggie and Joe Bob Maron, come to think of it. He used to brag that he could put together a whole baseball team. The widow in the last house you passed never had any children. Those are about the only folks who've been living here that long. The banks turned ugly some years back and foreclosed on a lot of folks' property. There were some politicians behind it who'd heard rumors that the interstate to Tucson was going through here and wanted to buy up the land for bedroom communities. Never happened, in case you didn't notice."

"Is that why you began this development?" I asked.

"Real estate agents hear rumors, too. Maisie and I owned the land, so we decided to go ahead and give it a shot. We got off to a good start, putting in the streets and utilities, completing a model home, but then the savings and loan where we'd arranged our financing failed. The auditors from the government descended like a pack of mangy wolves. There are more liens filed against us than there are crooks in the state legislature. We haven't called it quits, though; we sank every dollar we had in the Tricky M and the only way we're going to get back our investment is to borrow enough to continue the project. Maisie's at a bank right now, trying to arrange something."

"Was there a house on the property when you bought it?" I asked.

She frowned. "Yeah, but nobody'd lived in it for years and it wasn't worth saving. The first thing we did after we closed the deal was to burn it down. I brought the marshmallows and Maisie brought the champagne. I would have preferred beer, myself. We're not your classic peas in a pod, Maisie and me."

"Do you recall the owner's name?"

Trixie's frown deepened as she stared over my head. "An old guy, name of Rogers Cooper, who was real touchy if you called him Roger. Seems he was named after his father *and* his godfather. He'd owned the property for years, always dreaming of running cattle so he could play cowboy. Only obstacle was a lack of water. He was delighted to accept our offer. I saw him a couple of years back, driving a Mercedes and wearing a fancy white hat."

"Rogers Cooper," I said as I took out my notebook and wrote down the name. "I guess I'll stop at the houses along the road and see if anyone remembers the family, then try to find this man in Phoenix."

She jabbed out her cigarette, stood up, and held out her hand. "Good luck, Claire," she said as she squeezed my hand with enough pressure to make my knuckles pop. "If you ever decide to retire to Arizona, just give me a call and we'll have you in your own ranchette in no time. You can swim at the community pool, play pinochle in the recreation center, take classes in watercolor painting and macrame, and enjoy the companionship of—"

"Goodbye, Trixie," I said, then fled to the car before she could pull out a contract and a pen. As I drove away, I saw her truck bouncing down a dirt road behind the trailer. Hoping the gentleman in the barn was busily doing whatever one did in barns (nothing I cared to envision), I found my way back to the gate and stopped to contemplate what I'd learned.

Rogers Cooper could have been Fran's stepfather. Trixie had made no reference to a Mrs. Cooper, which was discouraging in that I was fairly sure wives had to sign documents when property was sold. It was possible that Fran had remained in contact with Cooper and he would know of her whereabouts. There might be a lot of Coopers in the telephone directory, but no more than one with such a peculiar first name.

The woman in the first house peered at me through a dirt-encrusted screen while I explained why I'd knocked on her door. In the background, I could hear the typically earnest conversation of soap opera characters discussing the ramifications of someone else's infidelity.

"No," she said, shaking her head, "I never knew the names of anyone out here. Didn't care, neither."

The door closed in my face. No one was home at the next, and the third had been vacant for some time. The few people I spoke to claimed ignorance of Rogers Cooper or a family with a daughter named Fran. Eventually, I arrived back in Phoenix and drove to the hotel.

Rogers Cooper was not in the telephone directory, and information did not have him listed. Those hiding under an initial proved to be Rene and Roseanne. It didn't much matter, I told myself as I closed the directory. The Rogers Cooper connection was as flimsy as Caron's excuse for the melange of dirty dishes under her bed. I'd merely speculated that he was the stepfather; he could have bought the property from Bea and her husband anytime in the last three decades.

But the idea of leaving without having spoken to him annoyed me. If I was finally forced to concede defeat, I wanted to be able to say I'd followed every lead, no matter how implausible. Wishing I'd read more private eye fiction, I took out all my notes and thumbed through them. When I arrived at the page Ronnie had written about Fran, I reread it carefully for some tiny clue I'd overlooked thus far—although I'd pretty well memorized it: petite, dramatic features, long hair, some Spanish, living on a ranch with her mother and stepfather when not in the grasp of the Sisters of the Holy Swine.

My eyes returned to the description of the stepfather. "Retired army officer and an alcoholic," I read aloud, then put down the page and tried to figure out how to utilize the scanty information. If he was alive, he still fit the first category and was apt to fit the second, too. Alcoholics Anonymous was hardly the sort of organization to offer the names and addresses of its members. A veterans' group, on the other hand, had no reason to keep secret its roster.

I opened the telephone directory and found a number for the local chapter of Veterans of Foreign Wars. Fran's stepfather (whether Rogers Cooper or someone else) would have been of an age to have participated in World War II, the Korean War, or even the early, unofficial years of the Vietnam War. All were distinctly foreign.

After concocting a charmingly simplistic lie, I took a deep breath and dialed the number. The man's voice that answered was gruff and exasperated, as if

I'd dragged him out of a hot tub where he'd been entertaining naked women. In his dreams, anyway.

"Is this the VFW?" I asked.

"Ain't the NCAA."

Rather than play games, I said, "I'm trying to find a dear old friend who lives in Phoenix. He's not in the telephone directory, but he may be a member of your organization. I was hoping you could—"

"What's his name?"

"Rogers Cooper."

There was a pause. "Don't know him, but the name's familiar. Hold on."

I held my breath as well as the receiver as I grabbed my notebook and a pencil. Rogers Cooper wasn't about to walk into the hotel room, but he was much closer than he'd been ten minutes earlier.

"Yeah," the man said, "I knew I'd seen the name. You want Cooper, look for him out on Hayden Road. I don't have a number, but you can find him right across from the Salt Cellar Restaurant and catty-corner from a place called the Auto-Plex or some fool name like that."

I babbled out my gratitude, hung up, and pulled out the map. Hayden Road was in Scottsdale, a suburb of Phoenix. It appeared to be a major thoroughfare, but surely I could find the restaurant and Auto-Plex without too much difficulty.

And I did, but across from the restaurant and catty-corner to the car shop was a sprawling green expanse with winding roads, well-tended shrubbery, and engraved marble slabs. If the joker from the VFW was to be believed, Rogers Cooper either worked at Green Acres Cemetery or was buried there. It wasn't much of a toss-up.

I drove around for a while, randomly searching for a gravestone with Cooper's name. There was no alphabetical order, but instead what seemed to be a first-come-first-served approach to the plots. The relentless sunshine had faded sprays of plastic flowers to near translucency, giving them an appropriately ghostly effect. A few framed photographs were bleached into blurs.

I finally acknowledged that my chances of happening on one particular grave were slim, at best. I found an office and asked the woman behind a desk for the location of Rogers Cooper. She consulted a file, took out a photocopied map, and drew a tidy X on a rectangle near one corner.

I eyed the file. "Would that have information about the next of kin?" I asked.

She was a good deal less forthcoming than the Reverend Mother. "Yeah, but you can't look at it."

I took the map and trudged back out to the car, wondering why carrots kept being dangled in front of me and then snatched away at the fateful second as if the entire citizenry of Arizona had entered into a conspiracy. The Mexicans were equally guilty. Just once, I thought as I drove toward the grave, it would be nice if someone simply handed me information that was accurate and comprehensive. It would also be nice if Caron voluntarily cleaned the bathroom and gave up speaking in capital letters, or if Peter stopped pressuring me to make a commitment.

My disposition was not sunny as I parked and went to find the mortal remains of Rogers Cooper. He was off by himself in a somewhat neglected corner, and no flowers or photos decorated his stone. He'd been born on December 12, 1916, and died on

February 27, 1966. Neither Fran Pickett nor her mother was kneeling in the grass, sobbing into a handkerchief.

I wrote down the dates and found a shady bench to sit and think. Trixie had made a mistake when she claimed to have seen Cooper in a Mercedes; unless the car had been used for a casket, he'd not been behind the wheel of anything for a long while. His house had been burned down with whatever had been left inside it. There were no ashes to be sifted, no half-burnt letters or address books to be reconstructed.

And I didn't know if he was the person I'd been seeking, or was just a frustrated cowboy from the city. At least Mrs. Cooper was not resting alongside him. I was too bruised from running into dead ends to deal with discovering that her first name had been Bea—and she was beyond answering my questions.

It occurred to me that I could determine if he'd been married when buried—if I could find a copy of his obituary. I took a final look at the headstone, then left him to rest in peace and drove out onto Hayden Road. I'd planned to go back to the hotel and call the local newspaper about their files (after all, it had worked so well in Acapulco), but I happened to spot a bookstore in a row of art galleries and souvenir shops. Its magnetic force was irresistible, as was the parking space directly in front of it. Rogers Cooper had been waiting since 1966; the particulars of his life and demise could wait a little longer while I replenished my reading material.

The Poisoned Pen, as the store was called, was exactly what I wished the Book Depot could be, but the limitations of the Farberville book-buying population precluded a store specializing in mystery fiction. After I'd found some paperbacks to keep me occupied on the flight home, I took them to the counter and asked for directions to the newspaper office.

"The *Arizona Republic*'s downtown," the woman said, spreading out a map. "If traffic is minimal *and* you don't get lost too often *and* you don't run into construction, it'll take about half an hour."

After listening to complicated and confusing directions, I said, "Maybe I ought to call first. I don't want to drive all that way and be denied access to their morgue. If they have one, that is."

"The public libraries have back issues on microfilm. Would you like directions to the nearest branch?"

I wrote down the information, paid for the books, and thanked her. It was tempting to linger in the genteel milieu and swap stories about the frustrations of dealing with the publishing industry, but I stoically returned to the car and drove to the library.

The back issues were on microfilm, as avowed by the sagacious proprietress of The Poisoned Pen. I scrolled to the issue most apt to have Rogers Cooper's obituary, tried the following one, and found it amidst lengthier accounts of more prominent citizens. Rogers, aged 50, had died at his residence from a self-inflicted injury. He had been a master sergeant in the army and served in Europe and Korea. After his retirement from the military, he'd owned an appliance store in Phoenix. He'd been a member of the VFW and a Mason. He was survived by his wife, Beatrice; a stepdaughter, Franchesca; and a brother, James F. Cooper, of Flagstaff.

"Self-inflicted injury," I said under my breath, provoking a dirty look from a pink-haired woman across the table. This injury had occurred less than two months after Fran and Ronnie had been snatched into the hostile clutches of the Mexican legal system. I scrolled backwards, searching for an article about his suicide.

It merited only a few sentences. Police officers had been called to the residence on Old Madrid Road by Mrs. Beatrice Cooper, who'd discovered the body upon returning home from a trip. The coroner had declared the death to have resulted from a single gunshot wound to the head. A handgun registered to Cooper had been found at the scene, along with a note. There was no evidence of an intruder.

Well, I'd found Fran's stepfather and knew his present whereabouts. I also knew where the family had been living thirty years ago, as well as Bea's legal name at that time. A librarian steered me to a collection of telephone directories from around the state. I wasn't especially surprised when I failed to find a listing for Beatrice Cooper—or James F. Cooper—in any of them.

The Reverend Mother at the convent had said she'd had no communication with Bea after the Christmas trip to Acapulco, so there was no reason to consider a plan to break into her office and rifle her files. The idea of breaking into the office at Green Acres Cemetery did not appeal; being nailed by a night watchman would lead to unpleasant complications with the local constabulary. And it was obvious I had no talent for such activities.

That left Trixie at the top of my list. She'd known Rogers Cooper to some extent, but not well enough to remember his wife's name. The sale of the property must have taken place sometime after Fran left to join her father in Acapulco in the middle of December of 1965 and before her stepfather's death at the end of February. If the latter had been delighted by the sale, his euphoria had faded when the proceeds went to bribe Mexican judges and wardens. Could his suicide have been motivated by Fran's involvement in the crime? It didn't make much sense, I decided. She hadn't disgraced *his* family name and there'd been no publicity in the United States. Her failure to return home could have been explained with a vague story about a new boarding school.

Trixie's partner Maisie might have better recollections of Bea Cooper. I mentally rearranged my list to reflect this, waved at the pink-haired woman, and left the library. I read one of my new paperbacks over a sandwich and a glass of iced tea, then drove out Old Madrid Road to the Tricky M (aka the Cooper homestead). Rather than listen to the radio, I entertained myself imagining Caron's reaction if I announced we were going to live on a ranchette in the Arizona desert, where we could have cowettes and sheepettes to mow the lawn. If Maisie's memory was no better than Trixie's, the opportunity to tease Caron might arise within twenty-four hours, I thought as my grin wavered. Ronnie would be forced to rely on a private investigator—or concede and pay the extortionist. Peter would be sympathetic but privately pleased.

As I drove past the model home, I saw movement behind a window. I slowed to a crawl to look more carefully, but if someone was inside, he or she had moved out of view. It might have been a workman, but was more likely to be teenagers up to some nefarious enterprise. I didn't park and go inside to investigate, since Trixie seemed capable of dealing with a trespasser without so much as ruffling her hair.

It was a good thing I was in the only car on the broad street, because I slammed on the brakes.

"Damn!" I howled. "How could I have been so stupid?"

Chapter 11

I was still berating myself as I parked between Trixie's pickup truck and a gaudy pink convertible that looked as though it had been purloined from Elvis's automobile museum. I gave myself a moment for absolution, then rapped on the trailer door and went inside without waiting for an invitation that might not be forthcoming.

Trixie sat behind her desk, a brown cigarette smoldering in her hand. Her lips tightened as she saw me, but she quickly produced a smile. "Did you come back for a tour, Claire? You're in luck because I can give you a great deal on one of our prime lots that'll be within spittin' distance of the pool."

"Not today," I said as I studied the other woman in the room. She stood in a doorway, motionless and without any of Trixie's phony congeniality. Her complexion was smoother and rosier than that of her partner, and her dark blonde hair was styled in a flip reminiscent of a sixties high school yearbook. She was taller and more slender, too, although her silk blouse strained across the noticeable contours of her chest. Despite her efforts, there were fine lines visible beneath her heavy makeup and a subtle capitulation to the force of gravity that made it clear she had celebrated more birthdays than I.

For a moment, I felt a surge of exhilaration that I'd found Fran Pickett, but it ebbed as I realized the woman had small, close-set blue eyes. Ronnie had been quite specific that Fran's were large and hazel, and one can only do so much with tinted contact lenses. "You must be Maisie" I said.

"That's right," she said, apparently willing to remain in the doorway for the duration of my visit.

I looked back at Trixie. "When I drove by the model home, I thought I saw someone inside it."

She stubbed out the cigarette. "Yeah, I sent the lazy son of a bitch over to take care of the dust and cobwebs. We don't have a parade of potential buyers, but we need to be prepared if one shows up. Are you sure I can't give you a short tour? There's not a lot to see, but we can go down to the barn where we're planning to fix up the stalls and put in a riding ring. If you don't mind a short hike, the hill behind it has a superb view of the Gila River."

"I'm not interested," I said as I sat down across from her and took out my notes. Rather than continue, I waited in silence, my expression mildly antagonistic.

Trixie began to fidget with a letter opener. "Did you ever find that box number you were looking for earlier?"

"No, but I did find Rogers Cooper. In his way, he was extremely helpful. That's why I'm here."

She dropped the letter opener and lit another cigarette. "I don't understand what you mean, Claire. Was he the fellow with a wife named Bea?"

"His wife's name was Beatrice," I said. "It took me longer than it should have to realize that 'Bea' is a nickname for Beatrice—and so is 'Trixie.' You're Fran Pickett's mother, aren't you?"

"Look at the time!" squealed Maisie, having miraculously uprooted her feet. "I told Grover down at First Federal that I'd be there at three to finish filling out the loan applications. Trixie, I'll stop by the model home and make sure everything's okay. Nice to have met you, Claire. I hope you'll reconsider buying a ranchette here at the Tricky M." Before we could respond, she wiggled her fingers at us and sailed out the door.

I turned back to the woman across the desk, not sure if I should think of her as Bea or Trixie. Both facets had played important roles in the case, so I at last settled on Beatrice.

"You're Fran Pickett's mother, aren't you?" I repeated. "Is your last name still Cooper?"

"A while back I thought about reverting to my maiden name, but it was too much trouble. Everybody in the real estate business has always known me as Trixie Cooper. I'd have been forced to get new business cards and send letters to all my previous clients."

She seemed eager to steer the conversation away from Fran, so I humored her for the moment. "I found your late husband's grave in Green Acres Cemetery. You didn't buy the property from him—you inherited it. Why didn't you tell me the truth?"

"I didn't know why you were asking," she said in a low voice, "and I was afraid you were a reporter. After Oliver's death, reporters from Los Angeles showed up, wanting to do interviews with his daughter and ex-wife. They didn't seem to know the details of his death, and I sure as hell didn't want to answer any questions about it. Rogers was furious that they'd dared set foot on our porch. He was a pious man who likened Hollywood to Sodom and Gomorrah. He forbade Fran from so much as mentioning her father. The child support checks went straight into a savings account for college."

"Why tell me Cooper's name at all?"

"Because you could find it at City Hall in a deed book, and my name would be alongside his. I figured if I told you he was alive, you'd try more ordinary channels, then get discouraged and give up."

"I'm not a reporter," I said, putting away my notes. "I'm here on behalf of Ronnie Landonwood. She desperately needs to communicate with Fran."

Beatrice's eyes widened. "She was sentenced to twelve years. I'm surprised to hear she survived."

"I've spoken with her on the telephone several times in the last two weeks." I was about to cite as further evidence the symposium in Brussels, then caught myself. The less anyone knew about Ronnie's personal life, the better. "Is Fran living in Phoenix?"

"I haven't laid eyes on her in twenty-three years. No letters, no calls, no nothing. I don't know if she got married and has a family, or is buried in some unmarked grave. Frannie was my only child, Claire. I won't pretend it hasn't been hard on me, especially after losing Rogers, too. Maisie's the closest thing I have to a family anymore. She can be a real pain in the butt, but for the most part, we get along real well."

"Let's stick to Fran," I said firmly. "I've been told what happened the night of Oliver Pickett's death and the trial afterward. Did you succeed in getting Fran out of Mexico?"

"Yeah, but only after two years of filing appeals and slipping money under the table," Beatrice said. Her hands had been trembling, but now they were lifeless on the desk. Her eyes clouded over and her face sagged like a crumpled paper sack. "I brought Frannie home and got her the best psychiatric care I could afford. She was in and out of hospitals for the best part of five years, being subjected to shock treatments and mind-deadening drugs. She knew what to say and do to convince the shrinks she was better, but then something would snap and she'd take a mess of sleeping pills or try to slash her wrists. During her good spells, she took night school classes. She was so intelligent that she easily could have been the top student at her school and been accepted at any college in the country."

I paused to ponder this, then said, "Ronnie told me she never saw Fran after they were transported to the prison. Was Fran transferred to another one?"

"Not to my knowledge. The few times I was allowed to visit her at that repulsive place, she refused to talk to me. I had to fight not to cry when I saw her through the mesh, getting thinner and pastier each time. After she got out, she never said one word about the prison. It must have been so—oh, God, I don't want to think about what my baby must have endured!"

"But you did win her release," I inserted soothingly. "You said she was periodically institutionalized over the next five years. Then what happened?"

"I honestly believed she was starting to do better. She worked in my office as a secretary and occasionally went out on a date, although never with the same boy more than once or twice. She'd even mentioned taking classes at a community college. In fact, we were talking about that the afternoon she got a letter from Ronnie. I never read it, but I could see how much it upset her. It must have been vicious."

"How strange," I said as I rocked back in the chair and stared at her. "I can't believe Ronnie would do that. There's been no animosity in her voice when she talked about Fran—only remorse."

"All I know is that Fran got quieter and quieter over the next couple of weeks. She wouldn't eat or go to work, and got to the point that she rarely came out of her bedroom. One morning she was gone. Later that day, the president of the bank called and said she'd closed out her savings account. A teller who'd just been hired screwed up and gave her a cashier's check instead of taking her request to his superiors. The president was worried because there was more than four hundred thousand dollars in the account."

"Four hundred thousand?" I said, gulping.

"Oliver was very wealthy, and had been ordered to pay child support of four thousand a month. For six years, every penny of it went straight into the account. Rogers and I used to fight about it like polecats. I wanted to fix up the house and buy nice clothes for Fran, but he said it was the devil's desserts. What's almost funny is that Oliver was just as prudish when it came to Frannie. He sent me money on the sly to pay for the convent school, and if he'd had his way, she would have entered the order when she turned eighteen and never set foot outside the walls. He was a real hypocrite, leading an amoral life in Hollywood, and then bitching at Fran if she filched a drink from his liquor cabinet. Rogers had a problem with his drinking, but he still had integrity."

"Why did he commit suicide?" I asked.

She lit a cigarette with hands that once again were trembling. "I suppose I was responsible. I was frantic to get hold of cash to bribe various Mexican officials. I'd emptied our checking and savings accounts. The college account couldn't be touched for two more years, and then only with Fran's signature. Rogers refused to sell the property because it had belonged to his family since Arizona became a state back in 1912. I couldn't sell it without his permission, but I found a way to mortgage it to the hilt. I was in Acapulco when he learned what I'd done. Guess he figured we'd never be able to keep up the payments."

It struck me as a little extreme, but I'd never owned so much as a square foot of property. Even the Book Depot was leased from the original owner's widow. "Let me ask you about something else," I said. "Did you arrange for Ronnie to receive monthly packages while she was in prison?"

"I swear, you sure as hell know a lot of things." She abruptly rose and went into another room, returning shortly thereafter with a glass of water. "You want something to drink?"

I looked at the lipstick smudges on the rim. "No thanks. What about the packages?"

"Yeah, I sent money to her lawyer every month. Oliver Pickett was a bastard and a bully. While I was married to him, I felt like I was living with a black hole that sucked in every morsel of my personality. When he got drunk, he had no reservations about slapping me around like I was his personal punching bag. I knew damn well he'd attacked Ronnie and she fought back in self-defense. It wasn't her fault. I didn't want her to know the packages were from me, though, because I was afraid that some day she'd show up to express her gratitude—and Fran might not have been able to handle it. Turned out I was right, didn't it?"

"Oliver's death certainly has had a major impact on a lot of people's lives," I said with a sigh, thinking of the lengthy list of casualties. Some were destroyed decades ago, others more recently—and possibly as a result of my snooping. Which was drawing to an end. I'd found everybody mentioned in my files with the exception of Fran Pickett, and doing so was well beyond improbable. She could be anywhere in the world, living in luxurious seclusion if she'd shrewdly invested her money. Or blackmailing Ronnie if she'd squandered it and needed a fresh source of income. Or even holed up in a convent with clones of Sister Jerome and Sister Mary Clarissa.

Beatrice cleared her throat. "You haven't told me why Ronnie wants to talk to Fran. It's a little late in the game for repentance. What's done is done."

"I'm not at liberty to explain," I said. I picked up my purse and stood up. "Thanks for your candor."

"Sorry about misleading you this morning," she said with a bit of a smile. "Maybe it did me some good to talk about this after so many years. Then again, maybe I'll crawl into bed with a bottle of tequila. Hard to say."

"Isn't it?" I opened the trailer door, recoiling as hot, gritty wind caught me in the face. The sky had darkened during the last hour, and a low rumble came from the west.

"We don't get much rain in November, but when we do, it can be a gully washer," Beatrice said. "You'd better hightail it back to town before it hits."

"One last question," I said, turning around. "What happened to the money from Oliver Pickett's estate?"

"You're standing on what's left of it. Oliver's will named me as trustee until Fran turned twenty-one. By the time that happened, her doctors backed my petition to remain her legal guardian until she was able to function. Never happened."

"How much was it?"

"Not as much as you'd think. Oliver was making a quarter of a million per picture, but he was living in a mansion in Beverly Hills and keeping coke-snorting bimbos like Debbie D'Avril in mink coats. He thought nothing of taking his devotees to Monte Carlo for the weekend. The total estate was around two million dollars, but a third went to taxes. I used some of it to pay off the mortgage and the loans I'd taken out to keep the lawyer working on the appeal. Over the years I invested what was left in real estate ventures. This place should have been a gold mine. I'd have doubled the investment if the dadburned savings and loan hadn't failed, catching Maisie and me with our pants around our ankles. Now we're reduced to sleeping here in the trailer and clipping coupons to keep us in beans and rice. We don't even have a telephone anymore."

"Why not live in the model home?"

"We've got to have something to show folks in case they're crazy enough to want to plunk down their life savings for a half-acre of rocks."

I went out to the car and drove back to Phoenix, watching the sky turn even darker as thunderclouds amassed in the broad valley. Beatrice had predicted a gully washer. I wasn't sure if the ditches along the road qualified as gullies, but I had no desire to be between them if they did.

Only a few drops of rain had splattered the windshield when I arrived at the hotel. I made a drink, then took out the files and added the particulars of the interview with Beatrice. There were several discrepancies. Fran had been at the same prison for two years. The co-conspirators might have been separated because of the nature of their crime, but it seemed odd that Ronnie never once caught a glimpse of Fran in the laundry, exercise yard, garden, or chapel. That same Fran who disappeared twenty-three years ago—after five years of suicide attempts. Had she ultimately been successful, or was she happily married and using her savings to put her own children through college?

Rain began to pelt the window like bullets from an automatic weapon. I closed the curtains, but I was as powerless to muffle the noise as I was to find Fran Pickett. Failure, even when diluted with scotch, was leaving an unpleasant aftertaste. Maybe this really was destined to be "Malloy's Crowning Flop." I wouldn't necessarily feel obligated to fling myself into a raging waterfall in the Sherlockian tradition. The Sisters of the Holy Shrine of San Jacinto had plenty of uninhabited cells, and surely Sister Ursala could use an assistant in the apiary.

I'd sunk to this unattractive level of despondency (replete with a generous dose of self-pity) when I resolved to call Ronnie and tender my final report. I'd been on the verge two days ago beside the pool at the Acapulco Plaza when Caron had made the fortuitous remark about the "shrine"; now I was teetering on the lip of the abyss. I found Ronnie's telephone number in Brussels and dialed it.

I was informed she'd left the hotel. After I'd located her number in a Chicago suburb, I replenished my drink as well as my strength of character, then dialed it.

"Hello?" she said groggily.

"Claire," I said. "I'm in Phoenix."

"That's nice. I'm in the throes of jet lag. I've been told it's worse going east, but going west always wipes me out for several days. Have you made progress?"

"I spoke to Fran Pickett's mother this afternoon," I said, hoping I didn't sound too smug. "It took some sleuthing to locate her, but I did."

"You did?"

Once again I'd anticipated at least a minimal expression of admiration. "The original house is gone, and she's living in a trailer on the same property. The problem is that she hasn't heard from Fran for more than twenty years."

"Or so she says. I don't remember much about her, but she looked as if she'd do anything to protect her cub."

"She told me some things that were inconsistent," I continued. "Fran was in the same prison with you for two years before her mother won her release and took her back to Phoenix. You said you never saw her."

"I didn't."

"How could she have been there for two years without your knowledge?" I asked.

"Shall I describe the horror of the daily regime?

Up at five in the morning, a breakfast consisting of bread and cold coffee, a fourteen-hour workday, followed by ten hours of listening to water drip and rats scurry across the floor—do you really want the details?"

I shuddered as the images filled my mind. "No, I get your point. There's more. After Fran had been back home for five years, she received a letter from you that had such an impact on her that she disappeared."

"I told you that I didn't know Fran's address in the United States. How could I have mailed a letter to her—care of General Delivery, Phoenix?"

I hadn't thought about that. "I guess you couldn't have," I conceded. "But who could have written it? Who in Acapulco knew Fran's address in Phoenix? Not Jorge, the limousine driver, and not Santiago, the innkeeper. Both lawyers, possibly, but what was the motive?"

Ronnie remained silent for a moment, breathing unevenly, then said, "I'd forgotten, but I did write her a letter after I was transferred to a hospital. I asked for her forgiveness, because I never believed I'd make it. All I wrote on the envelope was her name. How or why the letter ended up in Fran's hands is a mystery to me, too. Perhaps the prison authorities forwarded it to her after I was released and put on a bus to the border."

I wasn't convinced, but I had no other theories. "I suppose so."

"Fran's mother has no clue to her current whereabouts?" Ronnie asked with a trace of incredulity. "She didn't make any effort to find her own daughter?"

"She may have tried, but she never found her. I can't think of any way to find her, either. At this point, I'm not even going to suggest you try the private investigator. Fran could be a safari guide in Kenya or a homeroom mother in Dallas."

"Her mother has no clues whatsoever?"

"She claimed she didn't," I said, aware that my shrug could not be appreciated in Chicago. "Nor do I. When she left, she had a cashier's check for four hundred thousand dollars in her purse. That would have gotten her anywhere she wanted to go and allowed her to live however she chose."

"Indeed it would," Ronnie murmured. "If she's behind this blackmail demand, she's either very greedy or has decided to destroy me out of malice. You may as well go home, Claire. I'll find a way to deal with this."

I felt a chill similar to that when Caron first told me about Ronnie's call. "You're not going to . . . ?"

"Oh, no, I'll just comply and see what happens."

"A half-million dollars is a lot of money."

"Are you suggesting that I ignore the demand?"

"No," I said gently, "but you could, you know. The time will come when you're going to have to face all this, publicly or otherwise. I think people will accept your version and forgive you. Once this dreadful secret is exposed, you can put it behind you."

"I killed him, and I can never atone for it. It seems I will pay for my sins in half-million-dollar disbursements. That's not unjust, is it?" In that I couldn't pay for my sins in ten-dollar disbursements, I did not respond. "You've done everything you can," she went on. "Go back to Farberville and sell books. I'll be all right."

She hung up. I replaced the receiver and changed into a nightgown, but my newly acquired paperbacks had no allure. Damn it, I thought angrily as I punched pillows with the fury of a demented cartoon character, this was not supposed to be the way it ended. I'd located and interviewed every remaining player in the scenario: Pedro Benavides, Comandante Alvarez, Jorge Farias, and Beatrice Cooper. Others such as Zamora, Santiago, Rogers Cooper, and Ronnie's parents were unavailable, primarily because they were dead. Chad Warmeyer, Debbie D'Avril, and Fran Pickett had vanished, as had dear old Chico. And now Ronnie had told me to slink home and forget about it.

"Forget about it" was the hackneyed advice often given to divorcees and grief-stricken widows. It did not sit well in my empty stomach. I rolled around on the bed for a time, then acknowledged at least part of the problem, switched on the lights, and called room service.

I put on my robe and spread out my notes for the umpteenth time, determined to find some clue lurking within them like one of Ronnie's viruses: microscopic, but present and still lethal.

I was eating a hamburger when I found it.

Chapter 12

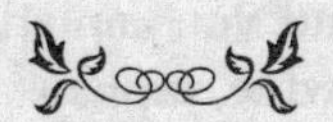

The rain had eased up as I drove down Old Madrid Road, but the air was sullen (and frankly, so was I). I pulled in next to Maisie's convertible. To my surprise, she and Beatrice were sitting in the front seat as if the trailer were a drive-in movie screen. A few beer cans were lined up on the dashboard, and a small cooler was on the seat between them.

"Going somewhere?" I asked.

Beatrice shook her head. "No, we're just sitting, enjoyin' the cool until the storm hits. We used to bring out folding chairs, but then we realized leather upholstery's kinder to the butt. Want a beer?"

I got into the backseat. "No thanks."

"Pretzel?" said Maisie, holding up a cellophane bag.

"No thanks," I said. "I would have thought you preferred champagne and caviar."

Maisie giggled. "I do, but we're living on Trixie's Social Security checks and she rules the budget. I'd just as soon kiss a wild pig as have to explain that I'd spent grocery money for champagne. As soon as we're back on our feet, I'm gonna spend a week in a spa, letting the staff pamper me. Gawd, I can't remember when I last had a decent massage."

Beatrice wiggled around until her back was against the car door and she could see me without twisting her neck. "Around here the massage parlors prefer a male clientele, and you can still find a tavern that refuses to serve wine coolers. It's getting harder, though. Maisie doesn't care, but I hanker for the days when BMWs were an oddity on the street and the mountains weren't hidden by smog."

"How long have you been partners?" I asked her.

"I went into the real estate business not too long after Rogers died. The hardware store was barely breaking even, and I had to keep up the fight to get Frannie out of prison. I married Oliver right out of high school, so I needed a job that didn't require a college degree or a long training period. I got my license and went to work for a friend of Rogers's. After Oliver's estate went through probate, I was able to open my own office. I could have quit working, I guess, but I didn't want to live off Frannie's inheritance—and I was having too much fun wheelin' and dealin'. Maisie came along about the time I decided to open a second office in Tucson. I sent her to a week-long crash course, and after she got her broker's license, she went down there. That would've been . . . oh, twenty-five years ago."

"Something like that," said Maisie. "The Tucson office didn't do well, so I moved up here after three years. I'm too softhearted to boss people around. Trixie sure as heck isn't."

I eased in for the kill. "That would have been about the time Fran emptied the savings account and left Phoenix, wouldn't it?"

Beatrice stiffened. "What does that have to do with it, Claire?"

"Well," I drawled, "Fran might not have reacted well if she'd known her most bitter rival for her father's affection had become best friends with her mother. Freud could have written an entire book about it."

"Have you been eating peyote buttons?" Maisie said as she turned around to glare at me as if I were an ill-mannered hitchhiker. "I don't know who this guy Freud is, but I can assure you I never met Oliver Pickett and nobody'd better be writing any books about me. Trixie got drunk one night and told me what happened in Mexico. That's all I know about it. Why don't you pack up your hallucinations and get the hell out of my car!"

I politely ignored the insinuation that I was unbalanced. "January, February, March, April—and then May. I can take a stab at doing it in French, but it's been twenty years since college. Let's see . . . *janvier, fevrier, mars, avril* That's *avril* as in D'Avril, followed by *mai* as in Maisie. You two sure are cute when it comes to nicknames. Is 'Junebug' next on the list?"

Maisie grabbed for the door handle, but Beatrice caught her arm and stopped her. "Let's hear out the rest of Claire's crazy story. That way she won't have to keep popping up like a prairie dog. In case you didn't know, a prairie dog's no kin to a poodle or a pekingese. It's a rat."

"Shall I tell you what I know about Debbie D'Avril?" I asked.

Beatrice opened a beer. "You're gonna do it anyway, so go ahead before the storm lets rip and the car fills up like a rain barrel."

I licked my lips, sorry I'd turned down her earlier offer of a beer. "After Oliver's death, Debbie returned to Hollywood and made low-budget porn movies until she was arrested for possession of cocaine in 1973. She scraped together enough money to make bail, then disappeared."

"So what?" snapped Maisie. "Plenty of people disappear. Go look at milk cartons in the grocery store. That doesn't mean I'm this missing person. I go by Maisie because my parents named me Maybelline and I got tired of jokes about mascara. The reason I ended up working for Trixie is that I was looking for a job as a secretary. She thought I was bright enough to get my license."

"Then you wouldn't object to having your fingerprints sent to the LAPD? There's no statute of limitations when someone jumps bail."

"What the hell difference does it make?" said Beatrice. "Even if Claire turns you in, the Los Angeles cops aren't going to bother to have you extradited over an old drug charge. These days they're too busy with driveby shootings and riots to get all excited about a couple of grams of cocaine."

"I won't turn you in," I said quickly. "All I want are some answers about what really happened in Acapulco on New Year's Eve. You were there."

"I was there," Maisie muttered, "but all I know is what I was told. Oliver went to the bungalow and that other girl killed him. Fran helped her throw the body off the balcony. They got caught and confessed."

"Let's back up," I said. "You knew about the party beforehand, didn't you? You and Fran had an argument, but for some reason you didn't tip off Oliver. Why not?"

"Because I wanted him to see how wild she was. I'd tried to tell him, but he insisted she was just going through a stage. She was smart enough to fool him, but she didn't fool me." She looked at Beatrice, who was slumped against the door as if each word had been delivered with a slap. "Come on, Trixie, you and I agreed she shouldn't visit Oliver and me in Beverly Hills. Sure, he'd order her to sit at home and watch television, but then he'd completely forget she was there and stay out all night, drinking with his celebrity friends at whichever club was the hot spot. When he'd stagger in at dawn, she'd be snuggled in bed with her teddy bear under her arm. I'm the one who found the empty vodka bottles and marijuana seeds in the trash."

"You two *agreed*?" I said. Ex-wives and girlfriends were usually contentious, if not combative. "When was this?"

Beatrice turned her head toward the trailer. I couldn't see her face, but her voice was pained. "Oliver initiated the divorce, but I was grateful for the excuse to get out from under his domination. I didn't care that I got screwed out of a fair settlement; I had my sanity and custody of my daughter. We moved back here because I'd grown up in the area and I had a few friends. One of them introduced me to Rogers. He was a hard worker and a practicing Catholic, and I figured Frannie would warm up to him as time passed. She was eight when the divorce took place, and ten when I married Rogers. Over the next six years, she never stopped begging to visit Oliver. She'd telephone him when I wasn't home and set it up, and I had to let her go because of the court order. She was always quarrelsome when she had to come home, and hell to live with for weeks afterward."

"So Trixie and I would talk on the phone," Maisie added, "and come up with ways to sabotage the visits. A couple of times I persuaded one of Oliver's high-powered friends to invite him on a deep-sea fishing trip in Baja or a weekend in Vegas to talk about a project. He was too wrapped up in himself to worry about hurting his daughter's feelings."

Beatrice sighed. "Once I lied to her and said he'd called me at the office to cancel her visit. She cried for three days. Maybe it was cruel, but I did it for her own good."

So Beatrice and Maisie had conspired just as Ronnie and Fran had, I thought as I gazed at their profiles in the dim light from the interior of the trailer. I'd been aware that my late husband had dallied with female students, but I'd never called one of them to volunteer his favorite recipes.

"How did you find out about the party?" I asked Maisie.

"I slipped the limo driver five bucks every few days. He wasn't real proud of himself, but he'd tell me what the girls had been doing. They hardly ever made their plans in advance. The New Year's Eve party was the first chance I had to arrange for Oliver to see for himself what he'd refused to accept."

"Did you push him into the swimming pool?"

She laughed unpleasantly. "I may have nudged him, but it was late in the evening and he was wobbly."

"He was terribly vain," said Beatrice. "He never would have stood around in wet clothes while people snickered at him. We once left a dinner party because I accidentally spilled my drink on his crotch. A very dreary dinner party, I seem to recall."

I wasn't interested in her past social life. "I still want to hear about New Year's Eve. After Oliver took a taxi to Las Floritas, what did the rest of you do?"

"Let me think," Maisie said, purring like a cat with a baby bird between its paws. "Margaret Landonwood lured the boy wonder, Chad Warmeyer, out to the beach and they took what turned out to be a very long moonlight stroll. She was a real knockout, which is the only reason Oliver invited her husband to come to Acapulco."

"Arthur didn't mind?"

"They had what was called an open marriage back then. As soon as his wife and Chad left, he tried to get me to go upstairs. When I refused, he put the make on a Mexican movie star who was staying at Las Floritas. I suspect he would have preferred her maid; he'd been trying for two weeks to get her to flirt with him. I stayed at the party in case Oliver came back. He didn't, for obvious reasons, and we took a taxi to the hotel after a couple of hours."

"You told the police all of you were together the rest of the night."

Maisie moved the rearview mirror and, after squinting at her reflection, realigned an errant curl. "So what? None of us had anything to do with Oliver's murder."

"Weren't you worried what might happen when Oliver arrived at the bungalow?" I asked. "You and Beatrice both knew he could be violent."

"I wasn't worried because I knew—" She took a

beer out of the cooler on the seat and tried to open it. "Ow, I broke a nail."

I was too intrigued to sympathize. "Knew what?"

Beatrice took the beer from her, deftly opened it, and handed it back. "She knew there were other people at the hotel that night," she said. "The restaurant was booked solid, and not everybody in the bungalows was going out. Oliver might have yelled and stomped around, but Maisie assumed the kids were agile enough to get away from a middle-aged drunk."

"That's right," Maisie said, nibbling at her broken fingernail. "Besides, I didn't want to be there and catch a stray fist. We were scheduled to go home in three days, and I had an audition lined up. The last thing I needed was a black eye or swollen lip."

I wondered why neither of them seemed to feel that Maisie was responsible for the ensuing chain of events. I would never have forgiven her if Caron had been one of the girls, but Beatrice had sent her to a real estate course, given her an office, and eventually taken her into a partnership. Clearly, she was more charitable than I.

Resolving to examine at a later time my otherwise flawless character, I said, "What happened after Oliver's body was found on the rocks?"

Maisie grimaced. "Fran got so hysterical she had to be sedated. After Trixie arrived, I was ready to fly home, but then the truth came out and I stayed on for another month to help her deal with the authorities."

"What about the other members of the group?" I asked.

"The girl's parents couldn't afford to stay at Las Floritas, so they moved into some crummy hotel down the hill. Chad figured out real quick that he was unemployed and moved to the same place. As far as I know, he was still there when I went back to Los Angeles."

"Did you ever see Chad again?"

"No," she said without hesitation, "but he was smarter than me. He must have realized he'd never get any decent work in the future. Oliver Pickett was like a god in Hollywood. People in the industry weren't about to hobnob with anyone linked to his death."

Beatrice held out her palm. "It's starting to rain. We'd better put the top up and go inside, if, of course, Claire's finished asking questions."

In that I could think of no more to ask, I got out of the convertible. "Yes, I'm finished," I said, then climbed into the rental car and sat for a moment, watching them struggle with the canvas top. They worked well together, perhaps from years of practice or perhaps because they were more like peas in a pod than Beatrice realized.

I was mulling over what they'd told me as I wound through the labyrinth of streets. Beatrice had been premature in her prediction of imminent rain, but she might have ended the conversation because she'd found it distressing. I certainly had, and puzzling as well.

As I drove by the model home, I saw a faint glow. It was rather late to be dusting, especially by what appeared to be candlelight. I pulled into the driveway and cut off the engine. I did not, however, go racing into the house to challenge the intruder. A nail file would not protect me from an armed escapee from maximum security.

On the other hand, I thought as my curiosity began to simmer, it was possible that Beatrice had told me a completely fabricated story about Fran's disappearance. Fran could have spent the last twenty-three years in a mental institution and taken an unsanctioned sabbatical. Beatrice, afraid I'd tattle, had told her daughter to stay in the model home until I'd slinked home.

Curiosity propelled me out of the car, but prudence kept me in the yard. I circled around to a patio in the back of the house and peered in a window. On the kitchen counter was a candle in a bowl, and beside it a messy pile of paper plates, a bottle of water, a jar of peanut butter, a plastic knife, and a loaf of bread. On the floor was a rumpled sleeping bag.

Someone as slovenly as Caron was living there, but he or she was not visible. Beatrice would not have tolerated a vagrant, whose presence might have an adverse effect on potential sales. I'd reported seeing someone several hours earlier, and Maisie had promised to stop by on her way to the bank.

If they had given permission to a friend to camp out for a few days, why hadn't they said so? It was their property, and they were entitled to offer hospitality to whomever they chose. Only if they were harboring a fugitive would they feel compelled to lie.

Said fugitive must have seen my headlights in the driveway and taken refuge in another part of the house. Or gone out the back door, I thought as I looked over my shoulder at the irregular terrain with bottomless pockets of darkness. I had no desire to play a round of hide-and-seek in a region fraught with reptiles, rodents, and prickly plants. I had no desire to go inside the house, for that matter, but if I waited until morning, I'd find nothing except the dirty plates.

My back was beginning to tingle as if I'd brushed up against a cactus. I continued around the house, looking through windows at rooms so dark that Beatrice could have stashed dozens of corpses of mendacious buyers. Anyone wishing to avoid being seen had only to stand next to the window or in a hallway.

I felt as though I'd spent much of the last two weeks in the dark, literally as well as figuratively—rescuing Caron at the seedy hotel, breaking into the convent of San Jacinto, and now inanely circling a model home in the middle of nowhere. Vowing to keep office hours of the nine-to-five variety in the future, I went to the car and took the disposable flashlight out of my purse.

I returned to the patio, switched on the flashlight, and tested the doorknob. Had it been locked, I would have been able to justify an expedient withdrawal. Instead, I eased open the door and listened for an indication of someone's presence. A gust of wind promptly put out the candle. I stepped across the threshold and again waited for a long, paralytic moment.

This time I heard a creak from another room. I took the plastic knife from the counter, turned off the flashlight, and crept to the doorway, across a hall, and into what was likely to be the living room. I risked using the flashlight long enough to determine that no one was there. I returned to the hall, halfway expecting to bump into the Minotaur.

"Fran?" I called softly.

The only response was a footstep behind me, followed by a forceful shove. I managed to maintain my balance (but not my composure) as I crashed into a wall. I dropped the flashlight and grabbed my shoulder, blinking furiously and willing myself not to whimper as pain shot down my arm.

A flash of lightning illuminated the spot where I'd been pushed. No one was there, and seconds later I heard the back door slam. Since I was alone, I permitted myself a small whimper, then hurried to the kitchen and out to the patio. There was no figure running across the yard and wasteland beyond it; if my assailant had chosen that direction, he or she had already found a hiding place. The sound of a car door opening caught my attention. I let go of my shoulder and ran around the corner of the house, keenly aware I'd left the key in the ignition. The door closed as I arrived at the edge of the driveway, but the overhead light had allowed me a glimpse of the assailant (and would-be car thief).

I made it to the car and jerked open the door before dear old Chico could make his getaway. I grabbed his shirt collar and waved the knife under his nose. It was not the most gracious way to treat a sickly man who was old enough to be Caron's grandfather, but it was a long walk back to Phoenix.

"Get out of the car," I growled.

"Or you'll slather me with peanut butter?"

"Just do it."

He mutely obliged. "Okay, now what?"

I took the key from the ignition and dropped it in my purse. "Now we talk, but we'd better go back in the house. It's going to start raining any minute." I pushed him in the direction of the back door. "No more nonsense, either. You came close to breaking my arm, which entitles me to try to do the same to you."

"Is this your best Edward G. Robinson imitation?"

I poked him in the back with the knife. "I'm really getting tired of you, Chico. If you don't cooperate, I'll stuff you in the trunk of the car and deliver you to the police department. Someone will get in touch with Comandante Quiroz in Acapulco. Better yet, I'll call Jorge Farias and suggest he send one of his men to collect you."

"Hey, I'm sorry about everything that happened down there," he said, glancing back at me and then wincing when I poked him in the same spot. "Take it easy, okay?"

We went into the kitchen. I told him to sit on the sleeping bag, found a matchbook on the counter and relit the candle, then positioned myself by the door.

"What are you doing here?" I demanded.

"After a rat ran across my foot in the barn, I decided the accommodations were too primitive for my taste. This is not to imply there weren't rats at Las Floritas, but we had an understanding about our respective territories. Arizona rats are too dullwitted to get the concept."

"What are you doing in a house owned by Fran Pickett's mother and her partner?"

"Well, this afternoon I dusted the windowsills and—"

I couldn't do a lot of damage with a plastic knife, but I was angry enough to find out exactly how much. "This is the last time I'm going to ask you to explain why you're here. I have the telephone number of the Farias Tourist Agency in my purse, and I also have a quarter, which should suffice if I call collect."

Chico kicked off his plastic sandals, then lay back and propped his head on his hand. "I happened to meet Bea when she came to Acapulco after Pickett died. She told me if I was ever in the area to give her a call. Due to circumstances beyond my control, I felt the need to leave Mexico, and decided to accept her offer of hospitality."

"Are you claiming that you remembered her name after thirty years?" I asked, shaking my head. "That's ridiculous."

"I suppose it sounds that way, doesn't it?"

"So try again, and this time put a little more effort into it." I tapped the knife on my palm, then wished I hadn't and scraped my hand on the edge of the counter.

"The day after the girls were arrested, she came over to my bungalow and—"

"You weren't staying in a bungalow. I found the guest register from that time, and none of the bungalows were occupied by two men."

"That was ingenious of you."

"I want facts, not flattery—and I don't want to stand here all night."

"Okay, after Pickett's death, there was a lot of gossip among the Americans. I couldn't afford to stay at Las Floritas, but I was curious enough to go there for a drink in hopes I'd hear more about it. I was doing my best to eavesdrop on conversations at other tables when Bea showed up."

"How did you recognize her?"

He grinned. "The bar got real quiet for a minute, then everybody started babbling about beaches and the weather. I invited her to sit with me, and we got to talking. She told me all about the divorce and how her daughter didn't get along with her husband. His name was odd enough that I wrote it down to use for a character."

"That doesn't get you to the Tricky M thirty years later," I said, not at all sure how much of his story to believe.

"She wrote down her address, and I hung onto it. After all, she had been married to a revered Hollywood director. You never know when a connection like that might become valuable."

"And on the basis of one conversation in a bar, she greeted you like an old friend and invited you to sleep in the barn?"

"She's a generous woman, isn't she? When I complained about the rats, she told me I could sleep here as long as I didn't set it on fire. She had the electricity on for a while, but had it cut off to save money when she had to stop construction."

"Did you run across any of the others in the bar at Las Floritas?"

Chico scratched his head, probably dislodging a variety of vermin. "I met that blonde actress," he said at last. "The only role she ever played with any profundity was in an elementary school production of *You Are What You Eat*. All the reviews described her as a particularly spirited enzyme. I thought I recognized her in a film once, but the camera wasn't exactly aimed at her face."

I dearly hoped my blush wasn't discernible. "Anyone else?"

"I was appalled how much bus tickets cost these days," he said. "And the rest stops were at places where the price of a plate of beans and rice was astronomical. Then I had to pay a guy to smuggle me across the border in his truck, and he had the nerve to pull a gun on me and drive away with my wallet."

"Chico," I said softly, "shall we go find a pay telephone?"

"I met the other girl's parents and an arrogant creep who'd been hired by Pickett to run errands and kiss ass. They took rooms at the hotel where I was staying. The mother would have been a real looker if she hadn't been so worried. She and the father spent most of their time talking to lawyers and trying to get through to the embassy in Mexico City. The creep tagged along with them."

"Were you still there when they had the wreck?"

"A terrible tragedy," he said blandly.

"A newspaper article said that their daughter was in the car with them, but she wasn't. Could the third person have been Chad Warmeyer?"

"From what I heard, the investigators at the scene found the charred bodies of two females and one male. Three passports were recovered, and because of either poor cooperation or incompetence no one bothered to tell the investigators that the girl was in prison."

I sat down on the floor and let my head rest

against the door. "Did you ever see the Landon-woods talking with a young woman in the hotel?"

"I realize you're not interested in my financial situation, but it's of prime importance to me. If you could find me, then so can Jorge Farias. He's probably already heard from the bastard who took my wallet just this side of Nogales. For all I know, the guy who gave me a lift to Phoenix is on Farias's payroll. I need enough cash to get to Canada."

I stared at him. "Do you truly know who was in the car with Margaret and Arthur Landonwood, or is this another of your lies?"

"I truly know," he said, holding up his hand as if being sworn in as a witness. "I may have been a little less than truthful in the past, but Margaret Landonwood told me before she left that she'd persuaded a crucial witness to go with them to the American Embassy."

"Who?" I demanded.

"How much?"

"I have about a hundred dollars. I would have had more if my purse hadn't been rifled in a certain hotel room in Acapulco."

"Hey, I needed to leave town. Farias is a very powerful man who trampled a lot of people to get to where he is. Santiago wasn't the only guy in town who couldn't utter Farias's name without adding a string of obscenities."

"Wasn't Farias sending him money every year?" I asked, remembering Gabriella's odd expression when I posed the question to her.

"Farias can be generous when it's in his own interest. He can also be more deadly than a scorpion." He nervously glanced at the window as if he expected to see a leering face. "Give me the hundred dollars and I'll tell you the identity of the third person in the car when it crashed."

Lightning flashed, and seconds later thunder rattled the house. What could have been more befitting than a dark and stormy night?

Chapter 13

Chico took the money and scuttled back to the sleeping bag and the camaraderie of his minuscule companions. "I don't remember the girl's name, but she was there at Hotel Las Floritas with a saggy old actress. She stayed in the bungalow for the most part, washing and ironing her mistress's clothes or whatever. She was pretty in a somber way, with good bone structure and almond-shaped eyes. She could have had some Indian blood."

"And on New Year's Eve, she was in the bungalow across from Oliver Pickett's," I said to prompt him. "What did she see that the Landonwoods felt was of such significance that they wanted her to accompany them to the embassy?"

"The same person Santiago saw, I suppose. He was too scared to admit he'd seen anything or anybody, but the girl had guts. It doesn't make much of an epitaph, does it?"

"No," I said glumly. "Are you sure Santiago never so much as dropped a hint about this person? A reference to sex or surprise that the person wasn't at a party elsewhere?"

"Even when he was drunk, he'd refuse to talk about that night. That's how deeply scared he was—and after thirty years. When I told him about you, he turned a delicate shade of green and bolted for the can." Chico stuffed the money in his pocket and began to roll up the sleeping bag. "Will you give me a ride to Phoenix? The bus station will be watched, so my best bet is to hop a freight train going any direction but south."

I nodded and stood up. After he'd put the bread and peanut butter in a backpack, I pinched out the candle and we trotted through rain to the car. Once inside, his body odor was overpowering, so I switched on the air conditioner before backing onto the street.

"You don't think it's rude to leave without thanking Beatrice Pickett for her hospitality?" I asked.

"I'll send her a thank you note from Canada."

I turned onto Old Madrid Road. "Did you meet her partner Maisie?"

"And recognize her? Yes, I knew who she was as soon as I saw her. She's held up better than some of us, but I don't think anyone from Hollywood's going to crawl across the desert to beg her to take an ingenue role."

This reminded me of something I'd neglected to ask him. "What did Chad Warmeyer do after the Landonwoods were killed?"

"I never saw him again. He left his clothes in his hotel room, and after a few days, the owner took them. They didn't fit very well, but he didn't seem to care."

The worst of the storm had moved eastward, and only occasional streaks of lightning took potshots at the eerie rock formations. This was likely to be the last time I could question Chico, but I was thoroughly bewildered. Margaret and Arthur Landonwood must have believed that the Mexican girl's evidence would vindicate their daughter—but how could it? Ronnie had steadfastly maintained her guilt since the day she'd confessed.

Chico took a grimy handkerchief from his backpack and blotted his face. "Do you know where the freight yard is? The longer I hang around, the better chance Farias's goons have of finding me. God, I shouldn't have come here in the first place. I'd be a lot safer in a guerrilla camp in Guatemala."

"They'd hardly look for you at the Tricky M Ranchettes," I said in a matter-of-fact voice. His only reply was a snuffle. "Come on, Chico," I continued, "Manuel is recovering from his injury and the limousine is back at the agency. Farias is not going to launch a full-scale manhunt for you. It might be wise not to go back to Acapulco anytime soon, but there's no need to worry about being tracked to the far reaches of . . . Manitoba or whatever."

"What's the weather like in Alaska this time of year?"

"Chilly," I said, then frowned as headlights bore down on us from the direction of Phoenix. The road was wide enough for two cars to pass, but the ditches were filled with muddy water and I had no desire to get mired on a shoulder.

Chico slithered onto the floor of the car and pulled his backpack over his head. "Don't let them take me," he said, apparently sharing none of my reservations about whimpering in front of witnesses.

I tightened my grip on the steering wheel. "People live out here, for pity's sake."

"Promise you won't let them take me."

I eased as far over as I dared and slowed to a crawl. "The only place they could take you is home with them, and I wouldn't count on any invitations for bed and board. The people I met weren't nearly as hospitable as Beatrice."

The approaching car stayed in the middle of the road, its headlights on high. Its driver braked until the car came to a stop, forcing me to do the same. Car doors opened on both sides and two men emerged. I couldn't make out their features, but I had no difficulty spotting the handguns they carried. They spoke to each other, nodded, and advanced on us.

It seemed I owed Chico an apology for the implication he was paranoid. It would have to wait, I decided as I jammed the car into reverse twisted around in order to see out the back windshield, and stepped on the accelerator. The car shot into the black vacuum. I couldn't estimate how far we'd come from the gate of the Tricky M; I'd been driving slowly in order to pelt Chico with final questions. Not more than a mile, I reassured myself.

"What's going on?" wailed Chico.

"I'll tell you later," I said, straining to see the pavement in the red haze of the taillights. I increased my speed as headlights bathed the interior of the car in a glare. My neck felt as if it were wrapped with barbed wire. Chico's high-pitched keening was almost—but not quite—loud enough to drown out my litany of profanities.

I saw the railroad ties. It was no time for thoughtful decisionmaking, so I careened beneath the gate.

The car pursuing us missed the turn, braked, and began to back up. I took the opportunity to turn around on the blessedly broad pavement and stomp the accelerator to the floor. I saw headlights in the rear-view mirror as I took the first corner I came to, and then the next. I hadn't explored the complexities of the Tricky M design during my previous visits, and I was terrified I'd find myself trapped in a cul-de-sac.

"Would you be quiet!" I snapped at Chico, then sent the car skidding around yet another corner. The headlights were no longer visible, but they would be before too long. The only exit from the development was through the gate. It was possible I'd achieved the minor advantage because they stopped to let one of the men out of the car. Unfortunately, they both had lethal weapons. I had a nail file. In a showdown, Chico would be as ineffectual as a faculty advisor.

I cut off my headlights as I circled around the boundary of a cul-de-sac. There was nothing to be done about the telltale brake lights, however, except reduce my speed to avoid using the brakes. The rain that I'd been cursing provided some camouflage; our hunters would have to be within a matter of yards to spot us.

Which might give me time to find the trailer, and more specifically, the barn beyond it.

I told Chico about the men, then said, "You have two choices. You can get out of the car right now and go hide in the desert—or you can help me look for the trailer. The road to the barn's not paved, so they might not notice it in the dark. That will give us a chance to alert Beatrice and Maisie. They don't have a telephone, but they do have rifles."

Chico sat up only far enough to peek over the dashboard. "Who were they?"

"Your friends, not mine. They both had guns and they acted as if they knew who was in this car." I coasted around a corner and saw the trailer. "The road's behind it, right?"

"Just past it," he said, kneeling on the seat in order to look out the back. "I don't see them."

"Well, I don't see the road and I don't want to turn on the headlights," I said. "You'll have to tell me how to get to the barn. I don't want to stray off the road and run over a cactus."

He stuck out a bony finger. "Turn here and keep going in that direction. The barn's about a quarter of a mile farther. Maybe it'd be better to stop and go knock on the door."

I looked at the road. "Here they come. I don't want to get caught outside the trailer. We'll hide the car in the barn and come back on foot." I yelped as the car hit a puddle and chocolate-brown water blanketed the windshield, momentarily eliminating visibility (which wasn't all that good to begin with; I do not recommend driving in the desert at night without headlights). Reminding myself to keep my foot off the brake, we bounced down an incline.

"Are you sure we're on the road?" I asked in what might have been a somewhat churlish voice.

He craned his neck to look behind us. "They went by the trailer and turned. Maybe this idiotic idea of yours is working."

We hit a particularly vicious hole. Once I'd gotten the car back under control, I said, "Idiotic? Would you prefer to walk back to the pavement and ask the nice gentlemen for a lift to the freight yard? I'd be delighted to stop and let you out."

"There's the barn. I'll open the doors so you can pull the car inside."

I waited while he did so, then drove into the barn and cut the engine. "Do you hear anything?" I asked him as I came to the barn door.

"All I hear is rain, and I don't see any lights. We ought to be safe for the time being."

I'd taken my flashlight out of my purse, and now I did a cursory examination of our hideout. It had served as a storage room in its later years; there were boxes of junk, tires, machinery parts, and a pile of rusted tools.

"We'd better wait for a while," I said, snapping off the flashlight. "If one of the men stayed at the gate, he'll know we're still somewhere in the development." I recalled Chico's remark about rats. "I'm going to sit in the car. If you prefer to sit elsewhere, feel free to do so."

He ignored my acerbic suggestion and climbed back in the car. "What did the men look like?"

"The lights were blinding. I saw their silhouettes and their guns." I rubbed my neck, hoping to ease muscles that were harder than steel cables. "I don't understand how Farias could have known to send them here to find you. He'd have to know where Beatrice lived, as well as the fact that you'd met her at Las Floritas. I'm convinced she sent him a substantial amount of money after Oliver's estate was dispersed, but she wouldn't have included directions to her house."

"He has contacts."

"But this is absurd," I said as I rolled down the

car window and took a deep breath. The air in the barn was damp and musty, but an improvement over that emanating from the passenger seat. "There's no way those men could have known that you were at the Tricky M, but they recognized my rental car."

Chico took the jar of peanut butter out of his backpack and stuck his finger in it. "Maybe they were your friends, after all." He transferred a dollop of peanut butter to his mouth, noisily sucked his finger, then thrust the jar at me. "Want some?"

The combination of body odor and peanuts was too much. I got out of the car and perched on the fender, careful to keep my feet well off the barn floor. Chico's blithe assertion could be true, I thought with a shiver. The men had seen me behind the steering wheel; they hadn't seen Chico. Either they wanted me—or they knew Chico was in the car. Both scenarios suggested that they'd been tipped off.

Tipped off by the two women in the trailer, obviously. One of them had driven by the model home, seen my car in the driveway, and continued to the nearest available telephone. But had I said anything to them to imply I'd encountered Chico in Acapulco?

"When you arrived here, did you tell Beatrice and Maisie about me?" I called.

"I may have said something about a reporter wanting to talk to people involved with Oliver Pickett's death," he said indistinctly. "Your name may have come up."

"Did Jorge Farias's name come up, too?"

"You sure you don't want some peanut butter? It's high in protein."

"I want you to tell me exactly what you said to Beatrice and Maisie, Chico. If you're not forthright, you're going to find yourself tied to a cactus in plain view of the street. I'll take my chances in the desert."

"Jeez," he said as he got out of the car, "all you do is threaten me. At my age, I deserve a little respect."

"Tell me," I said wearily.

"It took three days to get here, and I'll admit I may have been worse for the wear. I walked most of the way from Phoenix to here, except for a short ride in the back of a truck filled with hogs. Bea was in the trailer. She gave me a bucket of water, bar of soap, and a towel, and told me to leave my clothes in the garbage can. While I was getting cleaned up, she went into town and picked up some clothes at a thrift shop. Once I was presentable, she offered me food. I told her what had happened in Acapulco and how Farias was after me, then asked if she could loan me a small sum. She said it would take a couple of days to get the money together and offered to let me sleep here. You know the rest."

"I think I do," I said. "She called Farias and told him where you were. She also told him I was asking her questions about the case. What I don't know is why you and I are perceived to be so dangerous. Ronnie Landonwood killed Oliver. She confessed at the time. When I asked her if she was sure she committed the crime, she—"

"When?" he croaked.

"I talked to her earlier this evening before I came back here and had the pleasure of finding you making a sincere effort to steal my car. Considering the way things have been going ever since, I wish I'd let you have it." I felt a drop of water hit my neck, and scooted over a few inches. "Why do you care when I spoke to Ronnie?"

"I heard she died a long time ago. She caught some disease in prison and was taken to a hospital. Some guy who worked there as an orderly told Santiago, and he told me because . . . I don't know, because I was American and he thought I might be interested."

"She was in a hospital, but she didn't die," I said.

Chico leaned against the car, his back to me. After a long moment, he said, "The orderly must have been talking about another American girl. So what's she doing these days?"

"She has a successful career."

"Did she get married? Have kids?"

"I don't think so," I said. "She contacted me because someone made a blackmail demand. She had the crazy idea I could find the person and negotiate a deal to retrieve all the damning evidence of her involvement in Oliver Pickett's death."

"Any luck?" he asked, looking at me.

I couldn't see his expression in the darkness, but he sounded more than minimally intrigued. "Do you know anything about it?"

"Hey, I'm the one who thought she died in the middle of the 1970's. Am I going to waste my time writing blackmail letters to the cemetery?" He got back in the car and slammed the door.

I slid off the fender and went to the barn door to look out at the road. The rain had stopped, probably for good. No headlights were coming down the hill. I couldn't see the trailer from this vantage point, so I had no idea if I'd mentally slandered Beatrice and Maisie—or if they were showing Farias's men the road to the barn. The latter seemed likely.

I pushed open the barn doors, then got in the car and started the engine. "We're going to Phoenix," I announced as I backed out of the barn. "I am not going to sit here and wait for those men to materialize and cause undue damage to my anatomy. I've spent more time with you in the last week than with my daughter. She's cleaner, more entertaining, and slightly more willing to tell the truth. Do you want to get out here?"

Chico clutched his backpack to his chest. "I just want to go to Canada. Will you make sure I can go to Canada?"

"Sure," I said, lying through my teeth. I headed back up the non-road, crunching rocks and endangering whatever species were endangered in this environment. I was fairly certain that I qualified as one of them (homo snoopiens).

As I'd suspected, the car was parked in front of the trailer and lights were on inside. Maisie's convertible was gone, but Beatrice's truck was there. I eased off the gas pedal and let the car coast to minimize the sound of the engine.

"Watch the door," I said to Chico. I was going to elaborate when a fist rapped against my window.

Startled, I inadvertently hit the brakes. Beatrice's face hovered on the opposite side of the glass, distorted by the angular streaks of rain. The overall effect was ghoulish, to put it mildly, and all I could do was stare as she twirled her finger at me.

"What the hell!" gasped Chico.

My sentiments, too. I rolled down the window. "What do you want?"

"Please let me in your car!" she said urgently. "We've got to get away from here before they come back. I was on my way to the barn when I heard you coming. Please, help me."

The more the merrier, I told myself as I gestured at the back door. "Get in, then."

She threw herself across the seat. "Drive, Claire. They'll be back any minute."

I turned onto the street, drove a block, and then switched on the headlights. We flew past the model home, under the railroad ties, and out to Old Madrid Road at what may have been a somewhat reckless speed.

"I don't see them," Chico reported.

"They won't come after us," said Beatrice, sounding much calmer. "I threw the distributor cap in the desert and yanked out some wires. They'll have a helluva long walk back to town. Hope it rains all the way on the bastards!"

I slowed down, and after a quick glance in the rearview mirror, permitted myself a deep sigh. "Okay, Beatrice, explain. Where's Maisie?"

"She went into town a couple of hours ago, and hasn't come back. I was kinda surprised."

"Did she go in order to make a telephone call?" I asked. "To Jorge Farias, for instance?"

"Why would you say something cockeyed like that?" she replied. Conviction was missing.

"Because two of his men are looking for Chico, and they have a description of this car. I don't believe in coincidences, Beatrice—I prefer a more mundane cause-and-effect explanation. The men were following someone's instructions. Someone issued those instructions. In order for someone to issue those instructions, he had to have been apprised of the situation."

There was no response from the backseat. I listened

to Chico's ragged wheezes and kept an eye on the rearview mirror as we continued along the road.

Chico at last figured out what I'd implied. "She betrayed me?"

I smiled at the incredulity in his voice. "I suppose there's no honor among thieves anymore. I ask you, what's the world coming to if you two can't trust each other? The next thing you know, used car salesmen will be setting back odometers and televangelists will be making promises they can't keep."

"Let's not get personal," he said, then turned around to look at the figure cowering next to the door. "I told you that Farias was after me. Why would you tell him where I was?"

"Four days ago, one of his men came out to the trailer and gave me a number to call if you showed up," she said. "I was too frightened to ignore it, especially after Claire came sniffing around like a coyote tracking a lame calf. The man also demanded a description of this car, along with the license plate. I was too discombobulated to write it down, but Maisie got a good look at it tonight and went to a pay phone to pass it along."

We were nearing Phoenix. I considered heading for the police department with my two passengers, but I had not one iota of proof that they'd done anything illegal. Chico might be detained while a query was sent to Comandante Quiroz, who might prefer to leave Santiago's case closed. As for Beatrice, she was a longtime resident and well known in the business community. Accusations by a bookseller from out of state might not be taken with any seriousness.

I headed for the hotel. "What happened tonight, Beatrice? You and Maisie did as ordered. You shouldn't have had any reason to feel compelled to escape."

"They came to the door and said they'd lost your car, but were certain it was somewhere inside the Tricky M. I was about to tell them about the barn, but then they demanded to know where Maisie was and got real pissed when I said she hadn't come back. One of them made me give him the keys to the truck. I realized they were worried about witnesses. I sent them off in the wrong direction and was starting for the barn when you drove up."

"We should have left you," Chico said sourly.

"Don't push me," she responded.

"Snitch."

"Coward."

Listening to the two sixtysomethings squabble was no more bizarre than anything else that had happened lately. I let them hurl infantile insults as I drove across town and pulled into the hotel parking lot.

"Bring your sleeping bag," I said to Chico.

"You were supposed to take me to the freight yard."

I got out of the car. "I don't have any idea how many local thugs work for Farias, but I'm not going to drive all over Phoenix until one of them spots this car. You're welcome to take a hike. Good luck, and *adidós*."

"Is there any way he knows where you're staying?" Beatrice asked nervously as she got out of the backseat. She scanned the rows of cars as if expecting thugs to spring up like dandelions.

"Did you tell him?" I said.

"I had no way of knowing."

"Then he doesn't know" I said as I started toward the stairwell that led to the balcony. "If you're concerned, you can sleep in the car, take off with Chico, or stand there and twitter like the star of an aviary. It's well past midnight and I'm going to bed."

Once inside the room, I felt as though I were back in a college dormitory. Chico rolled out his sleeping bag, flopped down, and began to snore; the sound reminded me of a cropduster's plane. Beatrice grumbled at the sight of the king-sized bed, then stripped to her underwear and crawled beneath the bedspread. Her snores were as deafening as those from the floor.

I would have paced if I wouldn't have stepped on Chico. Was I babysitting victims or perpetrators? It was by far the goofiest position I'd put myself in, but there was no one else remotely responsible.

All of a sudden the desire to be back home swept over me with such intensity that I found myself unable to swallow. I wanted Caron's outrageous proclamations about Rhonda Maguire, I wanted Inez's solemn consensus, and I even—a little bit—wanted Peter's sarcasm. This heretofore unseen vulnerability sent me to the bathroom, where I wiped my eyes with a tissue and tried to interpret my expression in the mirror.

"Here comes the bride?" I asked myself, feeling foolish but searching for some clue as to my true emotions. The phrase failed to do much of anything; I did not envision myself in a gossamer veil, nor did I see my eyes welling with sappy tears. Perhaps the current situation was less than conducive, I concluded.

I was still pondering it when someone pounded on the door.

"Open up!" a voice said sternly. "Police!"

What I said under my breath warrants no mention.

Chapter 14

I must admit that the Phoenix Police Department's interrogation room was an improvement over the one in Acapulco, but I still wouldn't recommend it as a stop on the tour of scenic Arizona. The walls were dingy, the linoleum scarred, the amenities rudimentary. Having had little choice in the matter, I took a swallow of tepid coffee and numbly recited, "Please contact Lieutenant Peter Rosen of the Farberville CID. He'll vouch for my intentions, if not my methods. That's all I am willing to say until you provide me with an attorney."

Sergeant Prowell was unamused, perhaps because he'd heard this several times. "Mrs. Malloy, don't—"

"It's Ms."

"Ms. Malloy, you haven't been accused of a crime. We're only trying to determine what you're doing in Phoenix and how well you were acquainted with the victim. No one has suggested you have a motive. All we want is some basis for your involvement."

"Please contact Lieutenant Peter—"

"Rosen of the Farberville CID," he said. "The refrain pales, *Ms.* Malloy. Several of the officers are trying to set it to music to perk it up, but no one knows the melody."

I hummed a few bars of the theme song from *Gilligan's Island*.

Sergeant Prowell gave me an exasperated look. "What about this guy in your hotel room who claims he's a tourist from Mexico? He's got no identification, no visa, no nothing. Who is he?"

"If I only knew," I said sincerely. I finished the coffee, then examined the grainy remains in the bottom of the cup.

The sergeant was too young to be intimidating. He reminded me of Manuel, with his thick waist and wispy mustache. He looked more like an appliance repairman than a bona fide cop. Thus far I'd resisted telling him about my leaky washing machine.

"You don't know his name?" he said for the umpteenth time. "You allowed a stranger to sleep on the floor of your hotel room?"

"Yes, I did," I said, fighting back a yawn. If you want to tell me what concerns you, go right ahead. I am a bookseller. I am enjoying the weather here in Phoenix. Granted, it wasn't so pleasant last night, but it was splendid the day before and will be the same later today. You are aware that tourists come here, aren't you?"

He slammed the door as he left the room. I sat back and admired the decor, pea green and really pea green, then slumped in the chair and tried to coerce my weary mind into a more serviceable state.

It was well past three in the morning. Beatrice, Chico, and I had been separated at the hotel; I had no idea what they'd said. I wasn't so much protecting myself as avoiding the convoluted reasons for my presence. The only question I'd been asked of any significance concerned my whereabouts at midnight. Explaining that I'd been in a barn at the Tricky M, hiding from thugs sent by a man from Acapulco, sounded a tad improbable to even me, so I'd refused to answer. I easily could see the derision on their faces when I began, "My cousin, who's been dead for thirty years, called me and said . . ."

"Did she call collect, Ms. Malloy?" Sergeant Prowell would say, trying not to snicker. His associates would have no reluctance. Before I knew it, the entire police force would be guffawing like drunks at a comedy club.

"Are you charging me with a crime?" I asked Sergeant Prowell as he came back into the claustrophobic interrogation room.

"Maisie Wilk was found with her throat slit out in Scottsdale on Hayden Road," he said. "She had a license plate number written on a scrap of paper in her pocket; we got your name from the car rental agency, then called hotels."

"Was her body in the cemetery?"

"So you're familiar with the area?"

"I was at the cemetery yesterday morning," I responded. "I was hunting for an old friend. I found his grave, wished him well, and went on my way. I last saw Maisie about nine o'clock, out at the Tricky M."

"What was the purpose of your rendezvous?"

"It was not a rendezvous, Sergeant. She, Beatrice Cooper, and I sat in her car and discussed various events that took place more than twenty years ago. There was no hostility. She answered my questions, then went inside the trailer."

"And after that?"

I opted for a defiant stare. "I'm not answering any more questions until you tell me what's going on. That, or call Lieutenant Peter—"

"Rosen," he inserted, this time sighing.

"Did you try?"

"He says he'll be in touch tomorrow. Ms. Malloy, all you have to do is—"

"Tomorrow?" I echoed, outraged. "Peter can't bother to tell you that I'm not on the most wanted list, that I'm trying to help a family member—"

"He said he'd be in touch tomorrow," Sergeant Prowell repeated, sounding as fatigued as I felt. "How about a compromise? We'll take you to the hotel so you can catch some sleep, but at noon you'll tell us everything you know. We aren't accusing you of a crime, Ms. Malloy. We have a body. We have to determine what's going on."

"What will you do about Beatrice Cooper and Chico?"

"Trixie's been released. As for the guy, no way. He's our favorite lodger until we verify some ID. He doesn't have anything—no driver's license, Social Security, credit card, anything. We ran his prints by the FBI, but we haven't received a response. Until we do, he stays here and enjoys our hospitality."

"Trixie's been released?"

"She sold me a house after I got married, the same year she was named Woman of the Year by the Chamber of Commerce. The woman's a saint as far as I'm concerned."

"Then you, Sergeant Prowell," I said as I picked up my purse, "are a patsy."

"What's that mean?"

"My mind is in overdrive at the moment. Let me get a few hours' sleep, then you pick up Trixie and allow me to confront her. She's responsible for four deaths, maybe more."

"Trixie Cooper?"

"That's right," I said, heading for the door, "Trixie Cooper, Woman of the Year."

As soon as I got back to the hotel room, I called Peter's house. The phone rang a dozen times before he finally answered.

"Thanks a lot," I said. "I could have spent the rest of the night in a cell, you know. I'm sure they're cleaner than the ones in Acapulco, but I have a general aversion to bars."

"Did Prowell release you?"

"Cells are not equipped with cellular phones. I'm at the hotel."

"That's good," he murmured. "Sleep well."

"Wait a minute! Did you actually tell Sergeant Prowell you'd be in contact with him tomorrow? What if he'd refused to let me go until he heard from you? Would it not bother you in the slightest if I were locked in a six-foot room with—with a drug addict?"

He yawned. "I was confident that you could handle it without my intervention. I was right, wasn't I? I need to get some sleep, Claire. I have to testify in two court cases this morning, and I do better when I'm alert."

"So do I," I said, then hung up and did my best to sleep.

At noon a polite young uniformed officer drove me to the police department. I was led to a bench, where I had a view of miscreants in line to be booked at a counter. It reminded me of a fast food restaurant, although the menu was dissimilar ("Do you want handcuffs with that?"). Beatrice was escorted in by another teenaged officer and told to sit beside me. Her eyes were bloodshot and her eyelids were swollen. She was wearing the same clothes she'd worn the day before; they looked as though she'd slept in them. Neither of us offered a cheery greeting.

Shortly thereafter, Sergeant Prowell and an older man in a light gray suit approached us.

"This is Detective West," the sergeant said. "He's in charge of the investigation."

Detective West gazed down at me, his eyebrows arched. "I had a call this morning from a colleague in Farberville. He told me about your propensity for meddling in official investigations. Quite a history, Ms. Malloy. You ought to give up your bookstore and get a private investigator's license. At least you could charge for your services."

"Thank you for this bit of vocational counseling," I said, wondering what else Peter had been inspired to share.

"You said you were a reporter," Beatrice said accusingly.

"I never told *you* that," I said. "I told that to Manuel Estoban, Chico, and a lawyer named Pedro Benavides. Presumably Manuel told his brother-in-law; he told him everything else. Which of them told you?"

Sergeant Prowell cleared his throat. "Shall we continue this in a more private setting, ladies?"

Detective West took my elbow as we crossed the room, but I did not feel like a bride. In a low voice, he said "Lieutenant Rosen also alluded to your expertise in withholding information whenever you find it expedient. I hope you won't find it expedient today, Ms. Malloy. I've been on the force forty years, the last fifteen in homicide. I tend to become annoyed when witnesses fail to be forthright."

"That bugs me, too. The underlying problem in this case is that very few so-called witnesses have told me the truth. I can't remember when I've heard so many phony names."

Detective West harrumphed as we went down a hallway and into a room with a conference table. Beatrice sat on one side, her head bowed and her hands hanging limply between her legs. Sergeant Prowell was at the end of the table, tinkering with a tape recorder.

"Did you forget to invite Chico?" I asked the detective.

"Is there anybody else we've overlooked?"

"I don't think we have time for extraditions." I sat across from Beatrice and tried to stir up some pity for her. She'd just lost her partner and best friend, and she had to know she was indirectly responsible. Eventually she would lose the development, just as she'd lost her daughter and her husband more than thirty years ago.

"Now then, Ms. Malloy," said Detective West as he settled himself near the recorder and gestured at Sergeant Prowell to activate it, "this is an official interview. You're not under oath, but please bear in mind that it's a felony to hinder an investigation or conceal critical evidence. Neither you nor Ms. Cooper has been charged with a crime, so there's no reason for me to Mirandize you. You're welcome to have an attorney present if you'd prefer it."

I gave Beatrice a moment to respond, then shook my head. "I have nothing to hide," I said, then stopped to consider whether or not I wanted to allude to my unauthorized entry into the convent. The Reverend Mother hadn't filed charges, but there was no need to tempt her. "Lead us not into temptation," the Bible admonishes.

"Ms. Malloy?" said Detective West.

"Sorry, I was organizing my thoughts." I glanced up as Chico was brought into the room. He was wearing an orange jumpsuit and sandals, and appeared somewhat cleaner and tidier than when I had last seen him.

"You promised to take me to the freight yard," he said to me, his mustache twitching in disapproval. "I could have been in Salt Lake City by now."

The guard pushed him into a chair and told him to be quiet. Detective West repeated the suggestion, then looked back at me with a faintly carnivorous glint in his eyes.

I folded my hands and placed them in front of me. "Thirty years ago a famous movie director named Oliver Pickett decided to scout for locations around Acapulco. He took his secretary, a male assistant, and his daughter. Invited to come along were an ambitious scriptwriter, his wife, and their daughter."

"Once upon a time, that is," Chico inserted, then bit his lip as the guard jabbed him.

"Ms. Malloy," said Detective West, "what can this possibly have to do with the body found last night in front of a cemetery?"

"It's the latest addition to an extensive list," I said. "I haven't stopped to make a careful tally, but the total's at least seven."

"I thought you said four?" said Sergeant West.

"I was tired." I gave them a synopsis of what had taken place in Acapulco between the moment the girls had met and the ill-fated New Year's Eve party in the bungalow, concluding with, "The girls confessed and ended up in prison."

"Poor Frannie," Beatrice said in a husky voice.

"Indeed," I said. "All she wanted was for her father to love her. You and Oliver's secretary did everything possible to prevent that, didn't you? Furtive phone calls, lies, manipulation . . . and it was working." I looked at Detective West and Sergeant Prowell. "The secretary was using the name Debbie D'Avril back then. After she was charged with possession of cocaine and skipped bail, she decided to call herself Maisie "

"You have proof?" asked Detective West.

"She admitted it to me last night. You can confirm it by sending her fingerprints to Los Angeles."

"It's true," volunteered Beatrice. "Her nickname as a child was Maisie. She made up the last name, Wilk. We got her a forged birth certificate, and before long she had a new identity."

"How did you get the birth certificate?" I asked curiously. I was content with my identity, but someday Caron might do something so blatantly egregious that I might be forced to spend my waning years in the underground. It would be nice to be able to obtain a library card.

"From Mexico," she said.

"You can get any document you want there," Chico said, fluttering his hands. "Of course it'll cost you—"

The guard batted him on the head. "Keep your mouth shut, slime."

"Did you get it from Jorge Farias?" I asked Beatrice.

"No" she said, "from Pedro Benavides. One of his clients was a counterfeiter. The client resumed business after he was released from prison."

"Now who are we talking about?" demanded Detective West.

"A lawyer in Acapulco," I said obligingly. "He was a lowly public defender when he represented Ronnie Landonwood. I wondered where he'd found the money to go into private practice." I wished I'd brought my notes so I could proceed in an orderly fashion. Never before had I been involved with so many bodies; there were enough to merit an exclusive section in the Green Acres Cemetery. "To continue, what I related to you is what the police accepted. Since Ronnie and Fran confessed, there was no reason to question possible witnesses."

Sergeant Prowell snorted. "What witnesses?"

I pointed at Chico. "As loathe as I am to rely on anything he's told me, I've come to believe that a man named Ernesto Santiago, who was the owner of Las Floritas, and a Mexican girl staying in another bungalow both saw someone slip out of Pickett's bungalow approximately fifteen minutes after things quieted down. Santiago suffered a mysterious accident that resulted in a broken kneecap; after that, he wouldn't have told the police his mother's maiden name. The girl, however, was willing to talk, and Ronnie's parents were taking her to the American Embassy in Mexico City when they were killed . . . in a mysterious accident."

"That makes four," said Sergeant Prowell, holding up the appropriate number of fingers, "but I fail to see the relevance to Maisie Wilk's murder—or why you think Trixie Cooper has any responsibility. She wasn't there, Ms. Malloy."

"Yes, she was."

"The hell I was!" snapped Beatrice.

I shook my head. "Several people mentioned that you arrived almost immediately to take care of Fran. There are lots of flights to Acapulco these days, but I doubt there were all that many before the tourist industry blossomed. It couldn't have been that easy to catch a flight within hours of being informed of the situation, especially during the holiday season. Furthermore, you've admitted that you and Maisie were in constant communication. She told you about the party Fran had planned. You went to Acapulco, explicitly to be at the bungalow to protect Fran when Oliver Pickett walked in. You wanted to make sure he saw what a rotten father he was, didn't you? You wanted to make sure the already rocky relationship was extinguished once and for all. Did you make reservations so you could take Fran home the next day?"

Beatrice slumped back and looked at me with a vacant expression. Chico opened his mouth, then closed it when Detective West growled at him. Sergeant Prowell's hand was frozen above the recorder, his eyes rounded in anticipation.

No one seemed inclined to respond, so I opted to get on with it. "You arrived too late, didn't you?" I said to Beatrice. "The scheme you and Maisie concocted worked all too well. Seconds after Oliver sent the guests scrambling out of the bungalow, he turned on Fran. He must have told her that she was a slut, that she wouldn't be welcome to visit him in the future, that she was no longer his child. She couldn't take it, could she?"

"He caught her in bed with a boy," Beatrice said woodenly. "He wouldn't let her get dressed, but instead dragged her into the living room and started slapping her. She was high on alcohol and drugs, confused and frightened. How was she supposed to react?"

"She killed him, didn't she?" I said.

"She was defending herself." Beatrice covered her face with her hands and began to sob.

"Let's take a break," said Detective West. He told Sergeant Prowell to turn off the recorder and fetch coffee from the cafeteria.

"You're pretty good," Chico said to me.

"You're a pathological liar."

"I wasn't *always* one," he said, offended. "Living in the gutter teaches you some survival skills that are essential, but perhaps not commendable."

Beatrice's muffled sobs were making me uncomfortable. I told Detective West that I was going to the ladies room, then left the conference room and wandered down the hall, smiling politely at various officers and civilians. I finally found my desired destination. There was a small lounge area where I supposed distaff officers could powder their noses before going out on the streets to uphold law and order.

I sank down on a small sofa and thought over what Beatrice had said. Poor Frannie, yes—but poor, poor Ronnie. She'd spent the last thirty years convinced of her guilt. Her telephone number was with my notes; I resolved to call her the minute I returned to my room. I had no idea how she would react to this bombshell. I was debating if I should deliver said bombshell in person when the lounge door opened and a young woman entered.

"Detective West asked me to find you. He's ready to resume."

I wasn't, but I washed my hands and returned to the conference room. A tissue box had been placed in front of Beatrice, who appeared shaken but composed. Chico was slurping down a cup of coffee, oblivious to the dribbles accumulating on his chin like beads of dirty dew. Detective West and Sergeant Prowell were watching him with expressions of distaste.

"You're going to have to tell us about that night," I said to Beatrice as I resumed my seat. I heard a click as the recorder was reactivated, but I kept all my attention focused on the woman across from me. "After Fran realized what she'd done, she went into shock, didn't she?"

"She curled up in a corner of the room. I finally persuaded her to stand up so that I could wipe the blood off her face and hands and get her into some clothes. She was a zombie, unable to speak or assist me. I kept remembering how I'd bathed and dressed her when she was a baby. Happier times, even though I was married to that bastard." She snatched a tissue from the box and wiped her eyes.

"She was unable to speak," I said gently, "but she was able to understand you. You told her that her only chance was to put the blame on Ronnie, who was asleep in the master bedroom. Did you assure her that neither of them would go to prison, that they would be deported because they were minors?"

"Yes," she whispered.

Detective West tapped on the table. "Then why the need to involve the other girl?"

"Because," I said, continuing to address Beatrice, "you were aware of the laws of inheritance. You knew that if Fran confessed, she would not be able to inherit her father's estate. Oliver Pickett had no other heirs. It was logical to assume the bulk of his estate would go to his only daughter, whether or not he'd made a will. That was quick-witted of you."

"Yeah," she said bitterly. She crushed the tissue in her hand and dropped it on the table.

Chico giggled. "You ought to get on a game show, Bea. Is *I've Got a Secret* still on the air? I always wanted to be on it, but I never could think of a decent secret."

"When we get to you, I'll suggest one," I said without bothering to look at him. "Okay, Beatrice, you told Fran what to do and sent her out to the limousine, then soaked a towel or something with Oliver's blood and went into the bedroom to dab some on Ronnie. She must not have been awake or she would have objected."

"No, she was asleep. I . . . put blood on her shirt, face, and arms. She stirred a bit, as if on the verge of regaining consciousness. I murmured in her ear, telling her over and over what she'd done. I told her how Oliver had tried to rip off her clothes, how she'd fought back, how she'd grabbed the knife to save herself, how she'd stabbed him. When she began to cry, I put the knife in her hand and left the bungalow." She again covered her face with her hands. "It was a nightmare. I could hear the sounds of music and laughter from the terrace. Christmas lights were twinkling in all the trees. Everybody was so festive, so—"

"You didn't tell Fran that they should throw the body off the balcony, did you?" I asked her before she lapsed into sobs.

"No, only to go back to the bungalow, scream, and run to the lobby. She must have decided she could save Ronnie if they got rid of the evidence. Neither of them was clearheaded. If Frannie had done what I told her, she would never have been put through that horrible ordeal."

"This is an amazing story," said Detective West. "I don't quite see how you patched it together, Ms. Malloy, but you seem to have done so."

"A regular Sam Spade," Chico said.

Sergeant Prowell sighed. "That's it, buddy. Take him back to his cell and see that he's real cozy."

"No," I said, "we haven't gotten to the second act of this three-part melodrama. It's even more convoluted, isn't it?"

Chico made an unconvincing attempt to appear bewildered. "I couldn't say."

I gave him a moment to sweat, then said, "Sure you can, Arthur."

Chapter 15

The following evening I was back in Farberville, bathed in candlelight in the most expensive restaurant in town, and being wined and dined by a particularly handsome member of the Farberville CID (who'd had the perspicacity to meet me at the airport with an armful of flowers). I'd forgiven him for his disregard for my sticky situation in Phoenix, and he'd forgiven me for my admittedly peevish telephone call at four o'clock in the morning. This is not to say there was no tension between us as I paused in my recitation to take a sip of burgundy.

Peter waited until a waiter had removed our plates, then said, "Arthur Landonwood? Didn't you tell me that he was killed in an accident?"

"It wasn't an accident any more than Santiago's purported fall that left him permanently disabled. Beatrice finally admitted she realized Santiago had seen her leave the bungalow that night. The next day she paid Jorge Farias to make sure her presence was kept a secret. It's impossible to say if she dictated that degree of violence or if Jorge decided it was necessary in order to protect Fran." I shrugged. "Maybe it was the traditional way to communicate in those days."

"That doesn't explain why Arthur Landonwood is alive."

"No one was aware that the Mexican maid had been looking out the window at the significant moment. She went to the Landonwoods and told them she'd seen someone creeping away from the bungalow. The police wouldn't listen to her, however, so Margaret decided to take her to the embassy. When the girl's employer objected, Arthur was dispatched to her bungalow to distract her while the girl was whisked out of Acapulco. Chad Warmeyer agreed to drive the car."

"So he was a careless driver," Peter said with a grin, although he was listening intently.

"The car was rented from the same tourist agency that employed Jorge. Care to guess who delivered the car that morning?"

"Do you have any proof that he tampered with it?"

"No," I said, "and I don't think he'll come forward and confess. Beatrice must have promised him more money once she got her hands on Oliver's estate. It was enough for Jorge to buy the agency."

"This Beatrice must be a monster."

I thought about this for a moment. "She didn't actually kill anyone, although I did suggest to Detective West that Rogers Cooper might beg to differ if he could. Beatrice was trying to save her daughter. I personally can testify that maternal instincts can rage out of control. When I showed up in Acapulco with a list of potential interviewees, another instinct—that of self-preservation—came into play."

"Oh?" Peter murmured.

"Manuel took the list to Jorge for advice. Jorge had no difficulty associating those on the list with the thirty-year-old murder. He's the only person who could have known why I was there, who accompanied me, and where we were staying. He threatened me on the telephone, and when that was ineffectual, went to the hotel and killed Santiago. Placing my note under the body was the consummate touch. If the police hadn't come after me, he probably would have called in an anonymous tip—and if he hadn't been quite so imperious, I would have left Acapulco as soon as I had permission."

"A second monster?"

"I don't know if any of this will stick," I said. "So long ago, so few credible witnesses. Fran's out of the picture, and Ronnie's delusional. How am I supposed to tell her that not only did she spend eight years in prison for no reason, but that her father is alive—that he simply tossed in the towel and opted to become a bum on the streets of Acapulco?"

Peter caught my hand and squeezed it. "Not all parents are perfect," he said.

"No one's perfect." I paused to glower at the waiter, who seemed to presume he could wheel up the dessert cart and disrupt our conversation. He retreated. "At least Beatrice kept fighting to save her daughter. Arthur Landonwood could have done the same for Ronnie. The only reason she survived was that Beatrice paid to have packages delivered every month. He couldn't be bothered to let her know that he was alive. Or visit her. If he was so broke, he could have taken a bus to the prison."

"Calm down, Claire."

"I don't want to calm down," I retorted, confused and angry. At whom, I wasn't sure. At a father who'd abandoned his child? At those who'd knowingly let an innocent girl spend eight years in prison? Or at myself?

"Then don't calm down," Peter said in the velvety tone of a gynecologist. "Just try to relax."

I resisted the urge to put my heels on the tablecloth and lean back. It was a classy restaurant, after all, and I had no desire to be banned in perpetuity. "I'm relaxed—okay?"

"Have you told any of this to your cousin?"

"Not yet," I said, conceding a certain level of cowardice, "but she should be relieved to learn that she no longer has to worry about being exposed. Beatrice was the logical person to possess copies of the court transcripts and whatever else she needed to file all those appeals. An officer searched the trailer and found them stashed in a closet. Detective West has the evidence, but he said he can't file charges without Ronnie's cooperation."

"How did Beatrice find Ronnie?"

I finished my wine and set down the crystal glass. "She refused to say, but I think she must have kept tabs on her over the years because somehow it might have led her to Fran. Maybe she believed the letter that Ronnie wrote suggested the two girls meet. Oliver's estate would have provided plenty of money to hire a private detective to pick up the trail in Acapulco and follow it to San Diego. Ronnie's petition to change her name would have been a public record at the courthouse. At that point, it couldn't have been all that difficult to get information from co-workers, landlords, neighbors, and so forth."

"Then why didn't she do the same thing when her own daughter left?" asked Peter as he reached across the table to pour the last of the wine into my glass.

"I don't know, and she wouldn't say. She may know where Fran is—buried in the backyard, sucking her thumb in a mental institution, or making license plates in a less solicitous environment. Most of what I've told you is nothing but speculation. The men who came to the trailer weren't peddling Mary Kay cosmetics. Thirty years ago, Jorge was a respectful employee; these days he's nigh onto a mob kingpin. Beatrice acknowledged her own involvement, but then clammed up. I don't blame her for that."

"Is there any reason to blame yourself?"

"Of course not," I shot back automatically.

Peter gestured to the waiter to bring another bottle of wine. We'd been there so often that all of the waiters knew the label he preferred. A minor achievement in the realm of hometown aristocracy, perhaps.

"So what's next?" he asked, dimpling.

"I should have called Ronnie last night from Phoenix, but I was too overwhelmed," I said. "I took a couple of aspirin and dropped like a rock. She has to hear all this, though. She's suffered for thirty years. How am I supposed to tell her that Fran's mother made a mercenary decision to create those memories? That she's not a murderer, that she never should have been forced to spend those years in prison?"

Peter took an envelope out of his coat pocket and placed it on the table. "You need to put the ghost to rest," he said. "This is an airplane ticket to Chicago. Someone will pick you up at the airport and take you to the suburb where Ronnie lives."

"I have her home telephone number, but not her address," I admitted. "I suppose I could try to catch her at the research facility. It's not the place I'd choose to hear something of this magnitude, but I guess that can't be helped."

"Give me the number and I'll wheedle the address from the telephone company. Tell her what you uncovered, step by step. If she decides to get in touch with her father, that's her decision. It's not yours, Claire."

"I was too timid to call her," I said in a low voice. "The realities are so ugly. Thanks, Peter."

"All I want is for this to be behind you."

"I know," I said as I put the ticket in my purse. My throat tightened and my eyes began to sting. "When I get back, we'll talk."

"It might be time," he said.

Just in case I haven't made this clear, I am not an aficionado of sentimental movies and romance novels. "It might," I said, then waved imperiously at the waiter hovering behind the dessert cart. "The mousse looks good, doesn't it?"

There may have been a trace of discouragement in Peter's voice as he said, "Yes, the mousse. Looks divine."

Caron was waiting for me when I arrived home. Not exactly waiting for me, she explained, but staying by the telephone in case Inez called with an apocalyptic revelation. Waiting for me was a secondary activity.

I told her what had happened in Arizona.

"That's awful," she said. "Could Ronnie have really been persuaded to believe she killed someone?"

"It's called false memory. If you imagine how you would react in a situation and continue to embellish it with credible details, you eventually trick your mind into incorporating it into your experiences."

"Creepy."

"And destructive," I said as I went into the kitchen to make a cup of tea.

"What's going to happen to that nasty man?"

"Chico?"

"Yeah, Chico. Why On Earth didn't you hand him over to the men in the other car? I'd have dumped him on the road with a bow in his hair."

"He's close to seventy years old, dear. Sacrificial victims tend to be young and virginal. He's hardly either of those. He suffered as a result of what happened, too. His daughter was imprisoned, his wife was killed, his savings were depleted, and his career was ruined. He had nothing to go home to except vicious rumors."

Caron came to the kitchen door. "I'd like to think you wouldn't forget about me if I were locked up."

"Have you done something in the last few days that you'd care to discuss?"

She rolled her eyes at the absurdity of my question, but before she could voice her opinion, the telephone rang and she skittered into the living room.

As the teapot began to whistle, I heard her say, "No, trust me on this. All we do is keep telling Rhonda that she saw us in the parking lot when she pulled out with the guy. We'll remind her of what we were wearing and how windy it was and stuff like that. She'll let something drop."

I retreated to my bedroom.

* * *

It might have been more civilized to warn Ronnie of my impending arrival, but doing so would have led to questions that I did not want to answer on the telephone. I'd spent the previous night rehearsing my presentation, but I was not going to win a Nobel prize. The thick wad of notes was in my carry-on bag, along with the last of the paperbacks I'd purchased at The Poisoned Pen in Scottsdale. Other than those, I had only a single change of clothes, a toothbrush, and a nightgown; one night, either at Ronnie's house or in a hotel, would have to suffice. The bewildered retiree had accepted the news of his extended employment at the bookstore with a sardonic smile and an obscure reference to a new customer with "an untamed raven mane and emerald eyes that sparkle like a starry sky." I didn't recognize the source, but I had a feeling he wasn't quoting Shakespeare.

The late afternoon flight to O'Hare was packed with fussy babies and loquacious couples willing to share their innermost secrets with those of us in adjoining rows. As I emerged from the gate, I saw a young black man holding a sign with my name printed on it. Had it only been nine days since I'd looked around the airport in Acapulco for such a sign? What had taken place since then could never be made into a movie; even by Hollywood standards, it was too outlandish.

The driver took my bag and led me to a white Cadillac. Peter had called that morning with Ronnie's address. I shared it with the driver, then got in the backseat and tried to avoid fretting about the upcoming encounter by mentally casting the movie.

I was debating between Jodie Foster and Inez for the role of Gabriella as we turned down a street lined with century-old trees and imposing homes. Spotlights illuminated lawns that advertised the daily attention of gardeners. Rolling into driveways were Mercedeses, Rolls-Royces, Jaguars, and others of that variety. Every driver on the street had a cellular phone in his or her hand, most likely notifying a spouse of momentary arrival so a chilled martini could be presented at the front door. Even the perfectly synchronized joggers carried cellular phones. It was a matter of time before their pedigreed pets had beepers clipped to their collars.

The proximity of affluence did not make me nervous, but the conspicuous consumption was oppressive. The last time I saw Ronnie, she'd had braces on her teeth, acne on her forehead, and a stain on her blouse. Now she was more likely to answer the door in a tiara and silk dressing gown.

"This is it," the driver said as he stopped in front of a faux Tudor monstrosity and switched on the light above his head. "Shall I wait?"

I took out my compact and repaired my lipstick. "We may both have to wait. I'm not expected, and it's possible no one is home. I don't see a car in the driveway."

"The garage door is closed."

"I see that," I said sternly. "My vision is quite good for my age."

"There could be two, three cars in the garage."

"There could be a herd of camels in there, too."

The driver looked at me in the rearview mirror. "Yes, ma'am, there sure could be. I don't see any dung on the driveway, though."

"In *this* neighborhood?"

"I guess not."

At some point I was going to have to get out of the car, walk up the brick sidewalk, continue up the steps to the porch, and ring the doorbell. For some inexplicable reason, I felt as anxious about facing Ronnie as I had about the nuns at St. Martin's Academy. Possibly more so. I thought as my stomach began to churn.

I picked up my purse, then put it down. "I think it might be better to find a pay telephone and alert my cousin that I'm coming."

"Yes, ma'am," the driver said without inflection. "I've got a phone right here."

"No, I've changed my mind. Let's just sit here for a few minutes, shall we?"

"Suits me." He took a paperback out of the glove compartment and opened it.

After five minutes of silence, I said, "I'm going to go ring the bell now. If my cousin isn't there, we'll just have to hope she's on her way home instead of working late or going out to dinner."

"Don't see what else we can do, ma'am."

"Please wait here. No doubt I'll be back in less than a minute. You don't have plans, do you?"

"I'm at your disposal as long as you're here. I'll take you wherever you want, including back to the airport."

"Oh," I said. "Are you a Catholic?"

"Methodist." He got out of the car and opened my door. "I'll be waiting right here."

"Thank you," I said as I reluctantly stepped onto the curb. "I'm a little nervous."

"You're concealing it real well, ma'am."

There were lights on in several rooms, but the porch was dark and uninviting. I went up the steps, took a breath, and reminded myself that a seven-year difference in age was significant during childhood and adolescence; it was not a factor during adulthood. I repeated this several times, then rang the doorbell.

Porch lights came on. I made sure I was visible through the peephole and forced myself to smile like a wholesome housewife collecting donations for a charity.

The door opened a few inches. "Who are you?"

I recognized Ronnie's voice. "Claire Malloy," I said. "I have some good news for you."

"Why didn't you call?"

"I could have, but I preferred to explain things in person. May I come inside?"

"This is not a good time," she said slowly and carefully, as if she'd only recently mastered the English language. "It would be better if you called me at a later date. I'm busy at the moment."

"I spent more than nine days trying to sort out the truth about Oliver Pickett's death. Surely you can allow me a few minutes of your time, no matter how busy you are."

"I'm very busy."

"Polishing your next presentation—or your silver tea service?" I hadn't expected to be greeted with bells and whistles, but scotch would have been nice. When the door did not open, I said, "I don't suppose this is the sort of neighborhood where eavesdropping is condoned, so let's get this over with right now. For starters, your father is alive."

"No, he can't be! How could you say such a sadistic thing? Did you come here to torment me?"

The bells and whistles that had not been used to

herald my arrival now went off inside my head. I hoped she wasn't watching me through the peephole as I put my hand on the wall to steady myself. It was fortunate that the wind was cold; the steamy heat of Acapulco would have been my downfall (in the literal sense of the word).

I finally found my voice. "My mistake, cousin dearest," I said. "I was referring to Arthur Landonwood, not Oliver Pickett. It's very unpleasant standing here on the porch. May I please come inside?"

The door opened. I stepped inside and studied my hostess. Fran must have known I would never be fooled in a face-to-face meeting. Her hazel eyes dominated her face. In high heels, she would be several inches shy of Ronnie's stature; in slippers, she barely reached my chin. Her hair was more gray than blonde, and pulled back in a utilitarian bun. The unnatural paleness of her complexion was emphasized by her long, navy blue robe. The overall effect was that of a petrified porcelain figurine.

"Shall we sit down?" I said.

"Uh, yes," she mumbled, then went into a dim room and switched on a solitary lamp. "Would you like a drink?"

I requested scotch. She went into another room. I wasn't sure anyone had ever sat on the antique furniture, but I decided it was high time and picked a chair of Louis the Something vintage. The bells and whistles were fading, but I was still overcome with shock.

Fran returned with my drink. "I'm sorry you came here, Claire. It only complicates things."

"How does it do that?"

"You obviously think you know who I am—or

who I used to be, anyway. I'm no longer Franchesca Pickett. I suspect I never really was. My mother and stepfather forced me to comply with their ideal, as did the sisters. My father preferred a more glamorous version, although only at a superficial level. He wanted a sophisticated, charming daughter who could be paraded in front of his friends before being packed away in a convent until the next performance. Did you have Barbie dolls when you were a child?"

I shook my head. "I wasn't interested in dolls."

"My father sent them for Christmas and my birthday every year, even when I was much too old. It was partly because he couldn't bother to keep track of my age, but also, I always believed, because he subconsciously wanted me to realize this was his idea of a perfect daughter—well dressed, perpetually cheerful, and just the right size for a shoebox." She began to move around the room, picking up objects off the tables and then replacing them. "But you said you had things to tell me. I am busy, you know. I'm awaiting a call from a colleague in California. Our research has taken us in a similar direction, and we need to make arrangements to exchange data."

"Your mother told me what happened in the bungalow on New Year's Eve. I came here because I wanted to tell Ronnie that she didn't kill Oliver Pickett."

"Yes, I killed him—my own father. I never lied to you or denied my guilt." She made a fist and held it over her head. "I grabbed a knife off the bar. My arm went up like this, then I plunged it into his throat." She completed the pantomime and stared at me as if anticipating a compliment. When I failed to comply, she slowly uncurled her fingers, regarded them with a sublime smile, and sat down on the sofa. "So, did you have a chance to meet the Reverend Mother? She was rigid and uncompromising, but we had some fascinating discussions on the impact of feminism on contemporary theology."

I wondered if the driver outside would put down his book when the medics carried out my body in a canvas bag. "I met the Reverend Mother, and also Sister Jerome. She was gracious enough to allow me to look out a window at the convent grounds."

"She and I had tea in the garden on many occasions. Did she offer you tea?"

"No, but I was in a hurry," I said. I took a sip of my drink and listened to a clock chiming somewhere in the house. I also made sure there were no letter openers or other sharp objects within her reach.

"I did tell you a lie," Fran said abruptly, widening her eyes as she must have done in the Reverend Mother's office thirty-odd years ago. "Ronnie and I were cellmates for two years. To keep our sanity, we talked for hours every night about our families, describing in detail birthday parties, vacations, school, television shows—anything that allowed us to forget where we were."

"She must have been upset when you were released," I said.

"I was scrubbing pots one morning when a matron came and took me to the warden's office. My mother was there. I didn't understand what was happening until we were in a taxi, driving down a rough road. Even then, it seemed unreal. We went straight to the airport. As soon as we arrived in Phoenix, I was put in a hospital to be treated for malnutrition and internal parasites. Later, I was treated for depression and psychotic episodes." The sublime smile returned to her lips. "But I'm fine now."

"That's good," I said warily. "You don't need to worry about being blackmailed in the future. Your mother was responsible."

"My mother tried to blackmail me? I let her have the money from my father's estate. Criminals can't profit from their crimes, you know. She reminded me quite often that I had no moral right to the money. Why would she think she has any moral right to the money I've earned over the years? There are no bloodstains on it."

"She was about to lose the development. I don't know how she managed to find you after all these years, but—"

"Oh, she's always known where I was and what I was doing. My mother's not as crafty as she thinks she is, though. I used to catch glimpses of her on the campuses where I studied. Once I saw her peeping through my office window at the laboratory." She hesitated, then leaned forward and whispered, "She was in Brussels, too, standing at the back of a crowd of tourists at the flower market. She was wearing a disguise, but I recognized her."

I gulped down the rest of my drink. "Well, the police in Phoenix are now in possession of the old court records. I can give you a name and number if you want to press charges."

"And put her in prison?" Fran said with a giggle of delight. "That would make a wonderfully ironic finale, wouldn't it? But the Sisters of the Holy Swine always stressed the importance of charity, chastity, obedience—and above all, humility. It would be very egotistical of me to take pleasure in putting my mother behind bars. Besides, I am very busy."

I seized upon this as an excuse to put down my glass and rise. I may have done so with unseemly alacrity. "Thank you for the drink. I think I'll try to catch a flight home tonight instead of waiting until morning."

She followed me to the door. "I want you to know how much I appreciate everything you've done, Claire. If I'd been thinking more clearly twenty-three years ago, I would have sent you to the hospital in Acapulco to try to help Ronnie. She had tuberculosis, you know. She probably would have survived if she'd had access to proper treatment, but she was placed in a facility where needles were recycled and drugs were out of date. She told me in her letter that she'd never survive. Her death inspired me to go into medical research. I fully intended to dedicate my life to the study of mycobacteria, but there's just something so bewitching about viruses, isn't there?"

"Absolutely," I murmured, groping behind my back for the doorknob.

"There's one more favor I'd like to ask of you, if you don't mind."

"What's that?"

"If you happen to hear from Fran Pickett, ask her to call me. I want to tell her that I'm not angry anymore, and I will be more than pleased to give her a recommendation if she decides to live out her life at the Convent of the Holy Shrine of San Jacinto. Do you think she might like that?"

Incapable of responding verbally, I managed to nod, then went out to the porch and down the steps. The driver gurgled in alarm as I threw myself into the backseat and told him to head for the airport. As we pulled away from the curb, I looked back at the house. Fran was standing in the doorway with a string of rosary beads in her hand. I couldn't tell if her lips were moving, but I had little doubt that they were.

Chapter 16

I was sitting on the stool behind the counter, trying to take an interest in the mail that had accumulated in my absence. Envelopes with windows went into one pile, preapproved gold credit card offers (there's one deluded industry) in a second, and flyers trumpeting sales in the wastepaper basket. The bewildered retiree was humming to himself as he studied the new arrivals on the rack reserved for romance novels. He was the only customer in the Book Depot; the icy drizzle had pretty much cleared the street and sidewalks.

"I understand you actually knew Azalea Twilight," he said as he put half a dozen paperbacks in front of me. One of hers, *Sweeter Than Wine,* was on the top. "Was she as bewitching in person as she was on the printed page?"

There was no reason to spoil his fantasy with a description of dowdy Mildred Twiller. "Absolutely. Have you heard anything from your wife lately?"

"Only through her lawyer, but she's of no concern to me anymore. There's more to life than writing scholarly articles, taking that infernal cat to the vet's office, and growing tomatoes. I've never liked tomatoes; the seeds get under my dentures and cause sores."

I put his books in a sack and handed it to him. "Have you found a new hobby?"

"It would not be decorous to discuss my intentions with such a genteel woman as yourself. All I'll say is please do not be alarmed should you hear noises from my apartment in the wee hours of the night, when the moon blushes above the treetops and the breeze is redolent with the heady perfume of wisteria."

"Noises?" I said despite my better judgment.

"The pop of a champagne cork, the sensual strains of a tango, the murmuring of endearments." He gave me a rakish wink. "Or high heels being dropped on the floor."

I watched him as he sauntered out the door, not sure whether he fancied himself as Casanova or Farberville's newest addition to the transvestite community. Dismissing the question, I took the top bill from the pile and glumly opened it.

At noon, Peter arrived as promised with sandwiches and coffee. We went into my office, cleared off part of my desk, and sat down.

"I received some interesting faxes this morning," he said as he handed me a sandwich and a napkin. "They were from the detective in Phoenix. It doesn't look as if Beatrice Cooper will be charged with anything."

I stopped unwrapping the wax paper. "Do you realize how many people died because of her actions? If she'd called the police from the bungalow at Las Floritas and told them the truth, the body count would have stopped then and there. Fran might have been committed to a mental facility in Mexico, which surely would have been better for her. I wonder what would have happened if the party had broken up *before* Oliver Pickett arrived. He still might have ended up at the bottom of the cliff—after a push from his ex-wife."

"Detective West is as frustrated as you are, but there's no evidence that links her to any of the deaths. Jorge Farias isn't going to admit she paid him to tamper with the car. Why should he incriminate himself?"

I sullenly ate a dill pickle, then said, "What about Farias? Is he going to get away with killing Santiago and ordering Maisie's death? If those thugs had been any brighter, then Chico, Beatrice, and I would be on that same list."

"Detective West obtained a fairly decent description of the men from the agents at the car rental desk, and has an APB out on them. If they're picked up, they'll be offered leniency in exchange for testimony against Farias. Apparently, the comandante in Acapulco will do the same thing, although he's less optimistic that any potential witnesses would dare to testify. There is some justice, however. Farias had a heart attack last night and is in intensive care."

"Gabriella is more than capable of running the agency, especially with Manuel's assistance."

Peter smiled as he pulled the lid off a cup of coffee. "Does that mean you won't be sending flowers and a get well card?"

"Of course I will—right after Sister Mary Clarissa peddles up on a tricycle to buy a dozen copies of *The Joy of Sex*. What about Chico?"

"He was dropped off at a homeless shelter. It's not a crime to be without identification. He isn't an illegal alien."

I finished what I could of the sandwich, then pushed the wax paper aside and made a face. "He went to the Tricky M to engage in a spot of blackmail. Beatrice made it clear she was as broke as he, so they agreed on a few nights of lodging. She probably didn't call Farias until I showed up. I'd offered to pay him for information once, and might do it again.

"You certainly were a catalyst," Peter said. "Any chance you want to stir up a little something tonight?"

"Like spaghetti sauce?"

"I'll bring a bottle of chianti and candles," he said, then gave me a kiss that was a great deal more than perfunctory and left.

I cleaned up the remains of lunch and returned to the front room. Rather than opening bills, however, I went to the romance rack and studied the covers. I finally grabbed a couple, sat down on the stool, and randomly flipped through them, looking for a fictionalized "Hints From Heloise."

I was beneath the blushing moon, gazing up at his glistening chest as surges of heat washed through me, when Caron and Inez came into the store. I crammed the book into the top drawer, but not before they'd exchanged amused looks. In that I could concoct no credible explanation for being lost in the pages of *Daze of Our Love,* I said, "Have you found out about the defensive driving class?"

Caron ignored my question. "This time it Really Wasn't My Fault. All I did was make a deal with

Rhonda Maguire's brother. There was no way I could anticipate her reaction. I am not a psychic."

"What are you talking about?" I asked, thoroughly mystified.

Caron shrugged. "I offered the little dweeb five bucks to find out the name of the guy who's been riding around town in her car. He demanded ten, and we finally settled on seven-fifty."

"He's a miser," added Inez. "He has every penny of his allowance in a jar in the back of his closet, and is always looking under the cushions on the sofa in case—"

"That's irrelevant," Caron said curtly, "and we need to leave before Rhonda thinks to look for us here. She told Emily that she was going to rip off my ears and make me eat them. She also said her father would get a lawyer and sue me for public defamation. I don't think she can do that, but I may be wrong."

"What did you do to her?" I demanded. I had no view of the parking lot beside the store, and I was in no mood to have Rhonda storm in and mutilate my daughter. If nothing else, our health insurance carried a hefty deductible.

Caron made sure Inez was properly chastised, then said, "The little dweeb listened in on her calls last night. One of them was to a guy. She said something about getting him a check from her mother, so the dweeb took a look at his mother's checkbook."

"He's in the gifted and talented program," Inez said.

"And?" I said to Caron.

"Then he went and asked his mother who the guy was. She told him that was the name of Rhonda's algebra tutor. It turns out the guy is in ninth grade. Ninth grade! Rhonda has to pick him up and take him home because he's not old enough to drive. She's two years older than he is, but she has to let him explain her homework. Isn't that hysterical?"

"I still don't understand why Rhonda's so enraged at you," I said. "Did you broadcast this over the high school PA system?"

She thought for a moment, then shook her head. "No, but it's not a bad idea. All I did was walk into the cafeteria and ask Rhonda if she was going to invite her neonatal tutor to the Christmas dance next month. Inquiring minds wanted to know."

"The cafeteria was kind of crowded and noisy," Inez added, "so Caron had to shout to be heard. Everybody heard Rhonda's response, though. She's lucky the vice-principal wasn't there; she would have had detention for the rest of the semester."

"What color is Rhonda's car?" I asked innocently. "If it's red, she may have just turned into the parking lot."

"Here's what we'll do, Inez," Caron said. "I'll go to the back door and unlock it. You wait by the window. As soon as you see Rhonda coming, hurry to the office and we'll leave that way. We can stay on the railroad tracks most of the way to your house."

Inez shook her head. "Why should you get to wait in the office?"

"Because that's the plan."

"No, it isn't," she answered, "and you know why?"

"Why?" Caron and I said in unison, equally amazed by her defiance.

"It Wasn't My Fault."

"My mother was a very strange woman," the customer said, "and so was my father."

In that we'd done no more than make bland observations regarding the weather, I was not prepared for her abrupt pronouncement. I edged behind the counter, wishing there was at least one other customer in my dusty bookstore. As usual, there was not. Farber College had ended its fall semester and the earnest young students had fled home for the holidays. I was reduced to selling books to stray Christmas shoppers like the one standing in front of me on this dreary gray afternoon. "Stray" was an appropriate word; she appeared to be in her sixties or early seventies, with wispy gray hair in a haphazard bun, an ankle-length print dress, sandals, heavy wool socks, and a scarlet cloak. All she lacked to fit the stereotypic portrayal of a gypsy was a gold tooth.

"Oh, really?" I said.

"It was due, I should think, to her unconventional childhood. Mumsy was never quite at ease among the cannibals." She wandered behind the paperback fiction rack. "She remained a vegetarian until she fell to her death some years ago."

I resisted the urge to pinch myself as I watched the top of her head bobbling above the rack. "She fell to her death?" I said, futilely trying to come up with a scenario that entailed cannibals and trapezes.

"As did my father, as you must have guessed. Where do you keep the New Age books, dearie? All I'm finding are covers with buxom women in leather underwear and boots."

"You're in the fantasy section," I said, "but it's the closest I carry to New Age material. You might try one of the bookstores out at the mall."

This had to be the first time since I'd bought the bookstore in the old train station that I had discouraged a customer, and I could almost hear my liver-spotted accountant hissing in disapproval. There were months when business was adequate to pay the bills and make nominal contributions to the credit card companies, but there were also months when I endangered my relationship with the various publishers, as well as with the local utility companies, the above-mentioned accountant, and my daughter, who has a black belt in consumerism.

The woman reappeared and gave me a reproving look. "I do not patronize the merchants at the mall. The place is permeated by a negative energy field that makes me queasy. I have often suspected that the music blaring from unseen speakers masks subliminal messages. My name is Malthea Hendlerson, by the way. What's yours?"

"Claire Malloy," I said. "Would you like me to see if I can order books for you?"

"I have a list," she said as she began to dig through an immense cloth satchel. "This store, by contrast, has a very well balanced energy field. It must be situated on a ley line."

"Only if the railroad tracks qualify."

Malthea finally produced a scrap of paper covered with tiny writing. "See what you can do. I sense you have a very determined nature and will not allow yourself to be daunted by a challenge."

I put on my reading glasses and peered at the paper. "*Celtic Mysticism in the Second Century*? *Applied Magick*?

The Encyclopedia of Pagan Rituals and Initiations? Symbols of Irish Mythology? A General Introduction to the Fellowship of Isis? Pagan Spirituality in the New Age?" I looked up at her. "I'm not sure I can locate these. They're not exactly mainstream titles."

"Making the books difficult to acquire is an insidious form of censorship perpetrated by the religious right. After all, I am hardly a satanist."

I made sure the scissors and letter opener were not within her reach. Her expression was benign, almost twinkly, but during the course of my civic-minded attempts to aid the police in the apprehension of miscreants, I'd learned the wisdom of prudence. "Shall I call you if I have any success?" I asked.

"That would be very nice," Malthea said. Her hand once again plunged into the satchel. "Ah, yes, I knew I had a card in here somewhere. Here it is."

She put it on the counter, nodded, and sailed out of the store before I could respond. I picked up the dog-eared card and read: "Malthea Hendlerson, Arch Druid of the Sacred Grove of Keltria." Beneath this announcement were a mundane street address and a local telephone number—although, of course, the address might prove to be a vacant lot and the telephone attached to an oak tree.

I was somewhat pleased when my daughter, Caron, and her steadfast companion, Inez Thornton, came careening into the bookstore like a pair of dust devils. Caron has my red hair and fair, faintly freckled complexion, but at the moment her face was flushed with excitement. Inez was more muted; the two made a wonderful example of bipolar attraction. Inez is a placid lake, deep and sometimes unfathomable. Caron is, in all senses of the phrase, a babbling brook.

"We got the most fantastic job," she began, her hands swishing in the air. "You won't believe it! We not only get minimum wage—we get commissions, too! It works out to more than ten dollars an hour."

"That's a lot of money," I said mildly.

Inez nodded. "If we work ten hours a day until

Christmas, we'll make as much as six hundred dollars—less taxes and withholding."

Caron began to pirouette. "What's more, we don't have to wear dweebish paper hats and ask people if they want fries. We tried all the boutiques and department stores, but they weren't hiring. Inez wanted to try the shoe stores, but I wasn't about to spend eight hours a day bent over smelly feet and end up with hoof and mouth disease. The lady at the gift-wrapping booth said we'd have to come back when the manager was there and wrap packages so we could be rated on speed and aesthetic effect—as if some snotty little kid's going to sit there Christmas morning and admire the choice of paper and the color of the bow instead of ripping into it. Give me a break!"

Although I wasn't at all sure I wanted to know, I forced myself to say, "What's this fantastic job?"

Caron twirled to a stop and gave me the vastly superior smile she'd perfected on her sixteenth birthday in hopes, perhaps, of being conscripted into the British monarchy. "We're working for a photographer at the mall. The girls who were assisting her quit, and she was so desperate that she came up to us at the frozen yogurt stand and offered us the jobs. Starting tomorrow, we work from ten till eight. We each get a twenty-five cent commission for every portrait."

"In a department store?" I asked.

"Oh, no," inserted Inez, who occasionally found the nerve to undertake a minor role in Caron's melodramatic presentations. "We're assistants in Santa's Workshop. It's this gazebo kind of thing in the middle of the mall, with a bunch of fake snow, plastic elves, and Christmas lights. We collect money from the parents and steer the children up the steps to sit on Santa's lap."

"At which time," Caron said, regaining the limelight with practiced ease, "the photographer takes a shot, we stuff a candy cane in the kid's mouth and hustle him back to the rope, and then go for the next one. Santa gets regular potty breaks, but we can still run twenty to twenty-five kids through the chute every hour. Maybe more, if she'd let us use cattle prods. I don't think she will, though. She's anal."

"I should put in an application, too," I said. "Of course I'd have to apply for unemployment on December twenty-sixth unless I was offered a permanent position at the North Pole."

"Doing what?" Inez asked, blinking solemnly.

Caron grabbed her arm. "Come on, let's go to my house and look at fashion magazines. I am Sick And Tired of Rhonda Maguire feeling obliged to tell us the brand name of everything she wears from her sunglasses to her shoelaces. When school starts back up, she's going to look like a bag woman compared to us."

"Wait a minute," I said with a frown. "You are not going to spend every penny you earn on clothes. For one thing, you still owe me a hundred dollars for the traffic ticket and defensive driving course."

"I already explained it wasn't my fault," Caron retorted. "The whole thing was stupid."

"But also expensive," I said. "What's more, the other day I gave you ten dollars to put gas in the car. I did not intend for you to put in a gallon and pocket the change."

Her lower lip crept out as she considered her response. She eventually opted for pathos, one of her favorites. "Then you should have said so. I assumed you didn't want me to be the only student in the entirety of Farberville High School who has to stand in the hall and beg for lunch money—or root through garbage cans for crusts of bread and moldy carrot sticks."

"Or have pizza at the mall," I said, unimpressed by the performance. "The first one hundred and nine dollars of your wages have my name written all over them."

"That's a violation of the Child Labor Act."

"So report me." I made Caron hand over the car key, shooed them out the door, and went to find a guide to boarding schools in Iceland.

* * *

I wasn't exactly brooding, but I was feeling rather grumpy the following afternoon as I unpacked a shipment and found the books I'd ordered for Malthea Hendlerson. I flipped through them, unable to make much sense of the blithe references to metaphysical principals and festivals with peculiar names like Samhain, Imbolc, Beltaine, and Lughnasad. I was familiar with the less mysterious concepts of the summer and winter solstices and the spring and autumn equinoxes, although I had no idea what was de rigueur on such occasions. A photograph of naked bodies cavorting around a bonfire gave me a clue.

I found Malthea's card and called her. When she answered, I told her that her order had arrived.

"How splendid," she said. "Do you need instructions?"

"I don't think so," I said, staring at the photograph in the encyclopedia. If I were struck with an urge to dance around a bonfire in my birthday suit, I could figure out how to go about it on my own.

"Most people do."

"I'm not into paganism," I said tactfully.

Malthea chuckled. "Instructions how to find my house, Claire. My car is in the shop, awaiting a part, and it's a bit too far for me to walk to the bookstore. You may keep the books if you wish, and I'll come by when I can. However, I was hoping to get some decorating hints for the holiday season. I do so love to deck the halls with boughs of holly."

"You celebrate Christmas?" I asked, somewhat bewildered. "I wouldn't have thought Druids . . . did that."

"Why, of course we celebrate the birth of Jesus. We also welcome Dionysus, Attis, Mithras, and Baal with song and dance. We have an absolutely lovely ritual, then share a splendid feast, with my special 'Tipsy Tarts' for dessert. Why don't you join us this year?"

I took a deep breath. "Thank you for inviting me, but I'll have to check my schedule. I have a daughter, you see, and she and I always—"

"Rainbow and Cosmos will be delighted to make a new friend. Morning Rose and Sullivan believe in home schooling, and I often worry that the little ones miss out on opportunities to socialize with their peers."

I had a feeling Caron would not appreciate being cast in that particular role. "Well, we'll see," I said. "If you'll tell me how to find your house, I'll drop off the books on my way home this evening."

She obliged, and an hour later I pulled up in front of a one-story beige brick duplex in a neighborhood that had once been staunchly middleclass. Now the majority of the residences were rental properties that housed college students and marginal derelicts. Station wagons had been replaced with motorcycles, and porch swings with sofas salvaged from the local dump.

Malthea's duplex was tidier than the ones on either side, although the sidewalk was cracked and paint peeled from the trim. She'd told me her apartment was on the right, but as I raised my hand to knock, the other door opened and she said, "Over here, Claire."

I obediently went into a living room crammed with chairs, a loveseat, a bulging sofa, and a dozen spindly-legged tables holding potted plants of every description, from dangling vines to exotic cacti. The walls were covered with amateurish watercolor paintings and overly ambitious macrame hangings.

Malthea beamed at me as if I'd made it across a minefield. "This isn't where I live," she confided in a low voice, her eyebrows wiggling jauntily.

"It isn't?" I said.

"I have a cat."

"Do you really?" I murmured, wondering what on earth we were doing in someone else's home. I was not inexperienced in breaking and entering (I have an eclectic rap sheet), but I preferred to do so with adequate provocation.

"And a very fine cat she is," Malthea said. "Why don't you sit in this chair by the radiator and get comfortable? It's so drafty here that we might as well be outside."

It was indeed drafty where we stood, but I could feel a veneer of perspiration forming on my forehead. "Who lives here, Malthea?" I asked in a shaky voice.

"Her name is Merlinda. It's a play on Merlin of the Arthurian folklore."

"Merlinda who?" I persisted. "What are we doing in her home?" I did not add: and what have you done with her? I was glancing at the doorways, however, and remaining close to the front door.

"I don't understand, Claire," Malthea said, her smile fading as she approached me. Creases appeared between her eyebrows and cut semi-circles from the corners of her mouth. "I think you'd better sit down and have a cup of tea. I'd hate to think of you driving in this condition."

I kept the bag in front of me as I edged backward. "I promised my daughter that I'd—have dinner ready when she gets home from work, so I'd better be on my way. I'll leave the books on this table and you can mail a check when you get the chance."

"You need a cup of tea," she said sternly.

"No, I don't," I said, groping behind my back for the doorknob. "It's so kind of you to offer, but I must be going. As I said, I'll just leave the books—"

The doorbell rang. Malthea froze, but I'm embarrassed to say I gasped as if a slobbering monster in a horror movie had just leapt out of the bushes. I glanced wildly at Malthea, then spun around and yanked open the door.

The situation did not improve.